Dangerous Purpose

By

Geoff Loftus

Saugatuck
Books

Dangerous Purpose

© 2018 by Geoff Loftus

ISBN: 978-0-9983744-2-0

Dangerous Purpose is a work of fiction. Any resemblance to actual people is unintentional and coincidental. A serious attempt has been made to portray the details and geography of Massachusetts, Paris, San Francisco, Washington, DC, and the New York metropolitan area accurately, but the needs of the story may have driven me to exercise poetic license, including with some actual places and buildings. I hope the reader will excuse this.

Cover design by Tom Galligan, Green Thumb Graphics.

Cover photos by Barbara Brass.

Published by Saugatuck Books.

The purpose you undertake is dangerous; the friends you have named uncertain; the time itself unsorted; and your whole plot too light for the counterpoise of so great an opposition.

Hotspur in *The First Part of King Henry the Fourth*, Act II, Scene III

William Shakespeare

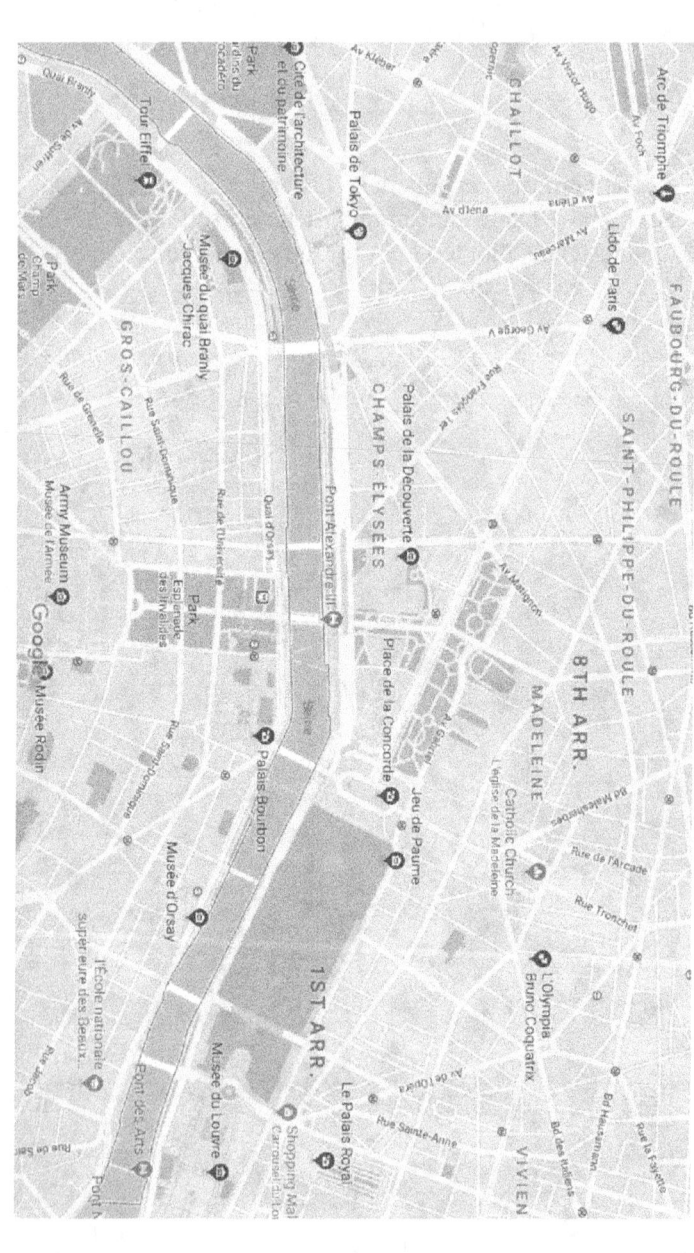

Prologue

Two men, without a good intention between them, were following me in Paris.

It was a late July evening, ten days after Bastille Day, and I was strolling down the Champs-Élysées, enjoying the night air and the glamour of the City of Light. I was wishing that I were the title character of Joni Mitchell's song "Free Man in Paris." That guy felt "unfettered and alive" with "nobody calling [him] up for favors and no one's future to decide." I was far from unfettered, and there were people's futures to save. I'm not saying that saving is the same as deciding, but saving feels like one hell of a heavy responsibility to me.

Anyway, as I was savoring the beauty of the tree-lined Champs-Élysées, I found myself twisting around to look at the Arc de Triomphe directly behind me, with the Eiffel Tower a little to my left. I was being a complete tourist, soaking up all the sights.

Several blocks later, I turned to look at the Arc de Triomphe one more time, and my internal radar pinged. Two guys with a killer vibe were tailing me. If these guys weren't ex-CIA and/or former SEALS or Delta—the type of henchmen that a nefarious spies-for-hire organization would employ—I was sadly mistaken. I would have gladly admitted to such a mistake. But my damn radar wouldn't go silent. These guys were bad news. Lethally bad news.

Picking up my pace, I continued walking, not pausing to twist this way and that to take in the sights. A few blocks ahead of me was the traffic roundabout where the Champs-Élysées met Avenue Franklin Delano Roosevelt. On the far side of the roundabout on the north of the Champs-Élysées, there was a public garden, the Jardin des Champs-Élysées. More parks to the south included the Theatre du Rond-Point, the huge glass-vaulted-and-domed Grand Palais, and the Petit Palais. If I was going to lose these guys, I would have my best chance in the *jardin*, although I knew there was a lot of open space between the rows of trees.

When I reached the rotary, I saw a tiny break in the swirl of traffic and dashed for it. Parisian roundabouts can be terrifying—all the drivers are playing traffic-circle chicken—and I *was* terrified, but my adrenaline rush gave me speed. I plunged across the four lanes of traffic, dodged a couple of scooters, jumped back to avoid being crushed by a small panel van, immediately resumed my rush forward, and felt the sideview mirror of a Citroen pluck at my sleeve. Brakes screeched, car and scooter horns honked, and the air was filled with Gallic cursing.

I made it to the small center of the rotary, a veritable island of safety in the midst of vehicular mayhem. I took a deep breath and plunged into the 4 lanes of traffic on the far side of the traffic circle. More honking, more cursing, and a helmeted scooter driver whacked my shoulder with his hand and shouted something that sounded like "*Piqûre stupide!*" I didn't ask him to translate.

As I reached the sidewalk, I heard a fresh burst of screeching, honking and cursing that I guessed was due to my pursuers, but I wasn't going to waste a second checking on their progress. I ran under the trees into the *jardin*, continued running across the walkways into a thick clump of shrubs, and ducked into them, hiding in the nighttime darkness. My pursuers had reached the sidewalk, stopped about fifty feet away from me, and turned toward the north side of the *jardin*.

I checked their position and saw two more men with the dangerous, *je ne sais quoi* quality typical of spies for hire, entering the *jardin* from the north side.

I still had a clear line of retreat down the Champs-Élysées. But I would only succeed in getting way if I were faster than all four of the guys chasing me. And only if none of them was armed. The chance that I could escape them if they were armed was *très petit*. I'm not without some serious skills of my own, but I was unarmed and at the wrong end of a 4-to-1 ratio.

The guys on the sidewalk began walking moving closer to me; their hands empty. Their team mates in the *jardin* were also moving slowly in my direction, but unless the dark was playing havoc with my eyes, their hands both held automatic pistols.

I double-checked the position of the sidewalk pair. They had stopped and were scanning the *jardin*. If they had a pair of night-vision goggles they would have spotted me in two seconds, but night-vision goggles are not particularly sleek and fashionable. In fact, wearing a pair of these goggles gives a person the look of an insect's head: the Goggle Mantis, which does not meet the fashion standards of Paris. Nor are they inconspicuous.

After a long moment, I noticed the sound of laughter, voices, and hurdy-gurdy music. I turned to the east and spotted a small carousel, the kind that gets towed into place by a truck and set up for street fairs. This carousel sat in an open space about two hundred feet away from me to the east. It was directly in front of the Théâtre Marigny, whose original architect Charles Garnier designed the magnificent Paris Opera House. The Marigny was nowhere near the size of the opera house, but it provided a nice backdrop for the carousel. Maybe I could ride to safety on a carousel horse. If only. It would have been so cool to escape the bad guys to the notes of the hurdy-gurdy machine.

Returning my attention to my pursuers, I noticed that the two spies for hire in the *jardin* had spread farther apart; no doubt to cut down on my escape path and to avoid shooting each other or catching the boys on the sidewalk in a crossfire. And unless I was imagining things, they were screwing suppressors onto their pistols. Good move, I thought. When you're going to kill someone in a public place, you don't want to make too much noise—it might disturb the carousel riders.

One of the men, with a pathetically wispy mustache and goatee, was getting very close to my hiding place. The other man, with a prominent hooked nose, remained in place to cover Mr. Goatee. Staying within the cover of the shrubs, I dropped to the ground and slithered silently toward Mr. Goatee. Yes, *toward*. This seemed like one of those moments when the best defense was a good offense. He obligingly came closer and closer, peering this way and that, doing his absolute best to find *moi*. Being the thorough type, he crouched down to check the ground. His stance wasn't balanced and his feet were tight together under him. Highly unstable. I swept my right leg in a hard kick, as hard as I could manage lying on my left side, catching him directly on the backs of his ankles.

Mr. Goatee flipped onto his back. I jerked myself upright and lunged on top of him, grabbing his gun hand, his right, with my left. I tore the gun away from him and fired at the other spy for hire in the *jardin*. It was a tough shot because Goatee's finger was still on the trigger—I missed. But the other guy scrambled for cover and aimed in my direction.

I slammed my right fist into Goatee's chin, and the back of his head bounced off the ground. He was out. I rolled again, yanking Goatee on top of me at the instant the other guy's bullets thudded into Goatee's back. I tugged Goatee's gun free from his now lifeless hand, pushed his body off me toward the shrubs, while I rolled in the other direction and fired. I fired six times, and I hit the other guy twice. He went down.

There was no sign of the sidewalk team. I wished they had disappeared into the night, running in fear from Tyrrell the Terrible. But they were pros. They weren't running away. They were staying hidden, guns in hand, moving closer to me for a kill shot. Damn.

I crawled on my belly to Goatee, checked again to see if I spotted the sidewalk team and when I didn't, and patted down Goatee's pockets, finding a phone and two extra magazines with ten rounds each for his Beretta M9. I hadn't fired this model Beretta since my time in the Army, but after the events of the last couple of minutes, I was still inclined to give it my personal endorsement.

Remaining behind Goatee for the cover his body provided, I tucked the phone and clips into one of my cargo pants pockets. It was a tight fit and not very comfortable. Running out of ammo would be much more uncomfortable, so I told myself to shut up and deal with it. I scanned the *jardin* very slowly, looking for the remaining two men. Still no sign of them. That was a problem.

The one dead man was about twenty feet away, closer to the carousel, which continued to turn while the hurdy-gurdy music played. More snaking along the ground for me. I reached him without anyone shooting me as I wriggled along. It's not easy crawling around on the ground, even Parisian ground, when your pockets are full of ammo and a phone, but it gets much tougher if someone is shooting at you while you do it. Sometimes, you just have to be grateful for the little things. And I was grateful for not having been shot. Yet.

The hooked-nose dead man's pockets also produced a phone and a wallet, both of which I took and was about to shove into my pocket, when I realized he was wearing a lightweight rucksack. Perfect for carrying guns, ammo, and spare phones. It took me a minute to get the rucksack off him—in my experience dead men are not very cooperative about someone looting their corpses—and loaded all the ammo, phones, wallet, and Goatee's Beretta into it. I had to paw around on the ground to find the other man's gun, a Sig Sauer P226 9mm, which I also packed inside the rucksack.

I crept into the nearest clump of bushes and checked the *jardin* in every direction. Still no sign of the two guys who had been on the sidewalk. Which meant, they could be near the carousel, enjoying the horses in their endless circling. Or, it meant they had departed the area to go enjoy some wine and cheese at a local bistro, which is what I would have done if I were them. Or, it meant . . . they were still lurking nearby, hiding, waiting for me to make a move.

If I had to bet, and it just so happened that I was betting my life, my spies-for-hire buddies were still lurking in the immediate vicinity. But since I had no idea where they were, I had no idea if I had a clear escape route. I scanned the area again, very slowly, and still couldn't find the twosome. I opened the rucksack, took everything out, and laid it all on the ground to take a quick inventory. I put the Beretta and its magazines back into the pack along with the phones. The Sig, with its large-capacity magazine, I kept in my right hand, and a spare mag went into my pants pocket.

I wriggled over to the hooked-nose man, rolled onto my left side, unscrewed the Sig's suppressor, pointed it at his back, and whispered, "Sorry about this, but you won't feel a thing." His body and my body would screen most of the muzzle flash when I fired, which I hoped would keep the two guys from spotting me. If, however, they were hiding only a few feet away from me, they would see the flash, and I'd be dead before I could relax my trigger finger.

I inhaled deeply then slowly exhaled. Now or never, Tyrrell. Now. I pulled the trigger three times. Lots of noise. The area around the carousel erupted in screams and shouts of fear and confusion. Feet pounded in every direction.

Two men jumped out of the bushes about fifteen feet away from me, between my position and the carousel.

I leapt to my feet and hurtled across the walkways under the trees and ran directly across the Champs-Élysées, a panel van barely missing me. The bad guys' bullets popped through the van's metal panels but I kept moving onto the Place Clemenceau then down the Avenue Winston Churchill, running as fast as I could past the elaborate facades of the Grand Palais on my right and the Petit Palais across the street on my left.

Bullets whined by both of my ears. One shot pinged off an ornate street lamp. Keep running, Tyrrell, the Seine's about three hundred feet in front of you.

My pursuers stopped firing and concentrated on chasing me. I raced across the walkways of the Cours la Reine and out onto the Pont Alexandre III, a Beaux Arts style bridge that—in my humble opinion—is the most extravagantly beautiful bridge in Paris.

A bullet ricocheted off the walkway near my feet. Another hit the railing to my right. I ignored them. I paused and peered down over the stone railing at the Seine. My prayers had been answered: A glass-enclosed riverboat was gliding east under the mid-span of the Pont Alexandre III. There was no time left to think or come up with another plan—there was no cover on the bridge, no place to hide.

I shoved the Sig into my pants pocket, planted both hands on the railing, and vaulted over the rail toward the glass dome of the boat—

Silly me. I had thought I would go to Paris, take in the beautiful city, enjoy the astounding food, make love to my beautiful girlfriend in a luxury hotel, and, in my spare time, stop a neo-Nazi terrorist attack. Instead, I was being pursued through the City of Light by a bunch of very nasty people with some seriously lethal skills. Put that down as the result of poor planning on my part.

All of which makes me realize you would probably

like to understand how I came to find myself trapped in this peculiar set of circumstances. Well. . . .

1

Eight days earlier . . .

"Ever since I caught Maggie's killer, which is something I've wanted to do for years, ever since I got him, I feel lost," I said.

Dr. Hoffman replied softly, "It's only been two months. Not a very long time."

"So you're saying it's just a phase? I'll grow out of it?"

"Are you still growing?" How did he manage to pack so much irony into a short comment and still make it sound neutral?

"Emotionally. I'm still growing emotionally."

"In what ways?"

I swallowed my immediate, smart-ass response and paused to think before speaking. See? I was growing more mature by the moment.

Dr. Hoffman was a good guy. For a therapist. He really was. I probably would have treated any therapist with a large dose of cynicism. To be completely honest, let's change probably to definitely. But Hoffman wasn't any therapist. He treated me with respect, ignored my cynicism, and deserved my cooperation.

"In what ways?" he repeated the question without anger or impatience.

I stared at the cream-colored walls of his office and the two large watercolors that reminded me of the Maine coastline. The furniture was contemporary and deliberately bland. An upholstered armchair for the good doctor and a couch for me. Hoffman's appearance was as calmly reassuring as his office: his medium height and build, gray hair combed straight back, and large brown eyes all said "trust me." He spoke with a slight, soft German accent. Very soothing. Very comforting. Given our differing roles in this session, we were both appropriately dressed. Hoffman was wearing a blue button-down shirt with an argyle tie over dark-gray flannel pants. I was wearing a navy blue polo shirt over khaki slacks.

"Please tell me in what ways you have been growing?"

"Ever since . . . Maggie's ghost appeared to me, I've been on a new path. She introduced me to Harry and told me that I'd have a chance to change my life." I stopped. No matter how often I thought about my reality, it was still overwhelming. The ghost of my dead wife had appeared to me the same way Marley's ghost appeared to Scrooge and told me I had an opportunity to change my life and that someone named Harry would show me the way. No wonder I'd ended up in a shrink's office.

"Who is Harry?" Hoffman asked.

"You know Harry—you work with him, too."

"Yes, but I'm asking you: Who do you think he is?"

"He's . . . he's my . . . guardian angel."

"And you work for him?"

"No, I work for the Chairman. So does Harry."

"And when you say 'the Chairman,' you mean God."

"Yes. You know that."

"Why do you refer to Him as the Chairman?"

"Because Harry does. Probably has to do with office politics in heaven."

Hoffman grinned then asked, "Is introducing you to Harry, and through Harry, the Chairman, the change in your life that your late wife was referring to?"

"Yes."

So simple. So astounding. So completely, off-the-wall crazy. My dead wife interceded with the Chairman to send my guardian angel to me and change my life.

"Humor me," Hoffman said with the tiniest of smiles—it was probably against the Therapists Code to smile at a patient. Against the code to display any emotion whatsoever. Then again, maybe I was transferring my desire *not* to express emotion to my therapist. Geez, Tyrrell, could you please just surrender to the damn process.

Hoffman continued, "Please review what happened to you and then explain what the change in you has been."

"Oh, boy."

"Please."

"Well, Maggie came to me on—"

"I'm sorry to interrupt you. But start farther back. I would like to hear your complete story."

"You've heard it."

"It may have *changed* since you caught your wife's killer. Please, just tell me your story."

"How much time do we have?"

He said nothing.

"Whether I shall turn out to be the hero of my own life, or whether that station—"

"Yes, thank you, David Copperfield. I do not need the Charles Dickens version of your life."

"Okay." I took a deep breath and then launched into my story, trying hard not to over think it or turn it into a lame standup comedy routine. "I came back from Afghanistan with PTSD. I was depressed but managed to function at some level. I joined the U.S. Marshals Service and met Maggie at about the same time. Things went all right with the Marshals and went extremely well with Maggie.

"Then we got married. But I never got any help with my PTSD, and I drank too much, and I hated my job, which I now realize was all about me and had almost nothing to do with the Marshals Service, and . . ."

"You took a bribe," Hoffman prompted.

"Yes."

"It's still hard to admit, isn't it?"

"Yes."

14

He was silent as he waited for me to gather myself and continue my story.

"So . . . I took a . . . a bribe. I never planned to deliver what I was bribed to deliver; in fact, I couldn't have delivered on it even if I wanted to."

"Why not?"

"Some Mafiosi wanted info from Witness Security. I didn't have any access to WitSec material. I rationalized that it was okay to take money from the Mob when I had no intention of delivering anything to them." I stopped. The result of my taking the bribe was too horrible, even now, to say out loud. I focused out of the office window on the top of a tree in Washington Square Park. It was wearing its full complement of green leaves, which swayed in a gentle breeze.

"You took the bribe, didn't deliver, and then?" Hoffman asked.

"I . . . I got my wife killed."

"How?"

I turned from the window and faced him. "You know damn well how I got her killed."

"Please."

"What is this? Pound of Flesh Day?"

"Please, just tell me your story."

"The Mafia guys who bribed me hired a hit man to kill her and wound me. They wanted to send me a message."

"Did you realize what they were communicating

15

when the attack first happened?"

"No, I was too drunk, too lost. I wallowed in grief and guilt and booze for five years. A complete waste case."

"But that changed."

"Yes. Maggie appeared to me the night of the fifth anniversary of her death. She had gotten me a second chance with the Chairman, who sent Harry to work with me. But every assignment is for others. I don't benefit in any way. I have to be selfless because for so long I was miserably selfish.

"Our first project together was some very dangerous business with the Russian Mafia. Then we dealt with a U.S. corporation that had teamed up with Chinese spies to sell defense secrets."

"Does the Chairman give you assignments directly? Or does Harry?"

"Harry introduces me to clients. So far they've both been beautiful women, which messed with my head to say the least."

"Why?"

"Why did it mess with my head? Are you kidding me? I'm a combat veteran, former Marshal, drunken, guilt-ridden loser, trying to stop a bunch of extraordinarily lethal people. Does that sound as if I'm actually capable of dealing with gorgeous, vulnerable women?"

"You may have a point." He permitted himself another small smile. "What about your last case?"

"I stumbled onto the hitman who killed Maggie. A

completely random event. I assumed the Chairman wouldn't let me go after him because that violates the code of selfless do-gooder."

"But the Chairman *did* let you go after him."

"Yes."

"And . . . ?"

"I caught the guy."

"Did you kill him?"

"No, I sent him to prison."

"Did you want to kill him?"

"Is the Pope Catholic?"

"Did you want to kill him?"

"Yes. Absolutely."

"Why didn't you?"

"It . . . I didn't think it was the way Maggie would want me to behave. Not to mention the Chairman."

"What about the men who sent the hitman after you and your wife?"

"I killed one. In self-defense. The other went to jail, thanks to my efforts, and an inmate killed him."

"Everything was wrapped up very neatly."

I glanced out his window. The tree's leaves were still dancing in the breeze. "I guess so."

"But you feel unresolved about it."

"No, not about Maggie's killer."

"What then?"

"I don't know, I'm . . . I feel so restless. I don't feel like I have a purpose or a mission anymore." I turned from the window to one of the paintings on the wall opposite me. But there were no more answers in the painting than there had been in the tree.

"Has Harry . . . redefined your mission?"

"No, not at all. I'm fine with the old mission. I want to do right by others. I went from being a . . . self-absorbed, drunken loser to someone who helps other people."

"Helps them selflessly, right?"

"Yes. They don't even remember me when it's all over."

"And you helped them even though you knew they wouldn't remember?"

"Yes."

"But now that's not enough."

"In my head, I'm convinced it's enough. In my head, I'm absolutely sure that's the right mission. That my purpose in life is to help. But . . . in my gut, it isn't doesn't feel . . ."

"Now that you've caught the man who killed your wife, you feel as if it should be mission accomplished."

"Yes, but it's not," I protested. "There are lots more people to help."

"But that's not how you *feel*."

"No, it's not. What do you call that?"

"You want a diagnosis?"

"It would be nice."

"A diagnosis that encompasses your intellectual embrace of an idea while at the same time your emotions are the opposite."

"Exactly."

"Your diagnosis is that you're normal."

I shot Hoffman a penetrating glare, which had no impact on him whatsoever. Then I found myself chuckling. "And that's that? I'm normal."

"At least when it comes to *thinking* one way and *feeling* another. Totally normal."

We sat in silence, and I wondered how he would react if I ever became a torrent of feelings. Probably prescribe horse tranquilizers.

After a long pause, Hoffman asked, "Do you feel any closure with Maggie?"

"Actually, yes. I still love her; I still regret that my actions led to her death. But I said goodbye to Maggie."

"How?"

"About two weeks ago, I went to her grave on Block Island."

"And spoke to her? At her grave?"

"Yes, out loud."

"That can be very helpful. What did you say?"

"I told her that the men who were responsible for her death had all been punished. I thanked her for interceding with the Chairman on my behalf. I told her that I still loved her and asked for forgiveness."

"Do you think you've been forgiven?"

"Yes. Harry appeared at the grave and told me that Maggie was proud of me. And that she was happy I'd found

Kim."

"How would you describe Kim?"

"About five feet six, glorious red hair, great smile, quick wit, warm, friendly, altogether wonderful. She's a marketing-and-communications consultant, who runs her own business from the second bedroom of her large apartment on the Upper West Side."

"You managed to tell me everything without telling me anything important," Hoffman sighed wearily. "But how would you describe her place in your life?"

"Well . . . 'girlfriend' sounds like someone I was dating in high school, but I guess that term captures the essence of the relationship."

"Do you love Kim?"

I hesitated before answering. "I'm not sure . . . we've only been together a very short time. A very short time. Then again, if she hadn't been going out with me, she wouldn't have been kidnapped by Mafia thugs. But I did make it up to her—I rescued her."

"These were the same Mafiosi responsible for killing your wife?"

"Yes."

"How did Kim feel about your putting her in jeopardy?"

"I don't know. Why not ask her?"

"Jack . . . ?"

"Oh, okay. But . . . I'm really not sure. Sorry, but I just don't know."

"Hypothesize."

"You're tough."

"You're evasive. Hypothesize."

I pondered Kim's kidnapping and rescue and what had happened since. "I'm pretty sure she doesn't blame me for the bad behavior of a bunch of gangsters. And she was grateful that I saved her. And relieved when I told her that Harry and I had spoken and the Chairman will keep her safe in any of my new adventures."

"Are you telling me that she's fine with everything that happened?"

"I'm not sure I'd say 'fine.' But I don't think she's worried about the past."

"What is she worried about?"

"Well . . . it's one thing to imagine the danger your boyfriend faces in his life. It's another thing entirely to experience it."

"And you feel that she's worried about your safety?"

"Yes."

"Has it caused any friction between you?"

"Not so far."

"Do you think it will?"

"I hope not."

Hoffman was quiet for a few minutes. He looked down at his notepad, then said, "So you managed to avenge your wife *and* save your girlfriend at the same time?"

"Yes."

"You've been through some pretty intense times with Kim. Do you love her?"

"I think . . . yes, I love her."

Hoffman let my answers fill the room. "Now that Maggie has forgiven you, and you've found someone new to love, how do you feel?"

"About Maggie? As good as I'll ever be able to feel. About Kim? As if I'm free and clear to see where the rest of my life is going to go. But . . ." I groped for the right words and found nothing but confusion. "I'm still lost. I don't have a sense of purpose. What do I do now? How do I deal with this *mishigas* of thoughts and emotions?"

"*Mishigas*?"

"It's Yiddish for nonsense, craziness."

"I know what it means. I'm just surprised you do."

"Hey, I may be an Irish Catholic kid, but I'm a New Yorker. We all know at least a few Yiddish words."

"I'm sorry, I didn't answer your question. You asked me how you should deal with your—*mishigas*—of thoughts and emotions."

"Yes, I did."

"What do you think?"

I lowered my head and stared at the bland carpet. "I should take action. I should go find someone who needs help."

"Yes. And that's Harry's department, not mine."

*   *   *

22

After I left Dr. Hoffman's office, I walked to the West 4th Street subway station and took a C Train uptown to 81st Street. I climbed the stairs from the subway platform to the sidewalk and faced Central Park. Immediately to my right, the American Museum of Natural History stretched downtown. I walked down Central Park West, past the museum's pillared entrance and its statue of Teddy Roosevelt on horseback in the middle of the front steps.

I turned on West 77th and strolled under the beech trees that lined the wide sidewalk on the southern side of the museum. This wasn't the most direct route to Kim's apartment, but I loved the southern facade of the museum.

"Harry?" I whispered so I wouldn't give any passersby a reason to think I was crazy.

He appeared, as he always did, instantly. I struggled to find a way to describe Harry's sudden appearances and disappearances. "Appear" gives the impression that there was a process of appearing. An extraordinarily fast process, but a process nonetheless. But there was no sensation of process with Harry's appearances. He didn't blink into sight. He didn't materialize or fade in. One second he was nowhere to be seen. The next second, he was there.

"Yes," he said. Harry was black, about 6-feet tall, slender, looked to be forty years old. I said black since, as an angel, Harry wasn't African American. I said he looked about forty, because he did, but I knew from what he had

23

told me that he was much, much older than that. As usual, he was in a suit and tie. As usual, I didn't really care about his wardrobe. If he wanted to overdress, that was his business.

"I think I'm ready to take another case. Assuming the Chairman wants to assign me another."

"He does," Harry replied. "I'll be back in a day or two to get you started."

"Am I going to get shot and stabbed and beat up again?"

"You say that like those are bad things."

I smiled. Harry's sense of humor was developing. When I was first met him, his level of humor was the equivalent of a dead fish's. He was unable to understand a joke. It's always possible that he just didn't appreciate *my* sense of humor, but that seemed highly unlikely. But continued exposure to me had changed him. Now he was quite capable of delivering a wry remark. He was especially adept at belittling me.

"You're immortal, you wouldn't understand how much a human being wants to avoid being shot, stabbed and beat up."

"I will mention your concerns to the Chairman."

"Doesn't He already know?"

"Would you prefer that I say nothing?"

"No, no. Please point out that I'd like to work on a safe, comfortable case."

"What would be the point of utilizing a

government-trained private detective cum troubleshooter on a safe case?"

"You do know that when Kim calls me that, she's teasing me. She's making light of my security consulting business—my regular way of earning a living. The paying gig that enables me to pay the rent."

"Teasing?" Harry's eyebrows arched microscopically, and he disappeared.

"Nice way to get the last line, Harry," I muttered as I resumed my course to West End Avenue, turning uptown for the three-block walk to the front of Kim's apartment building. Although I had my own apartment on West 76th Street where I kept my clothes and personal belongings, I found myself spending more and more time at Kim's home. Her building was twelve stories tall, the prewar building had a brick exterior and ornamental stone balconies that began at the fourth floor. I guess if you were on a floor lower than the fourth, you had no business pretending that you could step out onto your teeny weeny balcony. Kim's apartment was on the tenth floor and had balconies. Maybe we could have had a fire of torn strips of printer paper inside an empty coffee can out there and toasted marshmallows.

Every time I came to Kim's building, I felt a small surge of excitement. Every single time. And since I came to this building four or five or more times a week, that was a lot of excitement. But that's the kind of feeling she inspired in me. I admit to being prejudiced on her behalf, but in my opinion Kim Gannon was dazzling with her warm, funny personality and her long red hair and brilliant blue eyes. Her smile made my knees wobble. Harry had trusted her enough to appear and confirm for her that I worked for the Chairman. Despite my reluctance to tell Dr. Hoffman that I was in love with her, I suspected that, yes, I was in love with her.

I walked into the lobby. The doorman had grown accustomed to my face and waved to me as I passed him on the way to the elevator. I rode up to the tenth floor and sauntered down the floor to Kim's door. I was about to knock when I remembered I had a key—my having a key was relatively new, but I still had that teenage-boy-picking-up-his-date mentality when I walked to her apartment door.

As soon as I opened the door, I announced loudly in my best 1950s television-father voice, "Hi, Honey, I'm home!"

"I am not amused," Kim called. I found her in the kitchen, washing greens and cutting cucumbers, carrots, and mushrooms for a salad. "How was Dr. Hoffman? Are you cured?"

"Do you actually think that's a realistic outcome of my therapy?"

"No, but I can live in hope, can't I?"

"You can. But you might be better off hoping that you win the lottery."

"Then I'd have to buy lottery tickets."

"Yes, that is kind of a prerequisite for winning." I

stepped to the counter and gave her a kiss on the cheek. I waved at the salad fixings, "Anything I can do to help with the meal?"

"I reserved the rooftop grill and one of the tables. You're going to grill the steak, and we'll eat up there. Sound good?"

"Sounds great. Should I go prep the table?"

"That would be nice. There's a canvas bag full of picnic things in the front closet. Everything you need is there."

An hour later, we were seated under the umbrella of a large, cedar picnic table. It was one of three tables, all with umbrellas. Other areas of the roof were set up with lawn furniture and more umbrellas. Quite nice. Our meal—freshly grilled steak, baked potatoes, and salad—was on plates spread on a blue-and-white-check cotton tablecloth. We had paper plates and cups as well as plastic cutlery—all compostable, the forks and spoons were made out of corn resin—Kim was very "green". We even had citronella candles to keep the bugs away and for atmospheric lighting.

As it turned out, the sunset was all the lighting we needed, and a soft breeze kept the rooftop clear of bugs. Kim's building was taller than the buildings to the west, so we had a spectacular view of Riverside Park and the Hudson River. Because the sun was setting behind the New Jersey horizon, most of the town opposite us, Gutenberg, was in shadow.

Kim waited until I was chewing on a delicious bite of steak to say, "I'm really not trying to pry. But do you feel Dr. Hoffman is helping you? Just answer in a general way."

I chewed enough to be able to respond, "Omit all the details of my depravity?"

"Yes, please."

"Yes, he's helping me."

"Helping you in any particular way?"

"I thought you didn't want to hear about the details."

"Could you give me a general idea of how he's helping you? Or just tell me to mind my own business."

I held up my index finger to indicate that I needed a moment, finished chewing, and swallowed my bite of steak. "I'm not quite sure what to say. You know that I've been a little lost since . . ."

"Since you caught Maggie's killers."

"Yes."

"Why do you think you're lost?"

"Probably because I'm emotionally fragile and mentally feeble."

"Yeah, right. Why?"

"I'm not sure. I . . . never expected to catch Maggie's killers. When I first started working with Harry, he told me point blank that I would never get that chance. So it wasn't a goal for me, wasn't what motivated me. But then I got the chance . . . and now I have this unsettled feeling. As if I should be done."

"But you're not done, right?"

"No, I'm not. There are still people who need help. Maggie interceded with the Chairman for me so that I could help people. But . . . I don't know . . . anyway, Hoffman said if I felt like there were still people to help, I should help them. Regardless of my feelings. Just get going."

"Act as if."

"That sums it up. As I was walking here from the subway I had a chat with Harry and told him I was ready for our next case."

"Did he give you a new one?"

"No, but I think I'll have a new one soon."

"Are you happy you'll be going back to work?"

"Not yet. But I will be."

She smiled at my reply.

We ate quietly, enjoying the light as the sun continued to sink below the New Jersey horizon. On the Hudson, barges were pushed along by tugboats, their lights sparkling on the river's surface.

I was enthralled with the view, and I sensed rather than saw Kim turn away. I couldn't put my finger on it, but I felt something in her body English was off.

"What's the matter?" I asked.

"Nothing."

"Whatever it is will not get fixed if we don't talk about it."

"Oh? Is this something you can fix?"

"I won't know until you tell me."

"Not everything can be fixed."

She was right about that. But she was evading a topic that made her uncomfortable.

"Maybe I shouldn't have used the word 'fixed'." Come on, Tyrrell, what should you have said? I considered it for a few seconds and said, "How 'bout thinking in terms of 'help' or 'improve'? Or maybe I should have volunteered to listen. Just listen. No suggestions, no plans for fixing. Answering only direct questions."

"Speaking when spoken to."

"Yes."

"I can live with that. I think."

"Okay, then. What's wrong?"

Kim took a deep breath, looked directly at me with watering eyes, and said, "It's been two weeks since you went to Maggie's grave to say goodbye. I didn't think your trip was going to change everything, but I hoped it would change . . . somethings."

"Like . . . lovemaking?"

"Men always think it's about sex."

"Well, you've got me there. But didn't you mention that topic before I left to say goodbye?"

"I have to admit that . . . I did."

"So . . . maybe sometimes, once in a while, very occasionally, women think about sex, too."

"Yes."

"Is this one of those occasions?"

"Yes."

"At the risk of sounding as if I'm trying to fix things, would you like me to . . . uh, flirt with you?"

"What do you think?"

Holy moly, I thought. But what I said was, "I think I should take this conversation under advisement and follow a course of action in a natural, spontaneous way."

"That sounds good. And the spontaneity should occur soon."

"Oooooo-kay," I said and cut myself another bite of steak.

She wasn't willing to let it rest. "I've never been involved with someone this long and not become intimate."

"How many someones are we talking about?"

She made a face, "Two. All the other men in my life didn't last this long."

"Is that because you're so difficult?"

"Are you hoping to end this relationship before we get to dessert?"

"If it has to end, I'd prefer the end comes *after* dessert."

"I think I've mentioned this to you before: You are not as funny as you think you are."

"Oh dear."

She considered me for a long moment. Long enough to make me uncomfortable. "Are you nervous?"

"I guess. A little."

"Because it's been so long?"

"Yes. And just for you information, talking about being nervous does not in *any way* relieve the nervousness."

She smiled, "I have some ideas about how to relieve your jumpy nerves."

I wish I could tell you that her last remark was followed by kissing and caressing and nakedness and making love on the rooftop picnic table. Talk about spontaneity. However, that was not what happened.

We finished dinner and packed everything back into the canvas picnic bag. Once inside Kim's apartment, the leftover food went into the fridge, and the compostable trash went into a special container. All the while, my anxiety was building. I needed to make a move that wasn't obvious and heavy-handed. But the possibility of our making love loomed in my head like an obstacle course full of impossible challenges: a molten lava moat to cross, a mountain of sharp glass to climb, and a fence topped by razor wire. I hadn't been with any woman except Maggie in more than a dozen years, and it had been six years since she had died. On top of my worries about how rusty I was, there was Kim: a beautiful, sexy, smart, funny woman. Way out of my league. Right at that moment, I would have preferred to wrestle with a hungry grizzly bear or to grapple with a ninja. Get a grip, Tyrrell. She's a woman, and you are—theoretically speaking—a man. Let nature takes it course.

"Coffee? Dessert?" Kim asked.

Don't overthink it, Tyrrell. "Maybe later on the coffee and dessert." I put my arms around her waist and drew her close.

"Oh?" her mouth curved upward at the corners.

She stood on tiptoe and kissed me, her arms going around my neck. We stood in the kitchen, kissing, our bodies pressed close together. She clung tightly to me, and the feel of her body against mine was exhilarating. After a long, enthralling time, she took my hand in hers and led me to the bedroom.

And nature took its captivatingly wonderful course.

2

I woke up like a cliché in a romantic comedy, smiling from ear to ear. Kim, in a very large, gray T-shirt, was sitting on my side of the bed, holding a mug of what smelled like heaven. But it was just fresh-brewed coffee. She kissed me on the lips and handed me the mug.

"You look happy," she said.

"I, uh . . . that was worth the wait." I took a sip of coffee and a few of my cerebral cells kicked into action. "Let me rephrase: you were worth the wait."

"You, too." She stroked my cheek. "Might I interest you in a morning encore?"

"Yes, definitely yes. Just let me use the bathroom."

I took another sip of coffee as she stood up from the bed. In the bathroom, I rinsed my mouth with mouthwash, which was a terrible combination with the coffee, and splashed hot water on my face so that it began to feel like my own flesh and not a pancake composed of Silly Putty.

When I returned to the bedroom, Kim was in bed with the sheets pulled to her chin, her gray T-shirt lying on top of the sheets at the foot of the bed.

I yanked off my own T-shirt and shorts and slid next to her. Our encore was a wonderful repeat of the night before but different . . . less urgent and more giving. The first time making love had been spectacular. The second time was—somehow—even more meaningful, more amazing.

Later, we took a shower together, which led to an aquatic encore. My experience, limited as it was, was that once sex finally begins in a relationship, it's great music and fireworks and chocolate ice cream. It's intoxicating and overwhelming. Sex made me feel taller, cooler, and extraordinarily happy. Yes, Tyrrell, it's fantastic. Which begs the question: What the hell have you been waiting for?

I pulled on a maroon Fordham T-shirt and gray sweat pants while Kim settled back into her gray T-shirt for a simple—asexual—breakfast of coffee, eggs, toast, bacon, and more coffee. Kim went to the bedroom to change into clothes. I had the briefest impulse to follow her in and catch her in mid-change, but—

I found myself on a beach, with waves crashing on the sand. I wore the same T-shirt and gray sweat pants I'd been wearing a few seconds earlier in Kim's apartment. Sunlight blazed off the ocean. I didn't know exactly where this beach was, but I recognized it. This was the beach where Harry had held previous consultations with me—where he gave me my missions to right wrongs for other people.

I inhaled the wondrous smell of salt water as I watched the surf break and rush up the beach almost to my feet. Without looking for him, I said, "Hello, Harry."

"Hello, Jack." Harry was dressed in a charcoal-gray pinstriped suit. His black skin was unwrinkled and looked younger than my weathered, white skin. He had close-cropped dark hair, while I had wavy, light-brown hair that was long enough to go over my ears and collar. His eyes were brown and mine were blue. I've always been of the opinion that my eyes were nicer than Harry's, but maybe that was only *my* opinion. And hopefully, Kim's.

"Things are going well with Ms. Gannon," he said.

"Not that it's any of your business."

"I am glad that you are happy with her. That things seem to be . . . " he paused as he chose the precise term, "progressing."

"Are you taking charge of my general well being?"

"I am here to assist you in achieving happiness."

"I'm guessing that you don't mean happiness like a kid laughing at a stupid joke."

"There's nothing wrong with that kind of happiness."

"Of course not," I replied. "But I still think when you talk about happiness, you mean something deeper. More spiritual."

"You may well be correct." Another of his tiniest of smiles flashed briefly across his face. "Would you like to know why you're here?"

"You'll tell me when you're ready to."

"I *am* ready."

"Was that angel-speak for 'let's get down to business'?"

Harry said nothing. His tiny smile had departed.

I knew he'd tell me what he'd come to tell me in his own good time, so I continued to enjoy the waves and the white, foaming surf and the sun.

"Would you like me to brief you about the person you're being asked to help?" he asked.

"It's great that you say I'm being asked. We go through this every time. You tell me about someone with a problem, and I go help."

"No, the Chairman sends me to explain the situation to you, I explain, and you choose to help."

"Please, can I preempt you before you make a speech about the Chairman and free will? We all know that I will choose to help."

"Or not. You do have free will."

"Yes I do, and I've decided to help without hearing a single detail," I agreed. "Who needs me?"

"George Morita."

He waited for me to react.

"I'm sorry, but is that name supposed to mean something to me?"

"He worked for the CIA as an intelligence analyst at the same time as you were in Afghanistan."

"This may shock you, Harry, but there were a lot of CIA folks in Afghanistan when I was there. I only worked with a handful of them, and I don't remember any analyst named Morita."

"He's familiar with your work."

"He was a lot more likely to know of people like me, who were in ops, than I was to know him. Could we get to the point? Why does Mr. Morita need my help?"

"Have you heard of a firm called Privatus."

"Privatus? No, I don't think so. My Latin is really rusty, but I think 'privatus' means 'private.' I'm going to take a guess that this firm is exactly what it's name says it is: private. And since, once upon a time, Morita worked for the CIA, I'll make another guess that Privatus is a private security firm. Basically a spies-for-hire business. Corporations use these types of businesses for really nasty work against their competitors; governments use them when they don't want anything traced back to the government."

"Yes to your description of Privatus."

"Does Privatus employ a lot of former CIA, MI6, Mossad, BND employees?"

"Yes."

"All of them ops people?"

"Along with many intelligence analysts and cryptographers, too."

"Mostly former NSA?"

"And poor George Morita is not the Employee of the Month at Privatus."

"No, Morita is not in favor with his bosses."

"Oh boy, that could be ugly."

"Yes."

"So this is a dangerous bunch of people to have looking for you. And they're gunning for you."

"Yes."

I closed my eyes, inhaled the salt-water air, and listened to the crashing waves and rushing surf. My stomach was knotting in fear.

"Harry, I want to help, I really do. But . . . but going up against a private version of the CIA is not my idea of a good time. It scares the crap out of me."

"I seem to recall your saying that danger was your business."

"That was a joke when all I had to do was face Russian or Italian Mafiosi. Me fighting an army of guys with experience in black ops . . . that's a whole 'nother level of danger. That's insane."

"You said you'd help."

"False bravado. I'm sorry for Morita, I really am, but this is nuts."

"I don't think I have ever seen you this afraid."

I shrugged, having no response handy. I scanned the immediate area and picked up a flat, round stone the size of my palm. I judged the incoming wave and flicked the stone just over its crest, skipping it for five bounces before it disappeared into the water.

"I'm in love with Kim."

"I know."

"I have a lot more to lose now."

"Yes, a lot more."

"You're not helping."

Harry was quiet for a moment, glancing skyward and then a second later back to me. "Do you think you could be happy in a new life with Kim if you begin by betraying who you've become? By abandoning your sense of purpose?"

"You said I had free will. You said I could say 'no!' What the hell is all this crap about my betraying myself?"

"You can say 'no.' I just want you to think this through before you do. I'm urging you not to make a decision based on fear."

I looked down at the edge of the foamed-out surf was bubbling around my toes.

"I should make a decision based on faith."

"Yes." He put his hand on my shoulder, something he almost never did. "Remember you once said that you work for the Ultimate Power."

"I did say that."

"The only thing I would ask of you is this: remember your belief in that Power. Then decide."

I found another suitable-for-skimming stone. This one skipped eight times over the ocean's surface.

"Eight times? Really?" I turned to Harry, "Did you make it do that?"

"I merely assisted it. You threw it perfectly."

"Okay. Let's go talk to George Morita."

"First, we'll return to Kim's apartment so you can

change into some clothes."

In the tiniest speck of time, we were in Kim's kitchen again.

"Fine. I'll change. Although I haven't got a thing to wear to reassure a man who's got a private CIA gunning for him."

*   *   *

I changed into what was almost my uniform: tan cargo pants and a teal polo shirt. I slid a Walther CCP with eight 9mm rounds per magazine into the cargo pocket on my right thigh. It was a small enough gun to fit comfortably even with an extra magazine slipped in next to the pistol. I don't normally carry a weapon to my first meeting with a client, but I don't normally meet with guys who are trying to evade a firm of renegade agents.

"I'm ready if you—"

Harry transported us to the walkway next to the Reflecting Pool in front of the Lincoln Memorial in Washington, D.C.

"Holy moly," I whispered in awe. "That's your longest-distance whoosh ever."

"As I have tried to explain to you, concepts such as time and distance mean something very different to you than they do to me."

"Yeah, sure, but from the Upper West Side to Washington. That's a major whoosh in anyone's book.

41

Right?"

"I have also told you I do not appreciate you calling it 'whooshing.'"

"You have a term you'd prefer I use?"

"Yes. Travel."

"I can't do that. Travel is mundane. What you do is *not* travel, *it's* magic. Whoooooooosh!"

Harry shook his head then pointed toward the Lincoln Memorial, "The client is this way."

I glanced behind me to the east and saw the World War II Memorial, which from this viewpoint appeared to be at the base of the Washington Monument. Turning back toward the Lincoln Memorial, I could see the Vietnam Memorial to our right, through some trees. To our left, across the Reflecting Pool and past more trees, was the Korean Memorial.

As we moved farther west, I could see the large statue of Lincoln sitting in the center chamber of the majestic memorial. The statue captured Lincoln's fatigue and his noble spirit. He had wanted a united America and had been willing to do whatever he had to do to bring that about. I was confronting the greatest of American presidents, a man with an unwavering sense of purpose—and couldn't believe I was so pathetic that I had considered running from a few former spies. Although, to cut myself a break, Lincoln had been murdered for pursuing his beliefs—I was hoping to avoid that fate.

At the foot of the expansive stairs that led up to the

neoclassical facade of the memorial, an Asian-American man waited for us.

"Hello, Mr. Mitchum," he said and offered his right hand to Harry.

They shook hands, and Harry nodded at me, "This is Jack Tyrrell. Jack, this is George Morita."

"Nice to meet you, Mr. Tyrrell," Morita said. His handshake was firm but not macho-stupid crushingly firm. He had short, black hair and dark eyes. Unless I'd lost my touch for sizing people up, I'd say he was a slender five feet ten or eleven. In his mid-forties just like me.

"You, too." I smiled. "I understand from Harry that we were in Afghanistan at the same time."

"Yes, we never met, but I heard a lot about you."

"Don't believe everything you heard. Especially in the middle of a war."

"Ain't that the truth," he grinned.

"Not that I mean to rush things," I said, "but what can do to help you?"

"As Mr. Mitchum may have told you, I work for Privatus, a private security firm. We do intelligence analysis and black ops for anyone with the money to engage us. We are politically neutral."

"If the money's there, Privatus doesn't care."

"Exactly. If the money's there, Privatus does not care about its clients' policies or goals or whatever results from its activities."

"Fortunes lost, lives lost, it's all the same to

43

Privatus if the clients' money is green and plentiful."

"That's it."

"And you would like to resign your job?"

"Yes, very much."

"Why?"

"Because I can't stay neutral about many of the things we do. It's wrong. I wasn't naive when I took a job at Privatus. I'd seen plenty of shit in Afghanistan. But at least back then I thought I was helping my country. But not now—I had no idea how corrupted I would feel as part of a for-profit organization that produced pain and death anywhere and everywhere."

"And you can't quit? Just sign a non-disclosure agreement and resign from it like a normal job?"

Morita smiled bitterly, "I remember when I was recruited, one of the guys interviewing me said, 'we're not looking for workers to punch a clock; we're looking for employees for life.' I had no idea that he meant it literally. I've worked for Privatus for five years. All of the employees who have left the firm in those five years died."

"Died? Or were killed?"

"You got it."

"I see your problem." I stared up at Lincoln and then turned back to the white spire of the Washington Monument. Very inspiring, but not neither president was providing me the tiniest clue as to how I was to proceed. "I'm confused. How do I help you leave Privatus but not get you killed on your way out the door?"

"As long as the firm is in business, I'll never get out alive. I need you to take down Privatus."

I turned from Morita to Harry; my eyebrows arched as far up my forehead as possible. Which meant a millimeter below my hairline. Harry nodded and pointed me back to Morita. I wanted to ask Harry if he was kidding me. Actually the language I was using in my head was full of F-bombs in bold print with exclamation points. But I kept my mouth shut and stared at Harry. Who nodded again and continued to point me toward Morita.

"Do you really need me? Can't you just dump Privatus's files onto the Internet? Or send them to Wikileaks or *The Washington Post* or *The New York Times*? Expose them as a band of international criminals."

"I don't have the necessary hacking skills to break through the company's security. I'm an analyst—I sift through tons of facts and data points and create possible operations for guys like you. I can't crack our network security."

I asked Harry, "Do you have someone like that?"

"Yes."

"Then our problem is solved. We put Harry's hacker onto this issue, he does a gigantic data dump, and Privatus collapses when all of its dirty laundry is aired."

Morita shook his head, "Privatus stores data on different networks. If they stored everything on a secure Cloud it would be a lot easier. But to collect the data, you almost have to have physical access to the storage."

"Why?"

"Each network has its own security set up with encryption and multiple firewalls so each one has to be hacked individually, and that takes time. And it requires an extraordinarily gifted hacker to do this quickly and leave no traces—the minute Privatus thinks that any of its networks has been compromised, they'll shut them all down. Literally pull the plugs, cutting the power."

"Then there's no way to hack in from outside."

"Unfortunately."

"What if we only hack one network? Maybe we could do that fast enough that we could slip in, grab the data, and then dump it. Wouldn't that be enough to incriminate Privatus so thoroughly it would be stopped?"

"No. In addition to being brutal and amoral, the people at Privatus are very smart. All the data is encrypted. Even if you could hack the network and download data, you'd still have to break the encryption. That takes time. And, once you break the encryption, which would be incredibly time consuming. And then all you would have is one or two pieces of a larger puzzle. A couple of pieces of a jigsaw puzzle, which is rarely enough to know what the entire puzzle looks like."

"What about following the money?"

"Excuse me, but what does that mean?"

"What about trying to hack hack the financial data, only the financial data—wouldn't that be enough?"

"Maybe, but how the heck do you find the

financials in Privatus's digital mountain of data?"

"Shit," I said slowly, extending the "shhhhhhh" sound. "What about sneaking into the Privatus headquarters—where is the headquarters?"

George pointed past the Lincoln Memorial, "Across the river in Arlington."

"What about sneaking in there and grabbing physical evidence?"

"I don't see how you could do it. The place is impossible to get inside with double-locked metal doors, and access requires fingerprint and retinal scanning. Even if you managed to get past all that, there are cameras covering every inch except the secure black room. And—"

"There are armed guards patrolling everywhere," I said.

"Everywhere."

"What about dogs?" I asked. "I always think dogs are a nice touch."

George was nonplussed by my attitude. "Uh, no, no dogs."

"What a shame." I looked at Harry but spoke to George, "Assuming that somehow, someway, I could get inside undetected, would I find enough evidence to wreck Privatus?"

"I'm not sure. There's almost no paperwork and the couple of safes I know about are Grade-A, super-secure safes. Cracking one would be close to impossible. And I don't see how you could do it without alerting the guards or getting picked up on camera."

"Can you contact your old buddies at the CIA and tell them about all this?"

Morita was getting frustrated. "I have *no proof* of anything. Privatus covers its tracks incredibly well. I can't go to my CIA contacts and tell them I don't like my job and have a bad feeling about my employer. They can't take action based on my feelings. Not to mention they don't operate domestically."

"Well . . . this sucks," I moaned. "Do you have any suggestions for bringing Privatus down?"

"I'm not sure. There's a series of ops that will begin in a day or two. It's big and has something to do with global stock markets."

"Wait a minute, are you suggesting that it will be easier for me to break up an ongoing op than for us to hack into the computers?"

"Well, yes. You can't hide an op behind firewalls and encryption and armed guards. You need bodies on the ground, actively pursuing the goals of the op."

"Bodies on the ground with guns?"

"Yes . . . I think so."

"This gets better and better. But the only thing you know is that it involves international financial markets?"

"Yes."

"Where and when is it going to happen?"

"I'm not sure."

"Let me sum up: you don't know what the

operation is, you don't know where it's going to happen, and you're not sure when it's going to happen. But you think I could break it up in such a way that it exposes Privatus. Is that a correct accurate situation report?"

"Yes, I'm sorry, but—"

I turned to Harry, "You're the miracle worker here, not me. I have no idea what I can do." I turned back to Morita, "Sorry, but I honestly don't see how I can help you given so little information."

"I can get the information. Well, I'm pretty sure I can get it. I just didn't want to risk digging around for the info until I knew you agreed that we were going after Privatus."

Pretty damn smart. I should have realized this Morita was just knitting socks while he worked for the CIA.

"How soon do you think you can get what we need?"

"Twenty-four to forty-eight hours."

"Will that be fast enough?"

"I hope so. Does this mean you're going to help me?"

I checked with Harry, who said quietly to me, "You'll get what you need."

Remember, Tyrrell, you're the one who wanted to renew your commitment to the mission. You wanted a sense of purpose. And . . . you work for the Ultimate Authority when it comes to meting out justice. That

Authority will get you whatever you need. I sighed and turned to Morita, saying, "Yes, I'm going to help you."

"Thank you. Thank you very much."

"Harry knows how to contact you, right?"

"Yes."

"We'll be in touch."

George Morita walked toward the Lincoln Memorial, and we watched him until he disappeared in the crowds at the base of the memorial's steps.

A nanosecond later, we were in my apartment. I lived in a brownstone. A cozy one-bedroom place with an exposed brick wall that had been perfect for Maggie and me. Now, it was perfect for me. If only it wasn't crowded with memories.

"Would you consider whooshing me to my vacation destinations?" I asked. "It would eliminate jet leg and make it so much easier for me to enjoy myself."

"You are aware that we do what we do to help others and not to make life easier for you."

"Sure, I'm aware. I just hoped you could throw me the occasional whoosh."

His Mona Lisa smile flitted on and off his face so swiftly I almost missed it.

"I do need a favor for this job though," I said.

"And what is that?"

"There can't be any blowback from Privatus for Kim or my siblings or my nieces and nephews. I have to know that the Chairman will keep Kim and my family safe.

It's not fair for me to expose them to danger because I'm trying to help someone out."

"No, it's not fair. As I told you before, the Chairman recognizes that and will keep them safe."

"I'm guessing the Chairman's network is *not* hackable."

"As you might say: no way, no how."

"Thank you."

"You want some coffee? Or cappuccino?"

"No thanks."

"Well, I'm going to make a cappuccino for myself." I walked into my tiny kitchen, added water and espresso to the machine, and played barista, foaming milk with the machine's steaming spout and creating the perfect cappuccino.

"Why can't you just pluck George out of Privatus and erase their memory of his working there?" I asked. "Wouldn't it be easier than sending me in? Usually my presence results in a lot of . . . mayhem."

"Mayhem?"

"It sounds a bit less malicious and awful than death."

Harry pursed his lips but said nothing.

"Look, you've told me—and I've experienced firsthand—the Chairman makes people forget me and all sorts of information whenever He feels it's necessary. Why not do that for George?"

"The Chairman could do that."

"Great. Can you please ask Him to handle this problem that way?"

"You can ask," Harry replied. "The Chairman listens to you in much the same manner that He listens to me."

"Wait a minute," I sipped cappuccino, trying to absorb the significance of what Harry had just said. "He listens to me the same as He listens to you? Don't you communicate directly with Him?"

"Yes. So do you."

"Are you talking about prayer? 'Cause that's not the same thing at all."

"Yes, it is."

"No it's not. You get direct answers. I don't."

"Maybe you don't like the answers, so you don't want to perceive them as coming directly from the Chairman."

"This is heavy, Doc."

"Excuse me?"

I smiled, "It's what Marty McFly says to Doc Brown in *Back to the Future* whenever some significant thought penetrates Marty's consciousness."

"Ah, the wisdom of the movies."

"If I ask the Chairman to pull George out of Privatus and make them forget he existed, you think His answer will be 'no'."

"I would never presume to know the Chairman's answer. Why do you think He will say 'no' to you?"

"Because He enjoys messing with me."

Harry didn't respond.

"Because," I said after a long moment, "making the folks at Privatus forget George won't stop them from doing all the evil that they do."

"Messing with you and stopping evil sound like equally plausible answers from the Chairman."

"Yeah, right." I drank the last of my cappuccino, rinsed the cup, and placed it in the sink. I asked, "Will you know when George gets the information?"

"Of course."

"You'll be in contact with him instantly?"

"You have to ask?"

"Yes. I'm not divinely inspired like you. I have to work this stuff a step at a time. So . . . after you're in contact with George, you'll let me know?" I asked.

"Yes. And you'll immediately solve George's problem, correct?"

"Sarcasm doesn't suit you."

"But it's perfect for you." He whooshed out before I could reply.

3

PRIVATUS HEADQUARTERS, ARLINGTON, VA

THREE PEOPLE SAT IN LEATHER ARMCHAIRS at one end of a massive conference table in the "black room." There were no computers, no television monitors, no windows, and no phones in the room. A single, ultra-thick door with a black door lever was the only entrance. In the corner diagonally opposite the door was the only electronic device in the room: a black metal box with a glowing red light to indicate its power was on. This jammed all cell phone and radio signals, cutting the room off from the world. The ceiling, floor, and walls were cement with sound-dampening foam. Recessed lighting in the ceiling created the effect of a contemporary cave.

A woman, Desjardins, sat at the head of the table, her long blonde hair pulled into a neat ponytail. She had dark-gray-framed glasses, which emphasized her well-defined jawline. She wore a steel-gray pant suit that matched the athletic hardness of her body.

To her right sat Freund, middle-aged, with a tight suit and a thick body. He had tiny, cold blue eyes. His graying crew cut was not flattering, but then no hairstyle would have softened his face.

To Desjardins's left sat Hawkins. Well over six feet

tall with broad shoulders and a deep chest. Dark hair, dark eyes, and thin lips. He was more casually dressed than the other two, wearing slacks and a denim jacket over a button-down shirt. He looked lethal even doing something as simple as sitting ramrod straight in his chair.

Desjardins was the boss, Freund directed operations, and Hawkins actually executed the operations.

"You can have anyone you want for your team," Desjardins said to Hawkins. "Project Exchange is the largest scale engagement we've ever done."

"Not to be all about me," Hawkins grinned, "but what's my fee on this engagement?"

"Five millions dollars. Two million up front with the rest upon completion."

Hawkins's grin widened. "And who do I have to kill for that?"

Freund smiled. "There will be some high-profile targets in this engagement. Other than your assignments, you might want to keep the killing to a minimum." His English was precise although with a German accent.

"Less exposure?" Hawkins asked.

"Exactly." Freund turned to Desjardins, "Do we have the project scope from the client, yet?"

She shook her head, "Just the parameters." To Hawkins, "Your team will be attacking different organizations in various locations, including Paris. The result of your operations will be massive disruptions in European financial markets."

"A Parisian assignment? I can taste the food already."

"You may not have time to indulge your inner gourmet."

"I can dream, can't I?"

"Why not?" she asked lightly, but there was no humor in her voice. "I'll have the operational specs for you within twenty-four hours. I expect you to have a team and a plan within twenty-four hours of that."

"Forty-eight hours till Go Time. Copy that."

Desjardins gestured toward the door. Hawkins nodded, stood up from the table, and exited the room. The door made no sound as it shut behind him.

Freund waited a moment then he turned to Desjardins. "Are you sure about him?"

"Don't let his flippancy fool you."

"Americans," Freund muttered.

"This American was with the Delta Force, and then in the CIA's Directorate of Operations. More than fifty confirmed kills."

"I know all that."

"I know you do. Which makes me wonder why you continue to bring up the issue. Does Privatus have someone better qualified? Should someone better qualified to lead this engagement?"

"I'm sorry. He makes me uneasy."

"He makes everyone uneasy. That's why he's perfect for this job."

*　　*　　*

After Harry left my apartment, I ejected the magazine from my Walther, cleared the chamber, placed the pistol in its case, locked it, and put it on a high shelf in my closet. Since I live alone, this seemed like adequately safe gun storage.

I made another cup of cappuccino and relaxed in an upholstered armchair in the living room. I stared out the window at the lush leafiness of the trees along West 76th Street. I finished the cup and remembered that my departure from Kim's had been sudden and silent. She had no clue what had happened to me. I called her.

"Did Harry whoosh you away?"

"There's no fooling you, is there?"

"When you date a government-trained private detective cum troubleshooter who works for the Chairman, you have to accept sudden exits and entrances. Where are you now?"

"My apartment. Had to put away a gun."

"Wait a minute, you've only been gone about an hour—have you been shooting at people?"

"No, no, no. Not at all. No. It just seemed to be the prudent thing to do."

"To carry a gun?"

"Yes, sometimes my job requires a bit of firepower. This morning seemed like one of those times."

"Better you than me."

"It's so comforting to hear that you know your limitations when it comes to guns."

"Don't tempt me, buster."

"Buster? Have you been watching old movies again?" I shook my head. "Never mind. Would you like to spend the rest of Saturday together?"

"Yes. Definitely."

"I'll be there in ten."

It actually took me twelve minutes to walk to Kim's place. I had to wait out a couple of red lights then stopped to help an old lady get out of her taxi and carry her two bags of goodies from Zabar's to the doorman of her apartment building. It was worth the effort to overhear her tell the doorman what a nice *young* man I was.

Kim didn't comment on my tardiness. She did throw her arms around my neck and kiss me for a long time.

"I love you," she said.

"I love you, too."

"Is Harry going to involve you in something dangerous?"

"You know that's not how it works. I have to decide whether I want to get involved."

"Do you want to this time?"

"Yes. Reluctantly, but yes."

"Why reluctantly?"

"Well . . ." I sighed instead of replying. I wasn't

sure I wanted to tell Kim that I was terrified of Privatus, notwithstanding Harry's reassurances of the Chairman's help.

"Is this going to be long and complicated?" she asked.

"Depends on whether you want a bit of witty repartee or full disclosure."

"What do you think?"

"You want full disclosure."

"Yes. Let's get lunch, and you can disclose while we eat."

"Sounds good."

"Croque Monsieur at Truffaut's?"

"*Magnifique!*"

We strolled to the southwest corner of West 78th Street and Columbus Avenue and found an outdoor table at Truffaut's. We both ordered croque monsieur, which came with a small salad. As we waited for the food, I noticed a number of street vendors lined up along the iron railing that bordered the western grounds of the Museum of Natural History.

"Maybe we should go shopping after lunch," I pointed across Columbus to the street vendors.

"Oh no, you're not getting off. Don't think you can distract me with trinkets and baubles."

"Hey, trinkets and baubles worked for Peter Minuit when he bought Manhattan Island."

"Not me. I want full disclosure. What is it Harry

59

wants you to do?"

"The Chairman," I said emphatically, "wants me to assist someone with retirement planning."

"Really? Retirement planning? Why does someone need a government-trained private detective cum troubleshooter's help with retirement?"

"He works for the kind of organization that frowns upon retirement."

"Ooooh," she said, frowning. "What are you talking about? Mafia? Russian Mafia? Eastern European bad guys? Narco lords from Latin America? Chinese spies?"

"In some ways, it's worse than any of those."

"What could be worse?" she chuckled. "The IRS?"

"Well, yes, the IRS. But no, it's someone else. It's an agency of spies for hire. A privately owned, for-profit CIA."

"That doesn't sound good."

"It's not."

"Are a lot of their employees government-trained types like you?"

"All of them. Former CIA, Special Forces, Navy SEALS, Mossad, MI6. And the alumni of some other, equally dangerous groups."

"Sounds like a tough bunch of people."

I watched the people shopping at the sidewalk vendors and found myself wishing that the only decision in front of me was a buy/no-buy choice.

"Yeah," I said. "They're very tough."

Kim smiled, "But you're tougher right?"

"Believe me, there are people out there who are tougher than I am."

"Come on," she was making light of it, "I've seen you in action against a handful of Mafiosi. You're the real thing."

"You're right, I am. But . . . when I was in training for Special Forces, I had this sergeant who constantly reminded me and everyone else, 'You all think you're tough. You're all gonna be Green Berets. But there's always someone out there who's tougher than you are.' And one of the guys said, 'I haven't met him yet, Sarge.' And the sergeant smiled and said, 'Your time will come.'"

Kim was serious now, "Did he train you what to do when your time comes?"

"Yes. He told us that we had to refuse to lose."

"What?"

"Refuse to lose. Refuse to be beaten. No matter what."

"Does that really work?"

"It has so far."

She relaxed, dropping her shoulders. "So . . . you are the toughest guy."

"So far. But the people who work for this private security firm . . . well . . . they're mostly like me."

"And your client wants to retire from the firm?"

"Yes."

"Is that what the Chairman wants?"

"Yes."

"Is there a 'but' coming?"

"I'm supposed to help my client retire by bringing down the whole organization."

Kim leaned forward, wide-eyed in silence. I thought she was going to say "What?!?" but the waiter arrived with our food before she could express her surprise and exasperation.

After the waiter left, Kim leaned over the table and hissed, "You're kidding me, right?"

"No. But Harry assured me that I'll get whatever I need to do this."

"Does that mean you won't get killed?"

I shook my head.

"What?!?"

"If the Chairman decides He's done with me, than I'm done. But if He's not finished with me, I'll get whatever I need to do the job."

"You'll pardon me if I don't find that comforting."

"I don't find it comforting either. But if the Chairman is done with me, I could get hit by the proverbial bus on the way home today."

"I'm confused. Are we talking about predestination? When your time is up, it's up?"

"I don't believe in predestination."

"Well, how do you square that with your comment about the bus getting you?"

"What I meant is that if I make the seemingly safe choice and don't take on the scary renegade spies, I might end up dead anyway. You never know."

"But you said if the Chairman is done with you, you'd get hit by the bus. Are you saying when He's done, He's done? That your life is already mapped out."

"No. If it's already mapped out, then there's no need for free will. And believe me, Harry has made it clear that free will is very, very important to the Chairman."

"How does—" she made air quotes around her next phrase "—'if the Chairman's done with me' square with free will?"

"Before I answer, I just want to emphasize that this is just my opinion and not what Harry has told me."

"I understand."

"I think the Chairman understands that there are multiple paths that result from each and every decision we make, so He waits for our decisions—our choices—to play out in real time. It's as if there's an Option A and an Option B and an Option C to His will. Occasionally, He makes adjustments."

"Adjustments? You mean miracles?"

"When I look at what's happened to me since I began working with Harry, I have to believe the Chairman has worked miracles by allowing me to survive gunshots and stabbings and whatever."

"If He's adjusted things to save you in the past, why won't He keep doing that for you?"

"He might. Then again, He might be done with me, and then I'll die. From a bullet or a bus."

She considered all we'd just discussed for a minute. "So, if there are Options A, B and C, why choose the option that has you fighting with a super-dangerous organization? Why make that choice?"

I drank some of my water and wondered about her question. Why, Tyrrell? What the hell?

"Because this organization kills people. And I can help."

After a long moment when neither of us said anything, Kim pointed out, "Our food is getting cold."

It was impossible to argue with that. We both began eating. The croque monsieurs were wonderful. It wasn't inaccurate to say that a croque monsieur is just an open-faced grilled cheese-and-ham sandwich. But such a description was pathetically incapable of capturing the wonder of it.

We settled into a comfortable silence and enjoyed the warm Saturday afternoon, the chatter from nearby tables, and the view across to the museum. When we finished our meal, we both ordered café au lait and agreed to split a Napoleon. Perfection.

At that exact moment the dessert and coffees arrived, Harry appeared on the sidewalk next to our table.

"Would you like to join us?" Kim asked.

"He's here for me," I said. "Aren't you?"

"Yes. I'm sorry to interrupt, but we should be

going."

"Could I finish my coffee and dessert?"

Harry said nothing but continued to loom over us.

"Okay," I said, finishing the café au lait, then dabbing my mouth with a napkin. I reached for my wallet, but Kim waved me off.

"I've got it," she said.

"Thank you."

"You can make it up to me. Later."

"Sounds like a plan."

"That's my plan."

We both smiled. I turned to Harry and said, "I'm ready."

Faster than I could comprehend, he had whooshed me inside my apartment.

"You should prepare while I brief you on tonight's assignment."

"What do you mean by prepare? Tactical nukes? Maybe just some body armor and a bazooka?"

"Three men are going to attempt a kidnapping."

"And I'm supposed to make sure they fail in the attempt?"

"Exactly."

"Do I need to dress formally for the occasion?"

"No."

"Public place?"

"Outside a restaurant."

"I'm guessing the kidnappers will probably be

driving a van?"

"Yes."

I went to my bedroom closet and pulled a steel case and a wooden box from the top shelf. I grabbed a black, ballistic-nylon backpack off a hook at the back of the closet. I spread the case, the box, and the pack on my bed. Then I sent a text from my phone to a digital lock inside the closet. The right wall clicked open. Hiding behind the false wall was a cabinet about a foot deep, seven-feet tall, and two-feet wide. I swung the false wall back on its hinges and reached for a large duffle-pack. Like the backpack, it was black and made of ballistic nylon. What can I say? I prefer carrying my weapons in matching luggage.

I changed into a black T-shirt, black cargo pants, and dark-gray, crepe-soled shoes. Yes, it was a stereotypical cat burglar outfit, but it worked. And yes, now my black clothes matched my black luggage. The duffle was filled with lethal goodies—the official, master tool set of a government-trained private detective cum troubleshooter. I would select weapons from the duffle to fill my backpack, the specific tool kit for this operation. The duffle went on the bed, next to the other items. I took two steel cases down from the high shelf in the closet. From one case I took my shoulder holster, slipped into it, and placed a Ruger SR9 in the holster. I put an extra magazine of 9mm bullets into the left cargo pocket and put two more mags in a pocket in the backpack. From the other case, I took the Walther and one of its spare magazines went into my right-side cargo pocket. A dark-gray windbreaker went over my shirt. It was too warm for a windbreaker, but it covered my the Ruger, and that was more important to me than staying cool.

Harry had followed me into the bedroom and watched my prep.

"Am I ready?"

"You might want to add a little something—"

"Smokey? Percussive?"

"I would."

Looking through the duffle, I found mini-grenades. I took four: two were smoke grenades and two flash-bangs, which made lots of noise and light but weren't lethal. I held them up for Harry's inspection. He nodded.

"And, just to err on the safe side . . ." I dug through the duffle and pulled out an Uzi submachine gun as if I were a magician producing a rabbit from a hat. The Uzi and a pair of extra magazines for it also went into the backpack with the grenades.

"Finally, what could be appropriate parting gifts for our three kidnappers—" I showed Harry three plasticuffs and two small, magnetic GPS trackers. "Now I'm perfectly accessorized for a Saturday night out in New York." I considered that for a moment. "I'm guessing we're going to be operating in the city."

"Yes."

"But first, you're taking me to D.C. to see George Morita for a briefing."

"You're smarter than you look."

"Not really."

*   *   *

Harry whooshed us to the 17th Street side of the World War II Memorial. The Washington Monument towered above us to the east. To the west, at the other end of the Reflecting Pool, Lincoln sat in his memorial, visible even at this distance. Touring the DC memorials one at a time while having conversations about life and death would not have been the way I planned a visit to Washington, but sometimes the ugly realities got in the way of my best-laid plans.

Morita walked out of the World War II Memorial and joined us on the sidewalk. He seemed unaware that we had instantaneously materialized at our rendezvous.

"Why do we keep meeting in public?" I asked. "Do you think Privatus has bugged your home?"

"I think they bug all their employees' home. I was going to sweep for bugs then decided not to. What's the point?"

"Don't you feel that's a wee bit paranoid?"

"I'm pretty damn sure that I mentioned that no one leaves Privatus alive," George responded, looking askance at me. To be honest, I got that a lot. I needed to improve my people skills.

"Yes. You did."

Harry said, "Do you have something for us?"

George grimaced, "Just what I've observed. I can't ask a lot of questions, and as I told you there's no way to get files off the network without triggering alarms. There's no Internet use without oversight through real-time IP scanners. If you try to use e-mail, it sets off an alarm. When you leave, you do it through a body scanner and a metal detector."

I groaned softly, "I hope you have an amazing memory."

Harry said, "Could you give us the broad strokes?"

"Sure. Privatus is working for Waronov-Tybalt Investment Group, a private-equity firm, founded and now directed by a couple of billionaires. They're just like Privatus—if the money's there, they don't care."

"Sounds like a match made in heaven," I said.

"Really?" Harry grimaced. To George, "Please continue."

"I don't have all the details, but it looks to me like Waronov-Tybalt will be making a series of moves against several tech companies that provide cyber-security for stock exchanges and financial markets."

"Like firewalls?" I asked.

"Yes, but there's a hell of a lot more to it than firewalls."

"What's the goal?"

"I'm not sure. I think it's a bit like a VC firm: You invest in a lot of different things and hope that you get one or two big hits out of every twenty. But whatever it is, it's huge. Waronov-Tybalt's contract is the largest ever for Privatus."

"You said that Waronov-Tybalt is going to make moves against some tech companies. What does 'moves' mean?"

"I think there's going to be some kind of industrial sabotage. Maybe a kidnapping of a key player at one of the tech firms. I'm sorry, but I don't really know."

"And they're going to make multiple moves to increase the odds of success for their overall portfolio?"

"Just like a venture capitalist," George said.

"Couldn't Waronov-Tybalt just buy out the companies instead of attacking them?"

"I'm an analyst. I'm not paid to guess, but if I had to, I'd say that whatever is going on is huge: Waronov-Tybalt is trying to change international financial services. And they don't care what it takes to accomplish that. You don't engage Privatus if you're willing to play by the rules."

"You engage them for the opposite," Harry said.

"To break the law." I said. "To kill, if necessary."

"That's why I want out," George interjected. "That's why I have to get out. I left the CIA, yes, for the money. But also because I didn't want to be part of the black ops and the killing. But now my analysis is leading to the exact same thing."

"I can make some pretty good guesses as to how Privatus keeps its books secret. But how do the firm's clients hide the payments to Privatus?"

"Waronov-Tybalt is the perfect client for Privatus," George said. "It has no stockholders and a gigantic cash flow, which makes it very easy to hide the expenditures to pay Privatus. The normal fee structure is $10 million annually, plus operational expenses. If a client wants a very difficult operation, the retainer is increased or a special operation fee is charged."

"Can you give us an idea of what Privatus's deal with Waronov-Tybalt is?" I asked.

"Huge," George showed us a tight-lipped grin. "Absolutely huge. The annual retainer is $50 million. The operational fee for the current engagement is another $50 million. Plus expenses. The operations team leader is getting $5 million. That's for one guy."

"One guy gets five mil—I think I'm underpaid."

Harry replied, "It depends on your compensation metrics."

I wanted to come back with a truly snappy answer, but I couldn't come up with one. I resorted to muttering "Compensation metrics." I asked George, "Who is this $5 million man?"

"Ever heard of Daryl Hawkins? Six feet two or three, dark hair, brown eyes. Former Delta, then spent a bunch of years in the CIA. Fifty-three confirmed kills."

"Scar on his forehead just over his left eyebrow?"

"That's the guy."

"I met him in Afghanistan. He's not worth $5 million, but he's a very tough piece of work."

"The word is he was a lot more mellow back in Afghanistan."

"Can't say I'm looking forward to renewing this old acquaintance. I'm guessing that Hawkins gets to pick his own team."

"Yes."

"Any idea who?"

"No, sorry. Whoever they are, they'll all be just about as nasty as he is."

"Something to look forward to." I paused, thinking about my next question. "How does Privatus guarantee loyalty *to and from* a client? I mean, if I hire a bunch of people as deadly as Privatus, I want to know they're not going to come after me in a couple of years when my competitor pays them more money."

"Good question. Privatus offers a 100-year retainer program to guarantee loyalty to client. The client has to put funds into escrow to cover a minimum of ten years and then renews the escrow perpetually. The 100-year retainer protects both ways. If someone else tries to hire Privatus to "get" an existing client—Privatus alerts and protects that client. And the retainer guarantees Privatus a revenue stream. Since no client or Privatus that has been around more than a hundred years, it's virtually everlasting. Everybody wins."

"Except the people who get in the way of Privatus."

"That's true. Unfortunately," George agreed.

"Who runs Privatus?" I asked.

"The CEO is a woman named Desjardins."

"Desjardins? French name that means 'of the garden.' Is that her real name?"

"No. And I'm sorry, but I have no idea what her real name is."

"Can you describe her?"

"American, blonde, fortysomething, slender, five feet four. Former CIA."

"Anybody else I should know about?"

"A German guy named Freund."

"That's cute," I turned to Harry. "Freund is the German word for—"

"Friend," Harry interjected. "Likely another assumed name, correct?"

"Yes. I know, it's a lot of assumed names. These people are freaks for taking every possible security measure," George said. "And I don't know anything about Freund, other than he runs clandestine operations for Privatus."

"So he's probably a pretty nasty guy, whatever the hell his background is," I said.

"Yes, he is."

I contemplated the World War II Memorial's oval plaza, which had a large pool in the middle, surrounded by granite pillars. Triumphal arches rose on the north and south ends; one each for the Atlantic and Pacific theaters of the war. Many critics had spoken against the design, but I found it inspiring. I didn't know anything about the architecture and design behind the various memorials in Washington, but I knew what touched my heart. The World War II Memorial made me appreciate the sacrifices of my fellow vets—sixteen million of them—who fought in that war. I shivered involuntarily and turned back to George.

"What more do you know about tonight?"

"I wish I had more, but all I know is that Hawkins is supposed to kidnap a man named Alex Grayson from a restaurant. Grayson is the CEO of GraySecurFirm, which is a cyber-security company."

"Why kidnap? Why not kill him?"

"I don't know."

"Does Privatus have someone on the inside of GraySecurFirm? You seem to know when and where Grayson will be vulnerable."

"Inside? I don't know. Sorry."

"It's okay. Where's the kidnapping taking place and do you know when Grayson will be there?"

"At The Plymouth St. Grill in DUMBO. I think that's Brooklyn—"

"It is," I interjected. "DUMBO means Down Under the Manhattan Bridge Overpass. I know where it is. Any idea as to the timing of this snatch?"

"Sorry, but I don't know when."

"Okay, then," I said. To Harry, "Guess this means we're going on a stakeout."

"Yes."

"George, we'll be in touch. If you learn anything more, you'll let Harry know, right?"

"Right. Good luck. You're going to need it."

4

A Nissan NV cargo van was parked about fifty feet in front of us on Plymouth Street in Brooklyn. It was huge, the roofline must have been eight-feet high, and it was a dusty, dark green color. You could have squeezed a Porsche or Ferrari inside it, making it the perfect transport for your pampered sports car. Or for your high-speed getaway vehicle. The van was directly across the street from the Plymouth St. Grill, and if it wasn't full of a three-man team of kidnappers, my internal radar was malfunctioning.

Harry and I were sitting in a Ford Fusion with two cars separating our front bumper from the Nissan's rear. The Manhattan Bridge was visible through our windshield, looming almost directly over us. Behind us was the Brooklyn Bridge. A small park to our left was all that separated us from the East River.

"Where'd you get this car?" I asked.

"I rented it." He smiled a little furtively.

"Do you have a valid credit card? I mean . . . can you just rent a car like anyone else?"

Harry's furtive smile disappeared. "You find it easy to believe that I can 'whoosh' in and out of places or that I can keep us invisible, but you find it difficult to accept that

I am able to rent a car?"

"Well . . . when you put it that way. . . . Are we invisible right now?"

"We are. The car is not."

"This is the perfect stake out. Where were you back in my Marshal days?"

"Watching over you. You never noticed."

"It creeps me out when you say things like that."

"Nevertheless."

"Okay, I know, it's all my fault that I never noticed the Chairman's presence. That I never realized He was working—through you—in my life. It's my fault for being a spiritual troglodyte."

"Very well stated."

"Not to change the subject, but do you mind if we turn to the project at hand?"

"Not at all."

"Do we know why Privatus, working for Waronov-Tybalt, wants to kidnap Grayson?"

"George did not have that information."

"I was hoping that you might have more information than George. Seeing as how you are in the employ of the ultimate authority."

Harry, as he so often did, glanced upward for the tiniest fraction of a moment then turned to me. "Grayson's company handles cyber-security for many of the world's major stock exchanges and online retailers. He was about to pitch a major piece of business to Euronext Paris and the

Frankfurt Stock Exchange."

"And Waronov-Tybalt doesn't want that to happen, so they hire to Privatus to kidnap him."

"Yes. But maybe you can explain why they're kidnapping instead of killing. Wouldn't it be easier to murder Grayson?" Harry asked.

"This is just a theory on my part, but I'm guessing they want to paralyze Grayson's company. If he's killed, then the company would have to replace him, which might cause a delay in pitching their plan to Euronext Paris and Frankfurt, but pitch it they would. On the other hand, if Grayson is kidnapped, especially if there are ransom demands, then his company gets stuck in ransom negotiations. Grayson's second in command wouldn't know if he or she should become the new boss or wait and see if they can rescue the old boss."

"Is the ransom an important part of Privatus's operation?"

"No, it's small change compared to the money they're getting from Waronov-Tybalt. They're going to ask for ransom to stretch things out."

I dug into the side pocket of my backpack and pulled out a GPS tracker. I activated it and checked that my smart phone was registering it.

A black Chevy Suburban pulled to the sidewalk in front of the Plymouth St. Grill. The Suburban had darkly tinted windows, a deluxe trim package for the grill and wheels, and was almost certainly on limo duty. My inner radar was pinging madly—Grayson was about to be kidnapped.

"Is Grayson alone?" I asked.

"His wife is with him."

"Does he have personal security?"

"His driver and another man inside the restaurant, at the bar. Both are former NYPD detectives."

"Did one of these security guys sell him out to Privatus?"

"Yes."

"Oh . . . great."

The driver of the Suburban climbed out of the vehicle and walked around to the rear door nearest the restaurant.

I opened my door, stepped out of the Fusion, and walked down the sidewalk toward the rear of the Nissan van. The reflection in the large side-view mirror showed me that the driver was looking across the street at the restaurant. I ducked next to the rear bumper, lay down on the street, and placed the GPS tracker on the steel of the trailer hitch where it was out of sight. I got to my knees but remained crouched behind the Nissan.

From my vantage point it was hard to tell, but it looked like some people were about to exit the glass doors of the Plymouth Street Grill. I heard the doors of the Nissan cargo van open, leaned low to the pavement, and looked under the van. Two pairs of feet on the driver's side on the passenger side.

79

A man's low voice, coming from the passenger side of the van, said, "Keep the motor running, your weapon ready."

"Yes, sir."

I got to my feet, pulled the Walther from my pocket, and staying hidden in the shadow of the van's tall, bulky cargo area, watched two men cross the street. They were wearing dark windbreakers or sweat shirts, dark baseball caps with no logos, and thick, black-framed eyeglasses. As they approached the restaurant, they pulled bandanas up to cover their faces like bandits in an old western. I wasn't sure, but it looked as if both were carrying pistols with suppressors on them. There was no way for me to see if either man was Hawkins, but one of them was about my height, six feet two, and I was pretty damn sure that was Hawkins and he was going to snatch Grayson.

At the Plymouth St. Grill, a short, middle-aged man wearing a suit over a black T-shirt and a short, middle-aged woman in a black silk jacket and a flower-print dress exited through the glass door to the sidewalk, followed closely by the security who had been waiting at the bar. The driver of the Suburban opened the back door for the couple.

As the woman began to enter the Suburban, the taller Privatus man came around the SUV's hood and shot the driver twice. He bounced off the door and dropped to the sidewalk. Grayson's second security guy was reaching for his gun when he was shot twice and fell to the sidewalk.

The tall guy grabbed Mr. Grayson by his right arm, pressed his pistol into Grayson's ribs, and began tugging the short man across the street to the Nissan.

He called over his shoulder, "Kill her."

Grayson and his wife both screamed. The Privatus operative holding the woman aimed his gun at her skull, and—

Under my breath, I whispered, "Please help me, God." I stepped out from behind the Nissan and shouted, "Hey!"

Both Privatus men spun toward me. I raised my right arm, aimed the Walther, and fired as quickly as I possibly could. The man holding Mrs. Grayson was using her body as a screen with only the right side of his face, under the ball cap and bandana, visible. The shot needed to be a miraculous. I fired. Caught the man in his right eye. He spun backward, flopping to the sidewalk.

The tall man who had taken Grayson fired at me. He missed. By the time he fired for the second time, I had scuttled behind the Nissan, moving toward the driver's side. The driver was stepping out of the van. I shot him three times in the chest.

A low, harsh voice shouted, "Stop or I kill him."

I dove to the ground and checked the street from under the Nissan. There were two pairs of legs one close in front of the other. Hitting either man's legs was impossible.

"Throw out your gun or I kill him."

"Yeah, right," I muttered. I pushed off the ground

and slowly inched close to the driver's door. Carefully edging to the window, I cast a look through the van at the street. I couldn't see the two men, which meant they couldn't see me. I gripped the handle of the large, sliding door to the cargo area and pulled it open. I stepped up onto the van's floor and grabbed the upper hinge mechanism of the sliding door. I swung my right foot up, planted it on the door handle, straightened my leg, and pulled myself onto the van's roof.

I stretched flat on the roof and listened. There were no footsteps. No sounds from either of the Graysons. I inched to the far edge of the roof, the part closest to the tall kidnapper and his victims.

Mr. Grayson was being held in front of the Privatus man, who said, "All right, I guess we have to get dramatic about this. I'm going to count to three. If you don't toss your weapon and come out with your hands up, I kill Grayson. Got it?"

He waited a second, "One . . ."

From the van's roof I had an excellent angle on the kidnapper. I lined up my shot.

"Two . . . oh, okay, you're a last-second guy . . . thr—"

My bullet caught him in the upper chest. He staggered back then fell to the ground. Grayson ran toward his wife, who was still cowering near the Suburban. I was about to slide down over the nose of the Nissan when Mr. Tall Privatus fired. He was lying flat on his back, which is

82

not a great way to aim at anyone, but the bullet was close enough that I heard it whistle past me. I was forced to scramble down off the van the same way I had climbed up. Bullets thudded into the side of the Nissan but none came within a foot of me. Thank God—vans are not known for their bullet-proofing.

I ran past the rear of the Nissan and crouched for cover behind the small Toyota SUV parked immediately behind it. I could look up the left side of the van to the driver's door and through the Toyota's windows and see a large portion of the street.

Sirens announced the imminent arrival of the law. The tall Privatus agent came around the front corner of the van and fired several times at the Toyota. I ducked for cover as the glass in the SUV's windows shattered and rained upon me.

The firing stopped, the Nissan's engine roared, and the van pulled out of its parking space at high speed, heading toward the Manhattan Bridge.

I ran for the Fusion, jumped in beside Harry, turned on the engine, shifted into drive, and roared off in pursuit of the Nissan.

"Thanks for your help," I said.

"You're welcome," Harry replied.

"I was being sarcastic."

"That's obvious. Would you mind a question?"

Ahead of me, the Nissan made a tire-squealing right turn onto Pearl Street. Seconds later, I did the same.

"Sure, go ahead, ask."

"Do you really think you made the shot that saved Mrs. Grayson without any help?"

"Oh, yeah, well . . . when you put it that way."

The Nissan raced through a bewildering series of left and right turns as it maneuvered to get onto the Manhattan Bridge. Given the size of the van, the tall Privatus guy must have been one hell of a driver. I was having a hard time keeping up with him, and I was driving a small, agile car.

As the van roared onto the Bridge, I pulled my phone out of my pocket and handed it to Harry. "Please launch the GPS tracker app."

He did. The app's display showed the van on the bridge. I eased off my pace.

"Won't he be suspicious if he can't see you in his rear-view mirrors?"

"Yes, but he's probably desperate to dump that thing. It's standard operating procedure: steal a vehicle then get rid of it as soon as the job is done. Or as soon as things go bad. He might be suspicious about our dropping out of sight, but he's still going to abandon the van as soon as he can."

"And you can drive much more safely. Something Kim will be grateful for."

"I'm not that bad."

"You're not that good."

"What about Grayson's security team?"

Harry shook his head, "They're dead."

"Shit."

The van was nearing the Manhattan end of the bridge.

"Shit," I repeated in frustration. "Was one of the dead security men the one who sold out Grayson to Privatus?"

"Yes."

"That means Privatus was tying up loose ends when it killed them."

"Was Mrs. Grayson just another loose end?"

"Apparently."

"Is that why you started shooting?"

"I had to save her."

"Why? Your mission is to help George Morita."

"My mission is to help people who need help."

"You saved her life."

"With the help of a miracle shot."

"I do what I can. Although . . . to be completely honest, that was the Chairman. Not me."

We descended off the bridge as we reached Manhattan. The GPS tracker app showed the van had gone through Chinatown and was headed west on Canal Street.

But then the van stopped at the northwest corner of Canal and Lafayette Street.

"Shit!" I said. "There's a subway station there."

I accelerated as much as I could, but Canal is one of New York's perpetually busy streets, and it was difficult to drive fast. Two minutes later, I spotted the van, parked next to the green staircase that climbed from the sidewalk down to the subway. Two minutes was an eternity—the tall Privatus man could easily be on his way on a No. 4 or No. 6 Train. I jerked to a stop directly behind the van and hurtled out of our car.

At the exact second I shut the Fusion's door, the van disappeared in a fireball. The explosion threw m backwards through the air, and I crashed onto the hood of a passing taxi. I rolled off the hood and slammed into the pavement. And blacked out.

*　*　*

PRIVATUS HEADQUARTERS

HAWKINS WAS SITTING ON AN EXAMINATION TABLE. Desjardins and Freund watched as a doctor carefully took off the bullet-proof vest and cut away the black T-shirt. Underneath, Hawkins's upper chest was black-and-blue.

"You'll need a new vest," said the doctor. "Other than that, and some soreness, you're in good shape."

"Lucky me," Hawkins said.

"Doctor, could you give us a moment?" Desjardins asked.

The doctor stepped out of the room.

Freund said, "What happened? One man was able to stop three of you from doing your job?"

"That guy was some kind of magic warrior,"

Hawkins grunted. "The shot he put on Whitaker was unbelievable. Million to one. And going for position on me by climbing on the roof of the van—pretty damn smart. Guy should be working for us, not against us."

"Do you have any idea who it was?" Desjardins asked.

Hawkins shook his head. "Any surveillance video at the restaurant? Or maybe at Canal and Lafayette where I dumped the van?"

"The security video at the restaurant is focused on the outside of the front door. As for the traffic cameras at the intersection on Canal, all they show is a man getting out of a Ford Fusion and being blown backward when the van exploded."

"Can we run facial recognition on it?"

Desjardins shrugged, "The video was blurry."

"What about hospitals? Any man like that show up in an ER?"

"No."

"And the car?"

"Rented by a man named Harry Mitchum."

Hawkins grinned, "So, we got him."

"There is no Harry Mitchum. Fake address. Photo on the driver's license doesn't match any police or DMV databases."

"Who are these guys?" Hawkins asked.

Freund suggested, "Part of Grayson's security team, perhaps?"

Desjardins disagreed, "No. That's probably the story that will go to the press, but no. If Grayson had a larger team, it would have been obvious. And would have scared off any attempt at a kidnapping. Whoever Grayson's saviors were, they're new players in the game."

Freund said, "What now? Do you want me to set up another kidnapping attempt?"

"No point," Hawkins said. "We don't have anyone inside with Grayson, and he'll triple his security. Round-the-clock guards at his home and office, restricted travel—no, it's not worth it."

"I agree," said Desjardins. "We move our focus to our other operations."

"What about the magic warrior?" Hawkins asked.

"If I were you," replied Desjardins, "I'd make it a point to kill him the next time I see him."

* * *

A giant fist had punched me in my entire body. Every single joint, muscle, ligament, tendon, bone, and nerve ending ached. Even my hair ached. Really, I swear. Even my hair hurt.

I opened my eyes one eyelash at a time. I didn't want the movement of my eyelids to set off a cascade of pain throughout my dead body. Actually, if I had been a corpse, I would have been beyond pain. Guess I was lucky.

When my eyes were finally open and able to focus, I realized that I was on the couch in my living room. Harry was leaning over me and offering a mug of something hot.

"What is that?" I croaked.

"Cappuccino, of course."

"*You* can make cappuccino?"

"Of course."

"Am I capable of sitting up? My head won't fall off and roll away if I straighten up, will it?"

He reached out with his left hand, firmly but gently grabbed my right arm, and helped me sit up.

"Wow . . . ," I said slowly. "That van blowing up was no damn fun at all."

"No. Not for you."

"Was anyone hurt?"

"Just you."

"I'm guessing I'm not too badly hurt or I wouldn't be here."

"A headache and severe bruising. That's all."

"Are you practicing medicine now?"

"No, but I have it on Highest Medical Authority that you are fine and will feel much better very quickly."

I did the slowest neck roll in the history of neck rolls and felt several gentle pops. Then I flexed my shoulders back and forth, which produced the snap, crackle, pop of relief.

Harry handed me the mug. As I sipped, he stood up, fetched something from my bathroom, and returned to hand me a bottle of ibuprofen.

"This cappuccino is very good."

"Of course," he replied.

I popped four ibuprofen, swallowing them with the aid of Harry's delicious cappuccino, and felt my body inching toward normalcy.

"Your highest authority was absolutely correct, I'm already feeling a lot better."

"Good."

I savored more of my caffeinated beverage, felt the strength returning to my body, stood up, and walked across my living room to the window overlooking West 76th Street. Based on the angle of sunlight on the brownstones on the other side of the street, I guessed it was mid-morning on Sunday.

"Does Kim know I'm all right?"

"I told her."

"Thanks."

"How do you feel?"

"I told you, surprisingly better by the minute."

"I was not inquiring into your physical health—I already know that. How do you feel after last night?"

A gentle breeze was blowing through the trees. I pushed the windows up to open them and felt the warm July air flow into my apartment.

"I . . . I feel . . . pretty damn good."

"You killed two men."

"I haven't forgotten that. I could never forget that. But . . . I saved Mrs. Grayson's life. Probably Mr. Grayson, too. I . . . saved . . . their . . . lives."

"You did."

"I wish I hadn't had to kill anyone, but . . . I think I was . . . fulfilling the Chairman's mission for me. He wanted me to save the Graysons, and I did. It feels good to have a sense of purpose."

Harry nodded and smiled. "Are you going to ask me about what it means that the Chairman allowed you to kill two men?"

"As far as I'm concerned, it means their time was up. And I'm much more focused on the Graysons than a pair of dead bad guys." I finished my drink. "And who were they? Will the NYPD be able to tie them back to Privatus?"

Harry shook his head. "One's former Mossad, the other was former SAS. Both have cloudy backgrounds and worked for a fictitious security firm in Europe."

"And that fictitious firm is owned by another fictitious firm and another—like Russian nesting dolls."

"Yes."

"No easy way to trace back to Privatus."

"None."

"What about the van? Stolen?"

"Of course."

"And no DNA survived the fire. Any fingerprints?"

"No."

"Any trace of the guy who left the van on Canal St.? Maybe there's some video from cameras in the subway station?"

"There is. But he was still wearing the ball cap and the glasses, the collar of his jacket was turned up, and he kept his head down."

"He could be any tall guy wearing dark clothes in the subway."

"Yes."

"So, was Hawkins the guy who got away?"

"It was."

"Damn. He was wearing a vest, wasn't he? It's my fault he got away. I should have double-tapped him."

"Double tap?"

"Shoot him again, in the head, just to be sure."

"Far be it from me to presume anything about your mental processes, but I would imagine that—when you were in the moment—your primary concern was the welfare of the Graysons."

"It was, but I should have been taken Hawkins out of the equation. He started firing at me almost as soon as he went down. And that ain't easy after you've been shot in the chest."

"He was wearing a bullet-proof vest."

"Sure, but when you get shot in the vest, it's like being hit with a sledge hammer. It can break your ribs or collarbone. You can be knocked unconscious when the force of the bullet slams you into the ground the way it did him. But he was still able to shoot and shoot well enough that I had to scramble away to save my life. Letting Hawkins get away was a rookie mistake. I've been trained—by the U.S. government, no less—to secure a potential shooter, and I blew it. We all might have ended up dead."

We sat silently for a moment, then Harry said, "But you did save the Graysons."

"I guess I did." I swirled the tiny bit of cappuccino that remained in the cup. "Do we have any idea when the next Privatus op is going to happen?"

"Soon, but not in the next twenty-four hours."

"Good. My plan is to take a very hot shower, wash down even more ibuprofen, say hello to Kim, and then go to D.C. to see an old friend."

"Joanne Agar?"

"Yes, would you mind whooshing me there?"

"As much as I dislike your terminology, yes, I will take you to Washington."

I soaked in the shower for what felt like years but was really about twenty minutes. More ibuprofen as well as a breakfast of scrambled eggs and toast and cappuccino—all prepared by Harry and very good—had me feeling remarkably good for a man who had narrowly missed being blown to pieces the night before.

"You should call Kim," Harry said. "You disappeared after your late lunch yesterday, and she has not heard from you since."

"But you told her I was all right."

"Do you think my assurance is as meaningful as hearing from you?"

"When did you become my relationship guru?"

He silently handed me my phone.

I figure when your guardian angel tells you to call your girlfriend, you'd better do it. There's something cosmically sensible about following his advice.

"Jack? Where'd you go to?" Kim asked by way of answering her phone. "I thought I was going to see you 'later' as in 'later' last night."

"That was my plan, but . . . "

"Men plan; God laughs."

"Yup."

"Harry called to say you were okay. Are you?"

"Would Harry lie to you?"

"He wouldn't lie. But he might represent something as more positive than it really is."

I laughed. "Yes, he might. But not in this case. I got a few bruises but that's all."

"Harry said you saved two people's lives."

"Yes, that's true, too."

"No wonder I love you."

"And here I thought it was my baby blue eyes."

"They're part of the package. Am I going to see you later?"

"I think so. I have to do a bit of research for my current mission, but tonight looks good. Does that work for you?"

"Absolutely. Call me later?"

"Absolutely." I disconnected.

Harry smiled, "Aren't you glad you called her yourself?"

"Yes, Harry, I am glad I did exactly what you told me to do."

He was about to respond, but I was too quick for him—I had already dialed my old friend Joanne Agar at the FBI. We'd served in Afghanistan at the same time: She had been with Army Intelligence in Afghanistan; I was there with the Army Special Forces. I had saved her life during a special op we had run with the CIA.

"Jack?" she answered.

"In the flesh. How are you?"

"Not bad. Is there something I can do for you?"

"Brown bag lunch by the Reflecting Pool in an hour?"

She was surprised, "Jack, you do know it's Sunday, right?"

"I'm sorry, but this is urgent."

"Life and death urgent?"

"Yes."

"And you're going to be in D.C.?"

"I'll be . . . popping in and out. Only time for a meal."

"Just a meal? Or are you looking for some information, too?"

"I admit I do need information. But we could do that by phone or e-mail. I thought a quick, ultra-casual meal together would be nice."

She chuckled. "It will be nice. Before we get to your request for information—are you bringing lunch or am I?"

"I will."

"Okay. What information do you need?"

"I need the skinny on a spies-for-hire firm called Privatus."

"Oh," she groaned, "shit."

"What's the matter, have I asked for the wrong thing?"

"No, not as far as I'm concerned. But . . ."

"But what?"

"These are really bad people, Jack. Really bad." There was a long moment when neither of us said anything. Then Joanne said, "Look, I'll give you the lowdown on Privatus when you get here. Maybe you'll do the smart thing for once."

"And the smart thing would be?"

"Run away."

5

An hour later, wearing khaki slacks and a Nantucket-red polo shirt, I was sitting on a bench on the southern side of the Reflecting Pool with a brown-paper bag containing two genuine New York hot pastrami sandwiches. Looking past the southern end of the World War II Memorial, I saw a cab stop at the curb on 17th Street. Joanne stepped out and walked toward me. She was easy to spot: very tall, very slim, with long brunette hair. She was in a light-pink shirt dress that came to just above her knees, accentuating her long legs and her height.

"Hello, Jack," she said, beaming at me as she approached the bench.

"Hey, Joanne." I kissed her on the cheek.

"Security consulting must agree with you," she said. "You look good."

Given that I had barely escaped being blown to smithereens the night before, she had no idea just how good I actually looked. But, instead of being a smart ass, I replied, "I was thinking the same about you and the FBI."

"Thank you." She gave me a long, thoughtful look, smiled, and said, "You're in love."

"Holy moly, you're good."

"Always was. Congratulations."

"Thanks."

"How serious?"

"Pretty damn."

"Wow. Good for you."

"Thanks. What about you?" I asked.

"Still happily married to my wife."

"What would J. Edgar say about that?"

She shook her head and laughed, "Thank God that's not my problem."

We sat down, and I handed over a hot pastrami sandwich, a napkin, and a bottle of water.

"This sandwich is still warm," Joanne noted. "Where'd you get it?"

"Manhattan."

"What? How'd you get it here still warm?"

"I have resources you can only dream of."

"I'll say."

We ate in silence for a few minutes, enjoying the beautiful summer day and the impressive Washington scenery.

"This is a genuinely amazing sandwich," she said. "Thank you."

"You're very welcome."

"So . . . Privatus."

"Yes. Whatever you've got, please?"

"Like the name says: the firm's private security. World-class private security. Lots of ex-CIA, NSA, Mossad, etc. Highly trained operatives: men and women with successful track records and flexible morality."

"How long has the FBI been watching Privatus?"

"A while. Along with the CIA. I'm part of the FBI team; we're watching the domestic stuff. CIA is watching international activities, working with Interpol, Scotland Yard, and a few other agencies."

"Let me guess—so far, Privatus has done nothing illegal."

"So far."

"Do you know anything about a woman named Desjardins? Or a German named Freund?"

Joanne smiled, "Desjardins was CIA. Joined the Company right out of college, worked in operations for years, then managed ops, then made the switch to for-profit work. Desjardins is her mother's maiden name. She's now the head honcho at Privatus."

"What about Freund? I gather he's the director of ops for Privatus."

"Yes, he is. His real name is Reichel, but he hasn't used it in so long, no one remembers or cares. He cycled in and out of military intelligence and counter-intelligence. As you may know, the Germans have renamed and shuffled their agencies a few times. The important thing to know about the ironically named Freund is that he's without any redeeming moral features. He'll make sure anything Desjardins wants done is done."

"And what is it that?"

"Word is that Privatus has engaged a client named

Waronov-Tybalt. It's a private equity firm, and they're paying Privatus the largest fees the organization has ever received. We suspect Privatus is working some kind of stock-market manipulation on the European exchanges to benefit Waronov-Tybalt to the tune of billions of dollars."

"Billions?"

I pondered the events of the previous night. "Might there be a cyber-security angle to what's Privatus is doing for Waronov-Tybalt?"

"Maybe . . . ," she replied very slowly. "What do you know?"

"I know, but cannot prove, that last night, Privatus attempted to kidnap Alex Grayson of GraySecurFirm."

Joanne sat still and stared at me. After a long moment, she said, "Are you the guy who saved the Graysons?"

"Well, uh . . . yeah. I am. But that stays between you and me."

"Hey, as long as you're operating on the side of the angels, I don't care what you do."

I smiled, "I'm definitely on the side of the angels."

"You're either a lunatic or the luckiest man on earth."

"Or both?"

"Yes, both."

She took a small bite of her sandwich and chewed, mulling over my question about the cyber security angle. "We haven't heard anything about Waronov-Tybalt making a play for a cyber-security firm, but it would tie in quite neatly with what they might be planning regarding the European markets."

"Like how?"

"Well, this isn't my area of expertise, so I'm just guessing here—"

"Guess away."

"Okay, you asked for it. Maybe Waronov-Tybalt wants to acquire GraySecurFirm and they wanted to depress the acquisition price by kidnapping the key player. Or, they wanted to intimidate Grayson and his board into selling cheap."

"Or both."

"Yes, or both. If Grayson was willing to sell cheap, it might also help with any SEC and/or EU regulatory issues regarding the acquisition. I'm not sure about this, but I would think the regulators would be a little more willing to approve the sale if the GraySecurFirm purchase was considered a distress sale."

"If you're right about this, then kidnapping Grayson wouldn't really be necessary. Having him alive and scared shitless over his well being could be enough."

"Probably," she agreed.

"What about a guy named Daryl Hawkins? He was in Afghanistan same time we were."

"Daryl Hawkins?" Joanne appeared apprehensive at the mention of his name.

"Yes. He was the team leader for the Privatus

kidnapping of Grayson. I'm pretty sure he's the leader of whatever the hell it is that Privatus is doing for Waronov-Tybalt. I need . . . to stop him."

"Why do you need to stop Privatus from doing anything? Shouldn't you leave that to the FBI and the CIA?"

"I should, but . . . well, I can't. And I'm sorry, but I can't explain why."

"I get it," she replied. "Not your secret to tell."

"Exactly."

"You said before you had resources I couldn't dream of—was that just a typical Tyrrell wisecrack? Or was it for real? 'Cause you're going to need a hell of a lot of resources to go up against Privatus."

"It was for real. Believe me, I'm not happy that I'm messing with Privatus. Really and truly not happy. But, a man's gotta do—"

"Oh, please, not that hoary old cliche. Okay, I hope you really have amazing backup, 'cause you're going to need it."

"I have the best backup in the world." *In the universe*, for that matter, I thought to myself. "What about Hawkins?"

"He's you."

"Excuse me?"

"He's you. He's your doppelgänger. You're the same age, height, and weight—"

"Does he have baby blue eyes like me?"

"No. Jack this is serious. Hawkins was Delta, you were Special Forces. You both won medals in combat. You both worked special ops with the CIA in Afghanistan. Then you went to the Marshals Service—"

"And Hawkins stayed with the CIA."

"Yes."

"And exhibited extreme moral flexibility."

"Extreme. He's you, if you had gone over to the dark side."

"The road not taken."

"The Robert Frost poem?"

"Yes. The last lines are: 'Two roads diverged in a wood, and I—I took the one less traveled by, and that has made all the difference.'"

"I was never real big on poetry, Jack, but I can tell you, you don't want to go down the same road as Hawkins."

There was no adequate reply to that, so I finished the last bit of my pastrami. Joanne did the same with her sandwich. I tucked all our trash into the paper bag.

"One more thing, Jack," Joanne said. "With billions of dollars hanging in the balance and Hawkins's propensity for violence, you can imagine that a lot of people will be hurt or killed."

"Lucky me."

*   *   *

An hour later, after Harry had—at my request—

103

transported me to Washington Square Park, I walked into the (relative) safety of my therapist's office.

"Thank you for seeing me on a Sunday."

"Harry said to treat you with extra special care."

"Oh. That was nice of him. I guess he thinks I'm real mess."

"Are you?"

"I don't know. I'm not sure how I feel about the events of last night." I told him about the thwarted kidnapping, and my shooting and killing two men.

"Allow me to repeat back to you what you just said," Dr. Hoffman said in his soft German accent. "That way I can ensure that my understanding is correct."

"Repeat away," I replied.

"You are feeling a 'little bad'—as you put it—that you don't feel 'particularly bad'—as you also put it—that you killed two men. If you are feeling anything, you feel a sense of satisfaction. You have regained your sense of purpose. You are a man on a mission. Is that correct?"

"That's mostly it. It's important to note that I also feel good that I saved two lives."

"You've saved lives before and felt much more regret about killing. What is it different now?"

"That's what I wanted to talk with you about."

"Yes, go ahead . . . talk. Why are you more comfortable now than in the past?"

"I'm not sure comfortable is the right word—"

"Do you want to debate semantics with me?"

I gave him my charming, boyish grin. His expression spoke eloquently: stop using evasive tactics.

"Well . . . I guess I feel like I'm more . . . in tune with what the Chairman wants for me. More willing to take things as He presents them to me."

"And that worries you?"

"Well, yeah, like I said, 'it makes me feel a little bad' that I don't feel more remorse over killing those two."

"Why?"

"*Why* does it make me feel bad?"

"Yes, why?"

"Shouldn't I feel bad when I kill someone? I mean, shouldn't I feel pretty damn bad when I kill someone?"

"You tell me."

"I should. Or . . . I always used to."

"What's different now?"

"I know this sounds ridiculous, but I just feel like I'm doing what the Chairman wants, and that's more important than the results."

"The results? Two dead men?"

"Well . . . yeah."

"Tell me, Jack, do you pray every day?"

"Yes. Multiple times a day, actually."

"Do you ever ask for things when you pray?"

"Sure. Doesn't everybody?"

"What do you ask for?"

"Oh, the usual: money, power, sex, beachfront property in Hawaii—"

"Stop wasting my time."

"Sorry. Although I do pray for the property in Hawaii. But mostly I pray that He'll watch over my loved ones, and I pray I'll do the Chairman's will."

"So why does it concern you that—after praying to do His will—when you do something you *believe* is His will, you feel okay?"

I stared out the window at the thick, green leaves of the trees in Washington Square Park. Dr. Hoffman sat quietly and waited.

"I guess . . . I guess I'm not completely confident in my faith. In my relationship with the Chairman. I'm worried that I'm kidding myself."

Hoffman nodded and smiled. Which struck me as an outburst of enthusiasm that was strictly verboten in the *How To Be A Shrink* manual.

"Could I ask you a question, Doctor?"

"Yes. I can't promise to answer."

"Fine. Are you completely confident in your faith?"

"*Completely*? Without any doubt? Any tiny questions? No. That's why it's called *faith*. It's not fact."

"So . . . fact is easy. Faith is hard."

"Exactly."

When I left Dr. Hoffman's office, I stopped at a food vendor's cart, bought a bottle of cold spring water, then walked into Washington Square Park, found a bench in the shade of some trees, and sat down. It was a late afternoon in July in Manhattan, which meant people dressed in shorts and short skirts, in T-shirts and sleeveless tops, walking by my spot on the bench. I drank my water and enjoyed the view. I was blissfully aware of slender, tanned women and excited, playful children. The only men I noticed were guys walking dogs. I love dogs.

It would have been so nice if I could have kept my mind blank and soaked up some of the summer happiness of people strolling through the park. But I found myself focused on what the hell Waronov-Tybalt wanted and what kind of mayhem Privatus was committed to in order to fulfill its client's wishes. Were they going to make another move on GraySecurFirm? Was GraySecurFirm the only company Waronov-Tybalt wanted to take over? What other company or companies might be targeted? Was another attack planned against a different firm? It wouldn't be a kidnapping, that was way too obvious, but what else could it be? Assassination? Mass murder in a faux terrorist attack? If the only thing at stake was money—even billions of dollars—I would have been a lot less apprehensive. Hell, I'd be so serene, I might cut back on my sessions with Dr. Hoffman. But given the nature of the attack on the Graysons, it was absolutely clear that Privatus would not hesitate to kill to get what they wanted.

Was Waronov-Tybalt planning some kind of assault against a European cyber-security firm? Or against one of the European markets? Or maybe an attack on some kind of EU committee that oversaw financial markets? I made a mental note: Check what kinds of committees the EU had the oversaw any and all aspects of their stock markets.

And finally, my thoughts turned to my evil twin: Daryl Hawkins. Joanne described him as me, if I turned to the dark side.

But once upon a time, I *had* turned to the dark side. I had taken a bribe. After the mob had murdered my wife, I hired out as muscle for penny-ante criminals. Believe me, when you work as muscle for criminals, you *are* a criminal. In other words: living on the dark side. But I hadn't used all my government training to the murderous effect that Hawkins had. And I certainly hadn't earned the kind of money he had. Murder for hire was much more lucrative than what I had done.

All of my ruminating left me wondering: Why had my turn toward the dark side been such a long way from the evil depth of my doppelgänger's? What had separated me from Hawkins? What had saved me from turning to pure evil like Hawkins?

The answer was simple: My dead wife had interceded for me with the Chairman. I guessed that no dead people were pulling for Hawkins. Cursing him through eternity was a hell of a lot more likely.

I checked my phone and realized I had some time before I needed to head to Kim's place. I smiled at the thought of her. Not only did I have a wife who had interceded for me, but I had love in my life today. I bet that the closest to love that Hawkins experienced was the embrace of a prostitute. And he was way too savvy to confuse a sex-for-money transaction with love.

His loss.

I made a quick phone call to my friends and personal financial experts David and Valerie Berk. They had some free time and would be happy to have me visit. I walked east out of the park toward the Astor Place subway station and took the 6 train uptown to 59th Street. More walking east took me to Sutton Place, where the Berks lived.

David and Valerie, had made lots of money on Wall Street but never succumbed to the Masters of the Universe mentality that Tom Wolfe described in *The Bonfire of the Vanities*. They had worked hard, made a lot of money, and retired from the investment grind. These days, they lived in an apartment with an amazing view of the Queensboro Bridge, supported a number of New York-based charities, spent a lot of time at Lincoln Center, and traveled frequently to Europe and the American Southwest. Most important for my purposes: They were rabid arm-chair detectives, always eager to assist me with my cases.

David opened the door to the apartment. At six feet three, he was an inch taller than I, with broad-shoulders, dark-brown hair, and a graying beard. Valerie, a tall, slender redhead, stood at his elbow. She stepped past her husband to give me a kiss on the cheek.

"It's so nice to see you," Valerie said. "Are you

working on something juicy?"

"Yes, and I need your talent for explaining high finance."

As they always did, they led me through their living room with its floor-to-ceiling windows overlooking the East River, Roosevelt Island, and the pagoda-styled Queensboro Bridge to the den. We settled into the dusky-rose upholstered couch and matching arm chairs. Floor-to-ceiling bookshelves without an inch of bare space on them held a library ranging from financial tomes to great literature to mysteries and more mysteries, and finally a shelf full of books on baseball. David was as big a fan of the Mets as I was of the Yankees, but our shared love of the game overcame any interborough rivalries.

"Would you like a drink?" Valerie asked. "Water? Coffee? Tea?"

"Coffee, thanks." I sat in one of the chairs.

"Milk?"

"Black's fine, thanks."

Valerie left and David and I talked about how the season was going for our teams. The Mets had started hot, but the injury bug seemed to have bitten them again. The Yankees had begun the season slowly, but the bats had come to life, and the Bronx Bombers were bombing away.

"Here you are," Valerie said, handing me a cup of black coffee and settling onto the couch next to David.

"What do you need from us to help solve your latest?" she asked.

"What have you heard about Waronov-Tybalt?"

"Private equity firm founded by a couple of billionaire brothers," David replied. "The Waronovs."

"Where does the Tybalt name come from?"

"*Romeo and Juliet*," Valerie said.

"I know that, but what's the reason for it here?"

"Who knows? Probably a couple of hard-working boys attempting to seem educated. Apparently they don't know that Romeo kills Tybalt."

"Maybe they were sending a message about their lethal business practices," I suggested.

"If they were sending such a message, it would be consistent with their reputation. Although they should have picked a killer not the victim," David said.

I shrugged, "Tybalt kills before he is killed."

Valerie said, "The Waronovs should have brushed up their Shakespeare."

David followed up on his earlier point, "The Waronovs have never been caught breaking the law, but they have a reputation for a complete lack of morality coupled with absolute viscousness. If you get in their way, watch out."

"Yes, well, I may already be in their way." I drank my coffee. Rich and smooth. Nice blend. "I have some intel that they may be making some kind of play in the field of cyber-security. Maybe something to do with financial markets. Have you heard anything like that?"

Valerie and David looked at each other. He

shrugged, and she smiled.

"Currently, Waronov-Tybalt has nothing in its portfolio in tech, cyber-security, or financial-market services," Valerie said. "They tried to acquire a cyber-security firm last year, but the firm's founder mounted a vigorous defense and fought off the acquisition."

"But the Waronov brothers are not the kind of guys who take 'no' for an answer," David added.

"Would this firm happen to be GraySecurFirm?" I asked.

"You already know this, don't you?" Valerie asked. Then her eyes went wide, and she pointed at me, "Was that you last night? The late news had a story about a mystery man who saved the Graysons?"

"I can neither confirm nor deny that," I replied with a wink.

"Oh my God," Valerie said.

"The police described one of the mystery man's shots as a miracle."

In response, I cocked my head and arched my eyebrows. "Do you think that the Waronovs will keep pursuing GraySecurFirm?"

"Now more than ever," David said. "The stock prices dropped dramatically today. The GraySecurFirm board is probably going to pressure Grayson to sell while he still can."

"So the kidnapping worked, even if the victim was never actually kidnapped."

"Do you have proof that the Waronovs were behind the kidnapping attempt last night?"

"No. Believe me, my life would be much easier if I did." I had some more coffee. "Since it appears that the Waronov boys made a successful play going after the Graysons, are there any other cyber-security companies that they might want to go after? Companies resistant to selling out unless forcefully persuaded?"

"Hmm," Valerie replied, stood up, left the room, and returned with a laptop. She opened the computer as she sat on the couch with David. They spent a few minutes surfing and murmuring to each other about what they were seeing onscreen. I had no idea what they were so engrossed in. After a few minutes, both of them looked at me.

"We have two possible takeover targets for you," Valerie said.

"They both protect different aspects of security for large financial markets, and each one would make sense when combined with GraySecurFirm's product offering," David added. "Remember, if you already have one company, it makes no sense to buy another unless it is truly additive."

"I get it."

Valerie spoke, "Here's your list of lucky companies: Doberman Cyber in Boston and Intimidation Security in San Francisco."

"Intimidation? Doesn't sound very Californian to me."

113

"Probably why they went with the name."

"Putting the art of intimidation aside," David said, "if you're Waronov-Tybalt and you want to combine software security companies, you're going to look at firms with different security schemes to produce the most comprehensive product you can. GraySecurFirm provides an excellent array of security, but they have a different priority from the other three. GraySecurFirm detects intruders and goes after the hackers by back-tracing to the hackers' IP addresses. The others emphasize firewalls impervious to attack. Now, let me say again, all of these companies do everything pretty darn well, but their emphasis is on different priorities."

"So buy two of the companies, combine their security approaches, and the result is a super security product," I said.

"That's the idea," Valerie agreed. "Have you considered the possibility that the Waronovs might also be looking to sell conventional, human security services? Something like you?"

"There's nothing conventional about me, believe me. And no, I hadn't thought about that. But I already know who Waronov would use for that kind of security." I thought about my friends at Privatus and grinned.

"What's amusing about this?" Valerie asked.

"I think the Waronov boys are very ambitious and clever. They hire an extraordinary private security firm. That firm helps Waronov-Tybalt acquire cyber-security companies, which allows the Waronovs to create a super product. Then . . . the extraordinary security company stages an attack on a major market or markets, maybe one or more of the European stock exchanges. In the wake of the attack, the EU buys Waronov-Tybalt's cyber security, and hires the human security firm that the Waronovs recommend. Having the EU as a client would be a never-ending source of revenues."

"What security company is Waronov-Tybalt using?" Valerie asked.

"Better if you don't know. Private security. Extremely competent. Emphasis on *extreme*."

"This *extremely* competent security firm wouldn't be behind the Grayson kidnapping, would it?" David asked.

"Not that I can prove."

"No, of course not," Valerie nodded. "It would be one hell of a setup for a private security firm. It could collect fees from Waronov-Tybalt for its work on GraySecureFirm, Doberman and Intimidation and then receive more large fees for protecting the exchanges. Theoretically speaking."

"Yes," I replied. "Theoretically speaking."

6

I walked from the Berks on Sutton Place to Kim's home on West 81st and West End Avenue, cutting through Central Park. If you can't be at the beach on a beautiful July evening, Central Park is the next most perfect place. Softball games were being played in the pre-twilight on fields throughout the park. To the south, modern skyscrapers defined the skyline. To the west, I could see the landmark pre-war buildings lining Central Park West.

"Harry, could I have a few minutes of your ti—?"

He appeared before I finished my question. "Are you on your way to see Kim?"

"I am. But I was wondering if I could talk to George Morita."

"You want him to check out the tech-security firms the Berks mentioned to you?"

"Exactly."

Harry stopped walking, looked skyward for the tiniest instant and then back at me. "Are you ready?"

"Now?"

"Now."

"Sure—" as short a word as "sure" is, I was unable to finish it before I found myself in Washington, DC.

George Morita was standing in front of the

Franklin Delano Roosevelt Memorial with his back to the Tidal Basin. My back was to the FDR memorial, and I could see the basin and the Jefferson Memorial about five hundred feet away, across the basin from where we stood. The evening light was lovely in DC.

I whispered to Harry "Is he going to remember begin whooshed here from wherever he was a moment ago?"

Harry was disappointed in me, "I have done this before."

Ignoring him, I stepped over to Morita. "Hi, George, how are you?"

"Anxious. What the hell did you do in New York? I gather you stopped the Privatus operation in its tracks, but it's still being called a success."

"Too complicated to go into," I replied. "Listen, do you know if Privatus is launching any kind of operations against Doberman Cyber in Boston and/or Intimidation Security in San Francisco?"

"I haven't heard anything. As you might imagine, water-cooler gossip about operations is not encouraged at Privatus."

"Could you check? But don't put yourself in danger."

"I don't think so. Sorry. Security is beyond tight, right now. Where did you come up with those names? What are those companies?"

"They're all involved in marketing cyber security

for financial markets."

"GraySecurFirm competitors?"

"Yes."

"So you think Privatus is helping Waronov-Tybalt make a play in the tech-security field? And they're trying to force one or more of GraySecurFirm's competitors to sell itself? Waronov-Tybalt buys the pieces cheaply after Privatus manipulates the situation."

"Looks like it."

"Is there something else I can do for you?" George asked.

"Yeah, could you find out how the EU handles security issues for its stock markets? Is there room for Waronov-Tybalt to manipulate the EU's security needs?"

"As it happens, I already know about that." He saw that I was puzzled—Harry had his normal stone face of calm—and added, "I was assigned to do some analysis on the European Union and its many agencies that are working on security. I didn't realize it was for Waronov-Tybalt."

"What kind of security? For tech? Or industrial espionage? Anti-terrorism?" I asked.

"Every kind. The EU has a bunch of different agencies that are referred to as 'decentralized agencies' that handle a lot more than security. However, they have a few that deal with security: The one for network and information security is located in Greece. The one that oversees the financial markets is in Paris. It's called the European Securities and Markets Authority."

"Does it, by chance, have any committees of its own?"

George smiled like a teacher who appreciated an especially quick student. "Gotta love bureaucracies. Of course they have sub-units, and of course those sub-units overlap the focus of other 'decentralized agencies.' For our purposes, there are two that are relevant. One handles the information technology behind all market operations: stock trades, real-time stock pricing, and secured servers and networks. If it's digital and it has to do with a stock or commodities exchange, this committee is handling it."

"And the second?"

"It handles physical security of the exchanges."

"Mostly anti-terrorism, right?"

"Right. Despite the millions being traded in dollars and Euros, there are no large quantities of cash at the exchanges. You'd never go there to pull a robbery. But terrorists could think the exchanges would make good targets."

"Are both of these EU sub-units in Paris?"

"Yes."

"Any chance there are meetings for any of these agencies or sub-units scheduled sometime soon?"

"The European Securities and Markets Authority is having a three-day conference next week. All of its constituent committees and units will be there."

"I see baguettes and *fromage* in my future."

Harry's eyebrow arched briefly—so briefly that

George missed it.

"Listen, now that I know what I need to know, I think it's time for you to become very ill," I said. "George, can you call in sick tomorrow?"

"Yeah, of course, but Privatus will want me to verify I'm sick."

"Doctor's note?"

"I've never called in sick. I'm not sure, but yeah, a doctor's note at the very least."

"Maybe a blood test for common bacterial infections and/or viruses?" I deadpanned.

"Shit, I hope not."

"I'm kidding."

Harry said, "We'll take care of whatever you need."

George looked doubtful but said, "Thank you."

"Go home," I said. "We'll be in touch."

"Okay, thanks. Thanks for everything."

"Hang in there. I have a feeling that this will all be finished by next week."

"In Paris?"

Harry replied, "And anywhere else that needs fixing."

George nodded, reassuring himself, and walked north toward the Lincoln Memorial.

We said nothing until he was out of ear shot, then Harry asked, "I assume you have plans; what do you want from the Chairman?"

"What do I *need*, you mean."

"Yes. Need."

"First thing tomorrow, George needs to call Privatus and say he won't be coming in because he's sick. He needs to call from his company cell phone. Tells them he feels awful, something about diarrhea and vomiting—"

"Is it necessary to make his feigned illness disgusting?"

"Absolutely. Everyone is embarrassed and uncomfortable talking about diarrhea and puking. Gives the story more credibility. No one will ask questions about how bad it is, or how much puke or how much—"

"Yes, I see what you mean. Diarrhea and vomiting."

"Okay, he tells them he's going to the doctor at eleven o'clock."

"Will he actually go to the doctor?"

"No. This is where I need the Chairman's magic. After the phone call, you whoosh George and his family—does he have a family?"

"A wife and two children."

"Okay. In that case, they *all* need to be whooshed to a safe house."

"Would a hotel do?"

"As long as they are whooshed past any and all security cameras, there's no check-in where they have to show ID, nothing that could put them on the grid."

"I can make that happen."

"Perfect. Now, let's go back to George's Privatus-

121

issued phone. I'm pretty damn sure that when he calls in, the firm will ping his phone to confirm that he is at home. As soon as they do that, I need you to whoosh the phone to the doctor's office, where Privatus will ping it a few minutes after eleven o'clock to confirm that George is actually getting his intestinal issues checked."

"Then you want me to whoosh the phone back to George's now-empty house so that Privatus can ping it again to confirm that he is back home."

"Exactly."

"What's the point of all this phone magic?"

"It's an extra bit of safety for George and his family. Privatus won't begin looking for him until the day after tomorrow."

Harry's Mona Lisa smile flitted across his face. "You are actually quite competent at this sort of thing."

"I think that's why the Chairman hired me."

"It's so reassuring to know that He hires good people."

"Was that a joke at the Chairman's expense? That's borderline irreverent. Are you allowed to be irreverent?"

"I have free will like you. I can choose whatever I want."

"Careful, Harry. The next thing you know, you'll be fomenting revolution. Changing the subject, does Privatus have any insiders at Doberman or Intimidation?"

"Yes. The firm has negotiated the services of two men on the inside of Doberman and Intimidation."

"Probably the heads of security. Right?"

"Yes. How'd you figure that out?"

"If you're going to attack a corporation, who better to entice into your evil clutches than the heads of security?" I considered that for a second. "And security chiefs protect the physical premises. There'd be an IT guy in charge of security for the networks and servers. So Privatus's attack against Doberman and Intimidation will be against a location. What do you know about the attacks?"

Harry did his quick check with the Man Upstairs and said, "The attacks at Doberman and Intimidation are deliberately redundant. They serve as backups to each other."

"Because Waronov-Tybalt only needs one of these companies to become willing to be acquired."

"Exactly."

"Are the attacks redundant in method as well as in the intended result?"

"Yes," Harry said. "The attacks will take out each company's cooling system."

"The air-conditioning for the servers?"

"Yes."

"Nifty," I said appreciatively. "The air-conditioning goes down; the servers shut down when it gets too hot; the incident is incredibly disruptive, but no data is lost, and no physical plant to rebuild."

Harry nodded.

"And . . . being security firms, they won't admit

that it was sabotage."

"They will have to admit something—shutting down the server farm will almost certainly disrupt the delivery of at least some of their services," Harry pointed out.

"Sure, but they'll write it off as a fluke. Say it was a physical-plant problem, but now they're super-duper reinforcing their plants and this will never happen again. The reputational damage won't knock them out of business, but it will dampen their stock price and allow the Waronov brothers to acquire them a lot more easily."

"You seem to have a firm grasp of the situation."

I gave Harry my ice-cold, Deputy Marshal squint, but it had absolutely no effect on him.

"These will be dark-ops missions. Sneak in, sneak out," I said. "At night. Probably small teams. You wouldn't know when these attacks are scheduled, would you?"

"Privatus is working west to east: tomorrow night they will attempt to sabotage Intimidation Security in San Francisco. The night after, Tuesday, the attack will be against Doberman Cyber outside of Boston."

"And then three deep breaths and off to Paris, right?"

"*Oui.*"

My eyes went wide at Harry's bon mot, but I quickly forced a stone-faced expression. The last thing I wanted was to demonstrate my appreciation of his humor.

"Will you whoosh—sorry—transport me to each

place with enough time to prevent the attacks?"

"You mean with enough time for you to *attempt* to prevent the attacks."

"Yes, thank you. That is what I meant."

"Do you know the size of these teams?"

"Tomorrow night it's only two people. I would hazard a guess that if you are successful, they might add more people on Tuesday night."

"Oh, goody. Every time I succeed, I make it harder for myself."

"Indeed."

"Shall we meet at my apartment at 9:00 P.M.? I can get my equipment together while you brief me on the layout and security at Intimidation, and then we can whoosh."

Harry caught himself before his frown fully formed. "Yes, that sounds fine."

"Would you mind whooshing me to Kim's building now?"

"Yes, I would."

"Harry, come on, we're in Washington, DC."

He whooshed us to the front of Kim's building then frowned at me without any attempt to disguise his frustration. I started to say something, but he disappeared before I could get out any words. I was sure that if he had only given me a tiny fraction of an instant, I could have devastated him with a witty comment about his frown. Knowing Harry, he would say that he had saved me from injuring my brain.

*   *   *

PRIVATUS HEADQUARTERS

DESJARDINS, FREUND, AND HAWKINS SAT around the conference table in the black room.

"You leave tonight?" Desjardins asked Hawkins.

"Yes. Simkins will pick me up at the San Francisco airport. We'll prep tomorrow, go in tomorrow night, and both of us will return on an early morning plane."

"Are you sure you only need two people?" Freund asked.

Hawkins sneered, "This isn't an invasion. It's a covert operation. Stealth, not strength. But you already know that, so why the question?"

"Given what happened with the Grayson kidnapping, I feel it's my responsibility to ask such questions."

"Look, we got the results we wanted, right? And more team members wouldn't necessarily have helped. That guy had the element of surprise."

"Have you stopped referring to him as 'the magic warrior?'" Desjardins asked.

"I'll call him anything you like. Have we discovered who the hell he was or how he found out about our operation?"

"Nothing. No video, fingerprints or DNA at the scene to identify him. We've reviewed our planning and preparation and haven't found any sort of leak. Whoever he is, he has fantastic resources and a great skill set."

"Are you worried this 'magic warrior' will intervene in the San Francisco operation?" Freund asked.

"No, I'm not worried. But if the operation goes well, I'd kinda like another shot at the guy."

Desjardins smiled tightly, "As long as you prioritize the operation and not the 'magic warrior.'"

"A guy can dream, can't he?"

*   *   *

Kim and I ate a simple dinner of tuna salad sandwiches with vegetable chips on her building's rooftop patio as the last golden-red rays of sunlight faded over the horizon in New Jersey.

"Are you enjoying the sunset?" Kim asked.

"Very much. Did you arrange for it?"

"Of course."

"Speaking of enjoying, how 'bout spending a few days in Paris with me?"

"What? When?"

"I have to be there for business early next week, so I thought we'd leave for a long weekend this Wednesday night."

"Wow. Sounds wonderful. But I'll have to do a lot of rearranging of my schedule—this is kind of short notice."

"Yes it is, but it's Paris."

"That's a huge incentive . . ."

"How 'bout if I throw in business-class tickets?"

"You are the master manipulator."

"You can arrange for a brilliant sunset, but I'm the master manipulator for flying us business-class?"

"You are *soooooo* perceptive."

I watched a tugboat pushing a barge north on the Hudson River. Its progress was slow but steady. "Is that a 'yes' to Paris?"

"Of course, it's a 'yes' to Paris!"

"Is there anything for dessert?"

"You have a choice. There's a surprise dessert that comes on a plate. And a surprise that comes in a bed."

"Pun intended."

"What do you think?"

"Intended. I'll take the bed."

"I thought you might." She stood up and extended her right hand. I grabbed it and allowed her to pull me to the rooftop exit.

I wished that I could say we seamlessly transitioned from fully clothed dining to completely naked reclining, but when you've had tunafish for dinner, you must take a break for toothbrushing. Must. We managed the dental-hygiene portion of the evening quickly and smoothly, and in no time at all, found ourselves in each other's arms. I won't bore you with gratuitous details; all that you need to know is that our lovemaking was marvelous. Afterward, we lay on our sides, with me

128

spooning her. Spooning, especially naked spooning, might just have been the most effective way of being completely honest with each other. After all, you're extraordinarily intimate physically, but you can't see each other's faces so you don't get put off by facial expressions.

"What happens next?" Kim whispered.

"I don't know . . . maybe sleep? If you'd like to make love again, that's *very* okay, but nothing kinky. No S&M."

"You're an idiot," I heard a smile in her voice. "Where do we go as a couple? What's our next stage? Are we going to live together? Or . . . ?"

"The M-word?"

"Yes, what about that? Do you see us having that kind of future?"

I propped myself up on my left elbow, and she rolled back toward me. We could see each other's faces now.

"I . . . I haven't done a lot of thinking about our future. Actually, I haven't done any. But I love you, and I definitely want to have a future with you. With us."

She smiled and stroked my cheek with the back of her hand. "I guess we can settle on the exact details of our future later."

"Later. As in . . . *the future*."

"Assuming I don't come to my senses and leave you."

"No one would blame you if you did."

"Come here and kiss me."

I leaned down and kissed her mouth. Her lips were pillowy and sweet, despite her right shoulder digging into my Adam's apple.

"Now," she whispered, "what was that about a non-kinky round of lovemaking?"

7

Over coffee the next morning, I broke the news that I would be working the next couple of nights.

"Is this for one of your regular clients? The kind of thing I don't need to worry about? Or is this work with one of Harry's special clients—in which case I will worry."

"It's with Harry, but there's no need to worry. He always takes care of me."

"Given the amount of emergency medical attention you've needed since we've been together, I do not find your reassurances about Harry very . . ."

"Reassuring?"

Kim stifled a smile, "Seriously, Jack, a couple of times, you've barely made it back in one piece." Frown lines appeared on her forehead as her anxiety appeared on her face. "Why should I feel confident that you will be coming home safe and sound tonight or tomorrow or any other time? When you work with Harry, the odds don't seem to favor safe and sound."

"Well . . ."

"Don't make a joke of this. I'm scared by your work with Harry. Sorry, but I am."

"I . . . I have to help people. It's my purpose in life."

"Couldn't you volunteer at Big Brothers or a soup kitchen or something?"

"I hate to sound like Harry, but volunteering like that, while it would be helpful, would *not* utilize my particular skill set."

"Really? Your skill set?"

"Yes. Remember you're the one who called me a government-trained private detective cum troubleshooter. Not to mention that I work for the Chairman. In partnership with the formidable Harry Mitchum."

We sat quietly for a moment.

"I'm sorry," I said. "But I was called to this mission. I'm supposed to help people. It's just the way it is."

Kim remained silent, concentrating on her coffee.

"I wish I could give you a guarantee, but I can't," I reiterated.

"I think I need to speak to Harry myself," she sighed after a long pause. "Make sure he and the Chairman understand that I *need* you. Hasn't Harry always said you'll get what you need?"

"He has. But, not to make too fine a point of this, he was referring *to me*. It wasn't an all-inclusive friends-and-family package."

"Well, I'm going to renegotiate the terms of your package."

I held my hands up as if surrendering, "You should do what you have to do."

"I will." She drank more coffee. "Where are you going the next two nights?"

"San Francisco and Boston."

"Travel via Air Harry?"

"Yup. None of the inconvenience of airport security, checked bags, local transport to and from the airports, no jet lag—"

"No hassles about your weapons."

"Talk about *convenient*."

Kim chuckled then turned serious again. "Promise me you'll come home to me."

"I promise."

"I *mean* it, Jack."

"I might be returning to New York in the wee hours of the morning," I said.

"I don't care. I want you to come home to me, slip into bed, and wrap your arms around me."

I hesitated, then, "I think I can arrange that."

"Promise me."

"I'm dealing with some people, one guy in particular, who might have something to say about . . . whether or not I return."

"No. That's not how we're going to handle this. As far as I'm concerned you are the toughest man in the world, and you have Harry to back you up. You are going to promise me that you'll come home to me each and every night. Period. End of story."

"Well . . . since you put it that way, I promise."

"Really?"

"Absolutely." I stretched over the table and kissed her. "Absolutely, totally, and completely. I want a future with you."

She grinned. "Was that so hard? Couldn't you have given me an iron-clad promise at the beginning of this conversation?"

"Next time we have a conversation like this, I will make an iron-clad promise immediately."

"You better."

*   *   *

At 9:00 P.M., I was already dressed for the evening, again wearing what I thought of as my cat-burglar outfit: black T-shirt, charcoal-gray cargo pants, and black, crepe-soled shoes. I'd throw a black windbreaker on before I left. Even though it was July, the weather in San Francisco is notoriously capricious.

On my bed, I spread out my small, black rucksack, two Ruger pistols, mags of 9mm ammo, and criss-crossing shoulder holsters. Since Harry had told me the Privatus force was going to be two agents—this was a break-in, not an invasion—I felt no need to bring along heavier weapons like an Uzi or a shotgun. On the other hand, grenades were for any occasion. I added two flash-bangs and two smoke grenades next to the pistols. The finishing touches were a few plasticuffs and a balaclava to cover my face.

Harry appeared on the dot of 9:00 P.M. It was not

humanly possible to be more punctual than Harry. Then again, he wasn't human.

Unusually for Harry, he appeared with a laptop under his arm.

"Would you like to inspect the neighborhood and headquarters layout for Intimidation?" he asked.

"Yes, please."

He opened the laptop, clicked on the touchpad, and Google Maps appeared, showing the satellite image of the Mission Bay area on the east side of San Francisco, just south of AT&T Park where the Giants played baseball. Interstate 280, an elevated highway, was on the western side of the neighborhood, and San Francisco Bay was to the east. Harry zoomed in to Intimidation's HQ, a rectangular building at the corner of 3rd and South Streets. The whole area looked like warehouses and office buildings. Nothing too tall, all probably three or four stories high. To the northeast the San Francisco-Oakland Bay Bridge stretched to Yerba Buena Island before turning due east to reach Oakland. It wasn't as picturesque as the Golden Gate Bridge, but it wasn't bad at all.

"Do you have any pictures or any kind of blueprints for Intimidation's facilities?" I asked.

Harry shot me a look of scorn, opened a folder on the computer's desktop, and handed the laptop to me. I scrolled through pictures of the building's exterior and blueprints of the interior.

Intimidation's headquarters was a bland white

cement building with tinted windows in dark metal frames.

"The windows look as if they were installed pretty recently. Were they part of a total refurbishment?"

"Intimidation gutted the building. Leaving only load-bearing walls and floors. Trusses were added throughout to make the structure more earthquake resistant. Then new climate controls, digital networks, back-up generators for power, and state of the art alarm systems were built in."

"Which you will help me evade."

"Of course."

I continued looking at photos and blueprints. "Am I reading this blueprint correctly? Are the servers on the second floor?"

"Yes. Intimidation is about five hundred feet away from San Francisco Bay. They located the servers on the second floor, approximately fifteen feet above the normal high tides. In case of flooding."

"They aren't taking any chances, are they?" I peered more closely at the blueprints. "Are the AC units outside in back, near the parking lot?"

"Yes."

"The units are also on an elevated steel platform. I'm guessing it's also fifteen feet above water level."

"It is. As are the back-up generators, which are located on a platform on the far side of the parking lot."

"That way if there's some kind of fire or explosion at the generators, it won't take out the AC units."

"If the generators explode, wouldn't the air-conditioning stop working?"

"Yes, but there would be no damage to the AC. You could rush in more generators." I thought that over for a moment. "But with the generators out, there'd be no power and no AC. The servers would shut down."

"They would."

"Which means Intimidation must have backup servers somewhere else."

"It does."

"Where?"

"Iowa City."

"Is it going to be attacked tonight?"

Harry checked skyward, as he did every so often, and looked back at me, "Yes. A second team, which will go as soon as the primary team alerts them to success with this mission."

"So, if we thwart the attack at Intimidation, the secondary team won't go?"

"There'd be no point. The primary servers will still be operating and there will be no disruption in Intimidation's services to its clients. No data breach."

"Good." I returned to scanning the photos and blueprints. "It looks to me as if the entire parking lot is surrounded by a chain-link fence about ten-feet tall. On top of the fence is enough razor wire to stop a horde of orcs. The fence runs around three sides of the parking lot, terminating at the western corners of the building. In the photos, it looks as if the fence terminal posts butt up to the building. With no room to spare."

"They do. There is no gap between the final fence posts and the building."

"What fun. It looks to me as if the entire fencing and razor wire thing is repeated around the generator and the AC platforms."

"It is."

"Alarm systems covering the platforms? *And* . . . am I mistaken, but are there guard booths at each platform? And another at the gate to the parking lot?"

"Yes, there are alarms for both the generator and the AC, and yes, three guards on duty in the parking lot at all times, and another round-the-clock guard on duty just inside the main entrance of the building. Two guards patrol the interior of the building. Every two hours, the guards rotate to the next station. The night watch is 8:00 P.M. To 4:00 A.M."

"Lotta guards."

"I guess that would depend on how you define 'a lot'. But for our purposes, yes, a lot of guards."

"Not our purposes. Privatus's."

I stared at a photo of the parking lot, with its three guard shacks clearly visible. They were at least fifty feet away from each other.

"Are each of the guard shacks climate controlled?"
"Yes."

"Hard-wired phone lines, radios, and cell phones?"

138

"Yes."

I smiled as I continued to study the photo. "The Privatus boys are going to need a diversion."

* * *

At a few minutes after midnight, Harry whooshed us to the roof of the Intimidation building. There was a panoramic view to the north and east of the San Francisco-Oakland Bay Bridge as it crossed the bay to Yerba Buena Island and continued all the way to Oakland.

Immediately to our north there were some relatively new buildings, but none was high enough to block the view of San Francisco's financial district and the iconic Transamerica Pyramid.

The Intimidation building had a rooftop sports cage at the southern end—the one opposite the view—with basketball nets at either end of the cage. The rest of the roof had picnic tables.

I walked to the western side of the roof and looked down at the parking lot. It was your standard-issue parking lot. Except for the high fences with razor wire and the three different guard booths. If Intimidation added some machine gun nests and foot patrols with Rottweilers that would have been completely intimidating.

"Okay," I said to Harry. I pointed at a steel door that was probably at the top of a stairwell down into the building. "I'm guessing that's locked and alarmed."

"It is. Please, allow me to transport us to the fifth

floor."

"Well, if you in—"

I finished the word standing in the middle of a large, dimly lit, open-plan office floor. "—sist."

There were two conference tables with a dozen chairs around each of them to one side of us, and on the other side were about thirty desks almost but not quite standing in rows. I couldn't discern a pattern to the slight irregularity—it occurred to me that was what had been intended by the office designer. Maybe a trace of something off-kilter so the people who worked at Intimidation wouldn't feel as if they were being oppressed. It was interesting to me that a company named Intimidation would be concerned about the well being of its employees.

Before we explored any further, I reached inside my backpack and pulled out the balaclava. I put it on, but kept it rolled up above my forehead.

"It's July. Do you really think you need the mask?" Harry asked.

"I'm pretty sure I will recognize Hawkins. That means he might recognize me. And I'd prefer he not know who I am."

Harry replied, "We can't be seen or heard." In spite of that, he spoke softly.

"How 'bout infrared scanners?"

"What?" he seemed genuinely startled. "Do you know something I don't? Did you see something on the blueprints?"

I gave him a blank look. "You're sounding very insecure there, Harry. Very human."

"I spend too much time with you."

"I come with a warning label. Didn't you read it?"

"You come with a safety manual," Harry said.

"Full of photos and diagrams?"

"No, you're not all that complicated."

"Ouch."

"Are we finished here, or do you need to continue your scouting trip?"

Before I could answer, we heard footsteps.

"Remember," Harry said, "can't be seen or heard."

Two men walked into sight. They wore the de rigueur security uniforms: dark slacks, white button-down shirts, ball caps. They were not talking, just scanning the entire floor. One stopped at the large table to our right while the other walked within inches of my nose on his way to the windows. He gave a tug on a couple of windows' handles to make sure they were locked. They moved away from us, in parallel on opposite sides of the big room. They turned left when they reached the glassed-in conference rooms at the far end of the open space and disappeared from view.

"That guy practically bumped into me," I said.

"Impossible. And you know it is impossible."

"I know what I know, but I also know what I felt, and that guy was right on top of me. I could smell his after shave."

"Oh," Harry arched his right eyebrow, "what was it?"

"Brut."

"I gather that would not be your choice."

"It's fine. I'm just not an aftershave guy."

"Maybe you should reconsider."

"Ooooh, zing! If Don Rickles had ever wasted time on subtlety, he might have said something like that."

"Who's Don Rickles?"

"Never mind." I reconsidered what Harry had said about it being impossible for the guard to bump into me. "I have to be visible to interact with others, right? No Invisible Man stuff so I can punch someone out while he can't see me."

"That's correct, you have to be visible."

I nodded and grunted to myself, "Yeah, no point in making things easy." I looked at my phone. Only two out of four signal bars, but my only concern was that there was cell service not how many bars. I slipped the phone into my pocket and began walking in the direction the guards had followed off the floor.

"Are you expecting a message?" Harry asked.

"No. But I still have cell service."

"And the significance of that is?"

"It means Privatus isn't coming, yet."

"I despise having to admit that I know less than you do, but I find myself—"

"If I were Hawkins, and I were coming here, I'd

jam the cell service and radio just before I launched my attack. I'd also cut off the landline phones—there's probably a telephone exchange box near here."

"Wouldn't a sudden loss in cell, radio and phone service alert the Intimidation guards?"

"Sure, but what are they going to do about it? They'll be cut off from the rest of the world. The only way for them to communicate will be to get to someone who has a working phone. And my guess is, they won't have enough time to do that."

"You think the diversion will happen too quickly?"

"Yup."

Harry and I checked out the remaining four floors, most of which were variations of the fifth floor, but the third floor had a number of private offices at each end.

"Probably executive country," I pointed out.

On the second floor, a large, rear-corner space had been sealed off behind solid, cream-colored walls. "The servers," I nodded to Harry.

The first floor consisted of the main lobby with the guard's office just inside the front entrance. This guard showed no more awareness of us than her buddies upstairs had. There was a loading bay at the rear, or parking-lot side, of the building. But most of the floor was taken up by a gigantic cafeteria space, probably fifty feed wide by more than one hundred feet long. One end of the cafeteria had a movie screen; at the opposite end there was what looked like a TV studio control room, and there were speakers on the walls. The cafeteria could be converted into an auditorium for company meetings and events.

"Quite a set up," I said. "Intimidation must be doing well."

"That's why Waronov-Tybalt wants to acquire the company."

"At a Privatus discount."

"That is their plan."

As we moved along in our private, after-hours tour of the Intimidation building, I continued to check my cell phone service. Still no hint that the bad guys were on their way.

"No one's burning the midnight oil here."

"The last employee checked out about an hour ago."

"Checked out? Through an ID scanner?"

"Yes."

"Let's go out to the parking lot."

In less than the blink of an eye, we were standing in the mostly empty lot. A couple of nondescript sedans and pickup trucks were parked on the side of the lot nearest the AC platform.

"Those probably belong to the guards on duty."

Harry nodded, "They do."

I checked my phone again. No signal bars. Instead, there was very small type: No Service.

"Okay," I said. "The balloon is up . . ."

"Excuse me?"

"It's an old expression, meaning the operation has been launched. In this case, it means that trouble is coming."

We stood quietly, watching and waiting. I could see through the glass of the guard booth near the gate that the guard inside was checking his phone. Then he picked up a walkie talkie. No joy with either. He picked up the landline, listened, then hung up the receiver.

He stepped to the door of the booth and shouted across the parking lot. "Either of you have phones or radio?"

The guards near the AC units on one side of the parking lot and the generators on the other stepped out of their booths and shouted back that they had nothing.

"How the hell is that possible?" the guard at the gate muttered.

He barely had time to finish expressing his disgruntlement, when screeching tires and an over-revving engine filled the air. The sounds came from south of the Intimidation property, maybe from 16th Street, and grew louder as the vehicle making the noise raced up 4th Street. A medium-duty Mack dump truck—medium duty but still a monster—with a white cab and a steel dump box on its back, zigged and zagged north on 4th Street.

It banged over the curb and sliced across the sidewalk right into Intimidation's gate, smashing down the gate and a large portion of the chain-link fence. The truck's massive front end hit the guard booth, which crumpled as if

145

it were made of paper. The guard had been standing outside the booth, trying to pinpoint the sounds of the out-of-control truck, and when he saw the truck come over the curb, he had run for his life.

The other two guards met him in the middle of the lot, both with fire extinguishers in hand.

The truck came to a full stop atop the ruins of the guard booth. Hot water hissed and dripped from the broken radiator. The left-side headlight was smashed, but the right headlight was on, throwing a beam of light into the lot. The driver was slumped over the steering wheel.

The gate guard, who was in charge, turned to one of the others, a woman, and said, "Run out to 3rd Street and then head north until you get a cell signal. Then call 9-1-1."

She handed him her fire extinguisher and took off.

The gate man turned to the remaining guard and said, "We'd better check the driver."

I pulled the balaclava down over my face, adjusted it so I could see comfortably through the eye holes, and said to Harry, "Time for me to go."

"You're ready. Meaning you're visible."

"Thanks." Have to admit, I wasn't really sure I was sincere in my gratitude. I would dearly have loved to remain invisible.

I ran stealthily across the lot as the two male guards rushed around to the driver's side of the truck cab and struggled to pull open the door. I reached the passenger side of the cab unseen.

A man said, "Everyone freeze."

I would have gone under the truck, but the smashed guard booth blocked that possibility. Instead, I went around the back end, stepping quickly and silently on my crepe soles.

A tall man, about my height, in dark clothes with a dark balaclava pulled over his face, held the female guard in front of him with a knife to her throat. At the tall guy's right shoulder, the one nearest me, was another person in dark clothes and a balaclava. Given the shorter height and the smaller frame, I guessed tall man's partner was a woman. She was holding a small, black duffle.

The two guards were standing frozen, hands up in the air.

"Pull out your guns very slowly, using only your thumbs and index fingers," tall guy said. "Then hold them out to your side, barrels pointing down."

They did as they were told and held the guns far from their sides as if they were new parents dealing with horrendously dirty diapers.

The woman intruder collected the weapons. Tall guy handed her the female guard's pistol, which she tucked with the other weapons into her duffle.

"Lower your hands behind your back," tall guy said.

Once again, they did as they were instructed. The woman bound their hands with plasticuffs. The tall man turned the female guard around, and she was also plasticuffed.

Tall guy reached into the cab of the truck, grabbed the driver by his arm, shook him none too gently and said, "Get down. Now."

The driver must have been seeing stars. He cautiously stepped down from the cab. He was a scruffy young man. He wasn't African- or Asian-American, but other than that, I couldn't see him well enough to know anything about him. I could see, however, that he was unable to pull his eyes away from tall guy's knife. It had a six-inch blade that gleamed in the floodlights of the parking lot. If you intended to kill a man with a knife, you'd probably use something thin and sharp as hell. If you wanted to shock and awe, you went with something like tall guy's. It worked. The driver turned around without saying a word and allowed himself to be cuffed.

The female intruder handed tall guy a roll of duct tape and climbed into the Mack's cab, worked the controls, and the dump box tilted skyward. I scurried around the corner of the truck and crouched behind the right rear tires. Tall guy led his four hostages to the back, undid the gate on the dump box and allowed it to flop open, swinging on its hinges at the top of the box. Without much ceremony, tall guy taped the mouths of each of his captives, then lifted each into the dump truck's bay. Two of the guards and the driver were pretty slender, but the guard who had been on the gate originally had a substantial beer belly and must have pushed the scales at 230 or 240. Tall guy barely grunted when he tossed that guard into the bay.

Oh shit, I thought. A fitness freak with a big, sharp knife. The big knife being a sign of a bad attitude. I should have brought some help.

"Okay," tall guy grunted.

The truck machinery whirred, and the dump box lowered. Tall guy latched shut the box gate.

I edged around the truck again, saw the woman jump down from the cab, and step over to the tall guy. I drew my Ruger and stepped out from behind the truck.

"Daryl Hawkins, I presume."

"What?" He spun around and saw my gun.

"Drop the knife. Then hands up. Both of you."

He hesitated. Then he dropped the knife and slowly put his hands in the air. The woman did the same.

"Kick the knife under the truck."

He did what he was told. Surprisingly cooperative guy.

"Daryl Hawkins, right?"

"Who the hell are you?"

"Just a guy. Happened by. Isn't this a meeting of Ski Masks Anonymous?"

"Who are you?"

"Before we get to the question-and-answer part of this event, why don't you turn around? You—" to the woman, "cuff him."

Hawkins turned his back to me and extended his

arms behind him. The woman stepped toward him—

"Ah, ah, ah," I said. "Stay to his side, so I can see both of your hands."

Clever, Tyrrell. No one gets the jump on you.

As she reached toward him, he grabbed her, spun his right shoulder backward into her, and sent her staggering toward me. She fell to the ground. He continued spinning around until he was facing me, now with a pistol in his hand.

"I have to admit you're very good," I said. What I was thinking could easily be summed up by repeating the F-bomb multiple times. And then more times. I should have had them lie on the ground, disarmed them, then cuffed both. Instead I was staring into the barrel of what looked like a Sig Sauer P226 9mm pistol. Shit.

"Who the hell are you?" Hawkins growled. As the woman stood up, he spoke to her, "Take out the AC."

"Wait! Stay where you are," I ordered.

"Really?" Hawkins asked. "You're going to shoot someone to protect an AC unit? Yeah, right." To the woman he said, "Go ahead."

Her dark brown eyes blazed at me from the holes in her balaclava, sizing me up. She came up with the same decision as Hawkins: She was sure I wouldn't shoot her to protect an AC unit. She grabbed the small duffle then headed deeper into the parking lot toward the platform with the AC unit.

As she walked away, Hawkins and I continued to

stare at each other over the barrels of our pistols.

"This is cozy," I said.

"You're the guy who hit the miracle shot Saturday night in DUMBO, aren't you? The Magic Warrior."

"Yes. Don't make me do it again. Put down your weapon. Call your partner back."

"I don't think so—"

We both fired. His bullet caught me in the left arm, twisted me around, and sent me staggering against the truck.

My shot hit him in the chest. Or, if the night in DUMBO was any indiction, I hit him in his bullet-proof vest. Which would have been enough to put most men out of action for at least a few minutes. With this guy, I probably only had thirty seconds or so.

With a huge effort, I ignored my left arm, which hurt like hell, straightened up, and walked over to Hawkins. He was out. For the next few seconds, anyway. I kicked his gun away, rolled him over onto his belly, grabbed two pairs of plasticuffs out of my backpack and cuffed both his wrists and his ankles, then rolled him back onto his backside, which meant he was lying atop his cuffed wrists. To confirm the identity of my victim, I yanked off his balaclava and looked at his face. There was the scar over his left eyebrow. Yup, Daryl Hawkins.

I walked to the truck, reached under, and grabbed Hawkins's knife. I used the knife to cut his balaclava into a long strip, and tied it tightly around my left tricep, where his bullet had clipped me. The pressure of my improvised tourniquet was like being stung by a very large wasp. I sure hoped my improvised bandage was stopping the flow of blood.

A metal door clanked open behind me. I turned around and saw the guards I had passed on the fifth floor coming out of the building into the parking lot. They had weapons drawn. They spotted the woman above them on the AC platform.

"Hey, hold it! Stop!" the Brut-wearing guard shouted. They both ran toward the platform stairs.

The female intruder ignored them, intent on picking the lock of the metal-mesh door at the top of the stairs.

I tossed Hawkins's knife deep under the truck and scooped up his Sig P226, dropped it in a cargo pocket, and fell into a run behind the guards, knowing that if they threatened the intruder, she would kill them without hesitation. I wanted to de-escalate the situation extremely quickly. But the guards were a lot closer to the platform than I was.

They reached the bottom of the stairs, each standing at the bottom of one of the two steel railings that ran along each side of the steps.

"I said, 'HOLD it!'" the Brut guard growled. "Stop what you're doing."

The other guard said, "Put your hands up and turn around, slowly."

As the intruder slowly turned, I ducked behind one of the parked sedans in the lot. I was about twenty feet away from the standoff at the AC platform.

When the intruder finished turning, the other guard said, "Come down the stairs, slowly, one step at a time."

"No problem, officers," she replied sardonically.

She took the first two steps slowly, then her hands dropped to the railing, her feet swung up, and she braced herself atop the railing on her heels and palms. She slid down the railings like a surfer crouched over her board. She flipped off the end of the railing, and caught each guard with one of her feet.

The two guards were slammed backward, tumbling onto the parking lot blacktop. Their guns were jarred loose and skittered across the ground. The intruder walked to the nearest guard who was moaning and struggling to stand up and kicked him in the head, knocking him unconscious. The Brut guard had managed to get to his knees, but was unable to block the kick the intruder delivered to his head. Like his partner, he went down and out.

I ran from my hiding spot toward her, arriving a second after she finished kicking the crap out of the guards. Her head twisted in my direction, her brown eyes flashing as she began to spin to meet my attack.

I ducked my head and slammed into her with a full-body tackle. We crashed to the ground with my full weight on top of her. She grunted as we landed, the air being forced from her lungs. But she was tough. She threw some quick, hard jabs at my left kidney, forcing me to roll away from her.

We both scrambled to our feet extremely quickly, but she was faster than I was. Significantly faster. She launched a spin kick at me. Normally, I love it when someone pulls a Bruce Lee move like this. It's easy to defend: Block the kick with one arm while stepping inside the kicking leg and deliver a nasty jab to your opponent's groin. But her move was so swift there was no defense possible. Her foot caught me in the chest and smashed me off my feet, sending me backwards to a hard landing on the parking lot surface.

I was dazed. I had no time to react before she jumped on top of me, straddling my chest, legs pinning my arms, her fists pummeling my face. I rolled, avoiding a number of the blows, and her position on top of me didn't make it easy for her to get maximum weight behind each punch.

I yanked my right arm free from under her leg and punched her as hard as I could, catching her square on the left cheek and snapping her head back. She was stunned for a second but raised her left arm to parry my next blow. Now it was her turn to be too slow. My second punch landed in almost the same place as the first. Her eyes glazed over, and her head sagged. But she caught herself and jerked upright, so I hit her for the third time.

Lying on my back was far from the perfect way to punch someone. But I was a former Green Beret. A former

U.S. Marshal. (Okay, a deputy.) If I was able to throw three clear punches at you, even lying on my back, I was highly likely to knock you out. At the very least, stun you into submission.

Tough as she was, the lady intruder was unconscious. Out cold, she toppled forward onto me. I shoved her off. I could have been a wee bit more of a gentleman and carefully rolled her off of me. But my face was still stinging from her blows, and I was feeling far from gentlemanly.

I stood up and surveyed the damages. A crushed gate. A bunch of people trussed like turkeys in the back of a dump truck. Three people lying unconscious at my feet. But no damage to the operations of Intimidation. Job well done, Tyrrell.

The scraping sound on the asphalt was so tiny, I thought I might have imagined it. But I'm not a government-trained detective cum troubleshooter for nothing. I lunged to my right as Hawkins's knife whipped through the air and sliced through the balaclava wrapped around my left arm. His balaclava.

I grabbed the Ruger from the holster under my left arm, but Hawkins stabbed at me with his knife, and I had to parry the blow or die. Served me right for not tucking the knife into my rucksack. Now the blade was being wielded by someone who was harshly and lethally serious. As I knocked the blade aside, he punched me in the jaw with his left hand. His blow snapped my head back, made me stagger, and he dove at me again.

Enough of this shit, I thought. I clutched his right wrist with both hands as he stabbed at me, fell backward, rolling as I hit the ground and bringing my feet up into his gut. As I continued my backward somersault, I straightened my legs and launched him into the night air. I completed my roll, coming smoothly to my feet.

Hawkins had crashed into a parked car and was now slumped on the ground. With any luck, he had landed on the point of his nasty knife. But this guy was amazingly tough—he would have been a huge success in ultimate fighting. He struggled to his feet, the parking lot flood lights reflected off his damn knife blade.

Emergency sirens were screaming their way toward us—the harsh electronic sound of police vehicles and the booming horns of firetrucks.

I went for my Ruger again, but Hawkins threw his knife at me before I could clear my holster. I ducked and heard the knife whizz overhead and clatter to the ground behind me. I straightened up and yanked my gun loose. Hawkins had run to the woman intruder and picked her up. He was looking at her duffle bag, lying a few feet away.

"You'll never make it to the bag and get a gun out. Not before I shoot you or the police arrest you."

"Who the hell are you?" he asked.

"I'm the Magic Warrior. You said so yourself."

"Yeah, well, you're two for two with me. But they say the third time's the charm. I'll get you next time." He slung the woman over his shoulder and began running toward the smashed gate. It was his only escape route.

"Stop right there," I shouted.

"Fuck you," he laughed and halted. "You're the rescue guy. Not the killer." He ran right through the gate and out into the night. I took a few rushed steps after him, but the sirens were now very loud and there were flashes of red and blue light bouncing off buildings and parked vehicles.

"Harry . . .?"

Before another tick of the proverbial clock had ticked, I was standing in Kim's living room. Alone. No sign of Harry.

"Thanks," I whispered to the air.

8

The tally from Harry's and my Intimidation op was pretty darn good: no guards killed, no bad guys killed, and no damage to Intimidation's basic services. On the negative side: the bad guys got away. And my left arm was still on fire.

Kim's apartment had two bathrooms; one of which was off of her bedroom. The other bathroom, the guest bathroom, was off of the short hall that connected her bedrooms to her living room. I slunk silently to the guest bathroom. Even though I was only a frequent houseguest as opposed to a live-in boyfriend, I had taken the liberty of purchasing a top-quality first-aid kit and storing it under the vanity in the guest bathroom. I pulled out the kit and propped it open on the edge of the sink.

Before I began treatment of my wound, I swallowed four ibuprofen, drinking water from the tap. New York City tap water, cold and clean right out of the faucet. Now properly medicated, or as medicated as I was going to get, I undid what was left of Hawkins's balaclava from my arm. The balaclava and my shirt sleeve were sticky with blood. The pain of peeling off the balaclava strip, and then pulling off my shirt, made me see white. I panted for a few seconds, and normal vision and breathing returned as the pain faded.

The bullet had torn through the flesh of my upper arm, leaving a raw furrow about a quarter-inch wide by two-inches long. Sharply painful, and more than a wee bit of blood, but not serious. And it would make a nice addition to my collection of scars.

I washed out the wound with warm water and soap. Using a Q-tip, I swabbed the cut with anesthetic gel then used a lidocaine roll-on around the wound. When lidocaine first contacted the skin, it felt cold, which was just one more unpleasant sensation for my arm. But in a minute or two, the lidocaine began to numb the area. Bliss. After another minute, I applied some butterfly bandages then overlaid a piece of gauze that I taped down over the wound.

Sitting on the closed toilet seat, I closed my eyes and breathed slowly. After a couple of minutes the pain in had subsided significantly. Ibuprofen and lidocaine, beautiful together. I stood up, pulled off the rest of my clothes, sponged off with a washcloth, and tiptoed into Kim's bedroom. My overnight bag was in the corner. I grabbed a T-shirt and underwear from the case, pulled them on, and slid into bed next to Kim.

She was asleep on her right side, with her back to me. I lightly kissed her shoulder. She moaned.

"Are you all right?" she said in a husky, barely awake whisper.

"All in one piece. No worries."

"Good," she rolled over and kissed me. "I'm so

glad you're home."

"Me, too. I love you."

"I love you, too."

The next morning, Kim woke me a little after 10:00 A.M. She sat on the edge of the bed next to me, a mug full of steaming coffee in her hand.

"Hey, there," she leaned over, kissed me, and handed me the coffee. "I didn't think you'd want to sleep away the day."

"You were right."

"But of course," she smiled.

My reply was to sit up and sip coffee. It truly was the elixir of the gods.

"Would you like some ibuprofen?" she asked.

"You know me so well: yes, please."

She handed me two tablets.

"Only two?" I reacted in mock horror.

"I do not want to be responsible for your overdosing on ibuprofen."

"If you'd had the night I had, overdosing would be the least of your concerns."

"I bet." She handed me two more.

"You came prepared."

"As you said: I know you so well. And . . ." she reached over my legs, grabbed her open laptop, and showed me a news story. "Weren't you in San Francisco last night?"

"Uh, yes, but it was a very brief trip. I didn't have

time for anything. No jazz in North Beach, no food in Chinatown, no sightseeing at the Golden Gate—"

"But you managed to find the time to visit Intimidation Software, didn't you?" she asked playfully.

I could see a photo on the laptop screen: The Mack truck sitting atop the wreckage of the guard booth. I pointed at it and explained, "I didn't do that."

"Didn't do what? Crash the truck into the gate? Or subdue three people and leave them 'cuffed in the back of the truck? Or subdue two more guards and leave them on the ground in the parking lot?" Her tone was still playful, but I thought I heard a slight edge to it.

"I can honestly say that I didn't do any of that."

"So, were you the extra security measures that turned away a physical attack on the premises?" Yes, there was now a definite edge in her voice.

I nodded, "Yes, that would be me."

"You had mentioned a particular guy who might be a lot of trouble for you—was he there?"

"Yup."

"Did he give you that?" she pointed at the gauze pad and medical adhesive tape on my left arm.

"Yes, he did. Very thoughtful of him, wouldn't you say?"

"Tell me he looks worse than you do," she insisted.

"Well . . . he wasn't as cute as I was to begin with—"

"Does he look worse than you?"

"Uh . . . it's probably even."

"I'm going to have a talk with Harry about keeping you safe. It's not fair that you get beat up and—what is that?" she pointed at my arm again.

"Flesh wound. Bullet. He did try to stab me, but missed."

"It's not fair that you get beat up and shot and stabbed and everything else. It's not." Kim was angry. And worried. "If you're going to help people, then Harry has to take care of you."

"That's not how it works."

"Oh? How does it work?"

"Come on, Kim, you know how. Harry introduces me to people in need, I choose to help them, and I get whatever I need to fulfill my mission. But there are no guarantees."

"No guarantee that you'll be safe?"

"No. And no guarantee that I'll succeed."

"I thought the Chairman wanted you to help people."

"He does. But my help doesn't mean there's going to be a happy ending for everyone. Some nice people who were doing the Chairman's will and helping me have died."

"Died because they helped you?"

"Yes."

"That doesn't seem fair."

"It isn't. But—"

"Don't you dare say life's not fair."

"It isn't. Sorry."

She closed her laptop and stood up. "I'm beginning to dislike your work with Harry. Dislike it intensely."

"I understand."

"But you're not going to stop, are you?"

I shook my head. "I can't stop. It's my mission to help others."

"Volunteer at a soup kitchen if you want to help others!"

"A soup kitchen wouldn't utilize my skills as a government-trained detective cum troubleshooter."

Kim stood by the bed, looking down at me, then focused on my coffee cup. "You want a refill?"

"Yes, please."

"I love you, but I hate you, too."

"I know. I'm very annoying."

Her face softened; she grinned, leaned over, and kissed me. Then she took my coffee cup.

As she walked out of the bedroom, she called back over her shoulder, "Get out of bed. You're the laziest government-trained detective cum troubleshooter ever!"

*   *   *

PRIVATUS HEADQUARTERS

HAWKINS GINGERLY SETTLED himself into one of the leather armchairs around the conference table in the black room. Desjardins stifled a smile at his discomfort.

Freund snarled, "What happened in San Francisco?

163

How could your team fail?"

"The Magic Warrior was there."

"Who?" Freund was almost apoplectic. "Who the hell is that?"

"The same man who stopped us in DUMBO when we attempted to kidnap Grayson. Correct?" Desjardins asked.

"Yeah, correct," replied Hawkins. "Whoever the hell he is, he has some serious skills. He was faster on the draw than I was, and he took out Regina Mayfield in hand-to-hand combat."

"He probably has a similar background to you," Desjardins pointed out. "SEAL or Green Beret, maybe CIA after his time in the military."

"Yeah, sure, guys like him and me are a dime a dozen."

"I meant the opposite of that. How many of you could there be?"

"Almost three hundred meet those criteria," Freund said. "And they're all on our watch list."

"So if he's stupid enough to get caught on a security camera, we'll nail him with facial recognition," Hawkins said.

"Yes. Why do you say stupid enough?" Desjardins asked.

"This guy makes me feel real uneasy. How the hell did he know we were going to be in San Francisco, specifically at Intimidation? How did he get by all their security? We crashed the damn gate. But he was already inside, waiting for us—how the hell did he manage that?"

"You think he has an organization behind him," Desjardins suggested.

"He must. No one guy could have known enough to cut us off, first in DUMBO, than in San Francisco, beat the security at Intimidation, *and* beat us at both places. Not only is this guy good, but his organization is really good."

"CIA?" Freund asked. "Maybe the FBI?"

"Not the CIA. They can't operate domestically. And this guy just doesn't have that federal agent vibe."

"What makes you say that?" Freund asked.

"They would have staked out Intimidation," Desjardins replied. "Once Hawkins and Mayfield made their move, a large team of agents would have been all over our players."

Hawkins gestured toward Desjardins, his palm up in agreement, "Exactly. A lone wolf doesn't fit into the FBI playbook."

"So . . . which organization?"

Hawkins shook his head, "It's some outfit I don't think I've run into before. Maybe somebody private, like us. Whoever they are, they've got lots of resources and good people on the ground."

"That's not possible," Freund said. "At the very least, we would have heard rumors about another private agency of our size and resources."

"I don't know what to tell you," Hawkins

responded. "But I can't figure out who these guys are."

Desjardins had closed her eyes and was drumming her fingers very slowly and very quietly on the table top. The two men sat still and waited on her.

"We'll put aside the questions of who is the Magic Warrior and what organization he works for." Desjardins opened her eyes and looked from one man to the other. "We need to complete our missions, and our opponents will reveal themselves if they continue to fight us."

She stood up and paced the length of the room then back to the men. "We'll need to adjust our manpower requirements for the next op."

"Yes, indeed," Hawkins grinned. "Can I go in heavy?"

"Absolutely. But your priority is still to cripple Doberman Cyber. Secondly, you will capture the Magic Warrior if possible, kill him if not. And you will do this as quietly as possible."

"No worries, I only go ballistic if that's the only way to accomplish the priorities."

"Perfectly stated." She turned to Freund, "Let's return to the question of the Magic Warrior having advance knowledge about the Grayson kidnapping and last night's foray in San Francisco."

Freund nodded and said, "We think we have identified a leak: George Morita."

"He's one of our analysts, right?" Hawkins asked.

"Yes. I recruited him from the CIA," Desjardins

said. "Yesterday he called in sick, told us he was going to the doctor. We pinged his cell phone, and it was at the doctor's office at the correct time. Later we pinged it again, and it was at his home.

"But he never called in sick this morning. We pinged his cell phone and it's still in his home. We sent a team to check it out—no sign of him or his family. Morita's Privatus cell phone was on the kitchen counter. Both cars in the garage and the driveway. Home phone hasn't been used in twenty-seven hours. No credit cards used in the last forty-eight hours. We're still checking, but Morita and his family do not appear to have taken a train or plane or rented a car. They have not registered into a hotel or Airbnb."

"They're off the grid," Freund said. "Disappeared completely."

"Do you think the Magic Warrior's agency had a hand in this?" asked Hawkins.

"It's hard to imagine that an analyst—not an undercover agent—could vanish like this without some serious help," Desjardins replied.

"Most agents would have a hard time doing it," added Freund.

"Are we thinking that Morita gave up the information on Grayson? And Intimidation? And probably Doberman? Maybe even Paris?" Hawkins wondered.

"Probably," Desjardins said. "Unfortunately, we have no idea how much information he divulged. We have no idea what you're facing. That's why you can go heavy when you go against Doberman."

"And after I get the Magic Warrior, do I get to hunt Mr. Morita?"

"He's all yours. Let's hope you can wrap them up before you leave for Paris."

"That's my plan."

* * *

Tuesday evening found Kim and me at her dining room table, finishing one of the iconic meals of New York City: takeout Chinese.

"Do you want your fortune cookie?" I asked.

"Just the fortune." She grabbed a cookie and broke it open, pulling out the tiny piece of paper. "Oh crap. My fortune is: The people you trust are the people you love."

"What's wrong with that?"

"I prefer fortunes like 'You will win a million dollars' or 'You will find romance with a stranger.'"

"Hey, that hurts."

She smiled a glorious smile, "You were a stranger when we first met. That fortune already came true for me."

"Consider me somewhat mollified."

"How do I move you from 'somewhat' to 'completely' mollified?"

"Oh, well . . . would you be up for a late night rendezvous?"

"Late night? Do you have to work again tonight?"

"Unfortunately, yes." I pondered that for a moment. Would Privatus attack Doberman as originally planned? Or would last night change things?

"Actually," I said, "I'm not sure."

"You think last night might have changed things?"

"Maybe." I spoke into the air, "Harry?"

And . . . he arrived.

"Hello, Harry," Kim said. "I'm about to make some coffee. Would you like some?"

"No thank you."

Kim went into the kitchen.

"Are we working tonight?" I asked.

"I'm afraid so."

"Afraid? That's an interesting choice of words. Why are you afraid?"

Harry hesitated for a moment then said, "The situation may have changed."

"Privatus sending a larger team? Maybe some weapons that are bigger and badder?"

"Yes."

"Okay. Am I allowed to recruit some help?"

"Yes."

I mulled that one over for a moment. Who the hell was I going to get with only a few hours notice?

"I need to make a phone call," I said.

"Joanne Agar?"

"Of course. I need a ton of muscle fast, so I'm calling my buddy at the FBI."

"Are you going to want to be at Doberman?"

"Of course. Strictly as an observer. Will you whoosh me there?"

"Yes."

"What time should I suggest to Joanne?"

Harry glanced up and back at me. "Midnight will give the FBI plenty of time to set up."

"Thanks. See you around 11:30? My place?"

He nodded and disappeared.

Kim walked back into the dining room, with a mug of coffee in each hand. "Harry's already gone?"

"Yeah, he and I are meeting later."

"So you're working tonight?"

"Strictly observing."

"Really? You're only an observer?"

"I'm going to arrange to have dozens of big, powerful FBI agents handle tonight's mission while I observe. Then, when I get back . . ."

She handed me a mug. "Slip into bed next to me, kiss me, and we'll see what happens."

"I like the sound of that."

"Good."

"Now, unfortunately, I must make a business call."

"Strictly business?"

"Strictly." I stood up and carried my coffee to the living room windows that overlooked West End Avenue. I called Joanne's home number.

"Jack, please, can't this wait till tomorrow?" Joanne

asked when she answered on the third ring.

"Sorry, no. In fact, it can't wait at all."

"I'm about to go out to dinner with my wife."

"I am so sorry. Really. But that private security firm you've been investigating . . . Privatus? The folks there are going to make a move tonight."

"How do you know?"

"I have a most reliable source. Beyond reliable."

"I don't suppose this source provided you with evidence?"

"Nothing you can use in court."

"Why do you believe this source of yours?"

"Because that source led me to the right place at the right time to prevent Grayson's kidnapping in DUMBO the other night. And I was the 'extra security' that stopped the attack on Intimidation last night."

"What?" Joanne half-shouted into the phone. "Are you F'ing kidding me? Why are you telling me this now?"

"I know when and where Privatus is going tonight, but I don't know how many, and I suspect that they'll be loaded for bear."

"Which will be entirely due to your most recent efforts."

"Yes."

"So now you want me to come to your rescue by sending in a team capable of taking down Privatus."

"Well, when you put it that way . . . yes."

"Jack, if I didn't love you, I swear I'd find a way to

arrest you. Why didn't you tell me all of this before?"

"I didn't have any evidence to give you."

"Will there be evidence tonight?"

"Sure, you'll have the Privatus people to arrest."

There was silence on her end while she considered this. "You didn't think you needed help to handle the other two attacks, did you?"

"No, I didn't."

"You must be really worried if you feel you couldn't handle tonight by yourself."

"I am."

"And now that you've given me this gold-plated piece of information, I have to act on it."

"Sorry, but I think you do."

"I am not happy with you, Jack. Not happy at all."

"I'm sorry. I really am. Between my client's needs and my source, I didn't handle this the right way. If you want to throw me in jail overnight, I understand."

"Overnight? That's all?"

"You don't think one jailhouse breakfast is enough?"

"We'll see." She paused, "Okay, where and when?"

"Doberman Cyber, on the old Route 128, the Yankee Division Highway, near Woburn."

"You know, Jack, 128 is now part of Interstate 95."

"I'm lost in nostalgia—it was 128 when I visited my friends who went to one of Boston's gazillion colleges."

"You should seek professional help."

"I do."

"Really? From an honest-to-goodness shrink?"

"Honest-to-goodness."

"I find that very difficult to believe. But let's return to the issue of the Privatus op. When?"

"You'll need to be in place by midnight."

"Shit. I'm going to have to get one of the Bureau's jets—I have to get hopping. Any idea how many hostiles?"

"My guess would be between a half-dozen and a dozen. Very heavily armed."

"That's a lot. I'm going to have to contact the Massachusetts State Police."

"I think that's a good idea."

"One last thing," she said. "Are you planning to be there?"

"I was thinking of stopping by."

"Strictly as an observer, right?"

"Right."

"No weapons, right?"

"I was thinking of bringing a little, pearl-handled—"

"Jack," she said wearily. "No weapons. Right?"

"No weapons."

"Should we set up a rendezvous?"

"No need. I'll find you."

* * *

Kim hugged me close for a long moment at her

front door. Her head was tucked against my chest.

"You'd better come back to me."

"I will."

"Promise?"

"I promise."

She kissed me—a long, slow, open-mouthed kiss.

"Are you trying to seduce me into staying?" I whispered. I say 'whispered' because it seemed more manly than what I actually did: gasped.

"Is it working?"

"Almost." I kissed her, gently but quickly, and said, "I've got to go. Harry's meeting me at my place."

"Come back to me. Come back in one safe, solid piece."

"I will. I love you."

"I'm not sure how much of this I can take," she said. "I hate watching you leave to . . ." her voice trailed off.

"I'm . . . sorry. I . . . don't know what else to say."

"You have to go," she said resignedly.

"Yes."

"Go."

I walked to my apartment and tried to imagine how frightening it was for Kim every time I walked out the door. It was impossible for me to know how she felt, and other than quitting my work with Harry, there was nothing I could do to make her feel better.

The distance between Kim's apartment at West End

Avenue and West 81st Street and my place on West 76th is only a few blocks, but it was a muggy July night, and I had broken a sweat by the time I got home. It wasn't a dripping, just-off-the-elliptical-trainer sweat, but it did require a quick wash and toweling off. After performing my truncated ablutions, I pulled on fresh clothes that were almost identical to the previous night's attire: dark-gray T-shirt, black cargo pants, black crepe-soled shoes. I once again chose camouflage over comfort and put on a black windbreaker and tucked a balaclava in its left pocket. Finally, I dropped my Walther CCP, into my right side cargo pocket and an extra magazine into the left.

"You told Joanne you wouldn't have a weapon," Harry said, appearing, as usual, out of nowhere.

"Yeah, but, it's just a small weapon, almost nothing really . . ."

"Do you hear yourself rationalizing?"

"I hate it when you make me behave."

He shrugged. As with most of Harry's body movements, it was a minimal shrug.

I said and dug into my pockets and dumped the gun and the magazine on the bed. "Happy now?"

"Positively delighted," he deadpanned. "Are you ready?"

I cast a covetous glance back at the Walther on the bed then forced myself to turn away. I patted down my pockets to make sure I had my wallet and phone. I did. In the interest of full disclosure, I felt naked without a weapon. Please don't get me wrong, I don't normally walk around with a weapon on my person. I'm weapon-free about 99 percent of the time. But going on an operation without a weapon? Nope. Not my style.

This time would be the exception that proved the rule. "Yes, I'm ready."

9

Harry's Mona Lisa smile flashed on and off. And without being aware of any time passing, of any distance being traveled, I found myself at the edge of a parking lot about ten yards from a large dark trailer—a Massachusetts State Police mobile command center. Parked next to it were two Ford Explorers with U.S. Government license plates.

The command center and the Explorers were parked on the edge of the parking lot, immediately next to a grassy median bordered by high, asphalt curbs. The median had scrubby little shrubs and Scotch pines about ten to twelve feet tall. The median and parking lot stretched about hundred feet to my right, ending in a stand of trees. To my left, the median and lot reached out at least a hundred feet to what looked like a service road off Interstate 95. Behind me was a seven-story, modern glass building with no architectural character whatsoever. Just a big box. And not a window with a light in it—clearly no one was burning the midnight oil there.

On the far side of the median was . . . another parking lot. On the far side of that lot was . . . another nondescript, seven-story building surrounded by a chain-link, razor-wire-topped fence. Floodlights illuminated the outside of the building. Near the top of the building, in three-foot-tall letters, were the words: *Doberman Cyber.* Probably there so that if you were driving along Interstate 95 and had the sudden impulse to visit Doberman Cyber, you would know where to find it. You would spot the sign, exit the Interstate, drive to the capacious lot surrounding the building, park, and then attempt to talk your way through the guard booth at the entrance to the fence.

Or you could use the Privatus method and make a sneak attack in the middle of the night. Either way, the sign on the side of the building made it impossible to miss the place.

"Freeze, police!" A woman said.

Somehow, while surveilling the scene, I had missed the fact that two uniformed Massachusetts State Troopers were standing outside the mobile command center. Both had their hands on their still-holstered weapons. I guess one of the disadvantages of whooshing places with Harry is that you don't always notice every important detail of your new, suddenly whooshed-into surroundings. Especially in this case when Harry hadn't bothered to come along. The troopers could be forgiven for not noticing me—until a split second before, I hadn't been there to be noticed.

I raised my hands and said "I'm Jack Tyrrell. Special Agent Agar is expecting me."

One of the troopers backed to the door of the command center and banged on it with his fist. He kept his focus on me the entire time. The door opened a crack, and the trooper muttered something about someone here to see Special Agent Agar.

After a few seconds, Joanne stuck her head out of the door then pushed it open and descended the three steps from the command center to the parking lot.

"How the hell did you sneak past everyone?"

"I assure you, hell had nothing to do with it."

"Give me a straight answer, how did you get here?"

"Let's just say I still have some skills."

"Are you packing?"

"No. I told you I'd come unarmed, and I have."

"Hmm," she grunted and waved me toward the command center as she turned to go back up the steps. "Come inside." To the troopers she said, "Thank you."

The command center was a very long trailer with a bunch of wall-mounted monitors and communications devices. At one end of the trailer was a ten-feet-long, narrow table, surrounded by faux-leather banquettes. Seated around the table, with styrofoam cups full of coffee in front of them were a pair of Massachusetts State Troopers and a man in a light-gray suit with a white dress shirt and dark blue tie. He looked as if he had stepped out of the FBI's Dress For Success Manual, circa 1950. Quick introductions were made: Major Fitzgerald was in overall charge of the State Police presence in this operation, Captain Garnett was in charge of the STOP team, (STOP was the Massachusetts version of SWAT), and FBI Special

Agent Monroe was leading the Boston-based team of federal agents.

When it was my turn to be introduced, Joanne said, "This is Jack Tyrrell, former deputy, U.S. Marshals. He's consulting with us on this case. It was his informer that revealed this operation against Doberman."

Joanne pointed at a thermos on a countertop under one of the TV monitors and said, "Coffee."

I poured myself a styrofoam cup full. I ignored the small bowl with non-diary creamers in tiny plastic cups. Joanne and I sat down with the three men at the table.

"How good is your informer?" asked Special Agent Monroe smugly.

I wanted to tighten his tie for him and squeeze the smugness right out of him, but I refrained and said, "The best. He never fails."

"Never?" smiled Monroe woodenly.

"Never."

Monroe shrugged, turned to the State Police and smirked. They smirked in return.

"Did your informer happen to give you their plan of attack?"

"No."

"No wonder you think he's the best." Monroe turned to Joanne, "You jerked me out of my home for this bullshit?"

"I thought this was so important I arranged to fly here on one of the Bureau's jets. And believe me, it wasn't easy getting authorization for that. So, let's leave aside the credibility of Jack's source," Joanne said. She asked me, "Give us the details of the attack in San Francisco?"

"Only a two-person team. They arranged for a truck to crash through the gate as a diversion. I'm guessing they stole the truck beforehand and paid some lowlife ten grand to drive it through the gate."

"That's right," she nodded. "SFPD confirmed that the truck driver didn't know the names of the people who hired him, had never seen them before. Five grand up front to drive the truck, five grand after. Since he was arrested, he never got the second five."

"Poor boy," I said.

"What about the initial payment of five grand?" asked Major Fitzgerald. "Any luck tracing that?"

Joanne shook her head. "Completely clean. Dozens of partial and full fingerprints on the bills, but not a single print popped up in any law-enforcement databases except for the truck driver. The cash was used twenty-dollar bills, non-sequential serial numbers."

"Impossible to track back to anyone," the major added.

Joanne looked at me, "Last night a two-person team. But tonight you're sure they're going in heavy. Why?"

"My source says so. And . . . last night they went in with two but were stopped by one. They didn't accomplish their mission, which was to sabotage Intimidation's physical plant. And they didn't kill or capture me. They want to ensure that things go very differently tonight. And that means a larger team with heavier weapons." I faced Captain Garnett. "How are you set up?"

First Garnett glanced at Joanne, who nodded in approval, then he replied, "I have two teams, totaling a dozen troopers, ready to go. Six are positioned—" he pointed to a map that was on the table— "here in an old Chevy van near Doberman's parking lot driveway, about fifty feet from the smaller of the two gates in the fence that forms the security perimeter of the building. And here, a second team of six is taking cover in the woods at the back of the parking lot, also about fifty feet from the larger gate that is the entrance to the building's loading dock."

"What's on the far side of the woods?" I asked.

"Another parking lot. For a shopping mall. There are no twenty-four hour retailers in there. The mall's shut tight."

"May I ask what equipment your teams have?"

"Sure. Assault rifles, flash-bang grenades, tear-gas grenades, 9mm pistols, body armor. They're ready." Garnett paused and scanned the map spread out on the table. "Do you have any idea how the bad guys will launch this operation?"

"I'm sorry, I wish I knew. If I were going in, and going in as heavy as they are, I wouldn't waste time being subtle. I'd crash through one or both of the gates, blast my way to the AC or whatever they're planning to destroy, then get the hell out."

"You think they're going after the air-conditioning?"

"A tech company like Doberman has to run a bunch of servers to support its networks, store its data, etc. And servers require a lot of cooling capacity. A lot. Any building with air-conditioning, especially one with a lot of servers, requires large condenser/compressor units outside, which are much more vulnerable to sabotage then something inside the building."

"Take out the AC, and you take out the servers," Garnett said.

""Take out the servers," Joanne finished for him, "and you take out the company. At least temporarily."

"*Temporarily* is all that the bad guys are hoping for," I added.

Major Fitzgerald had been staring at the map while we had been talking. "No disrespect Deputy Tyrrell—"

"It's just Tyrrell."

He smiled, "For the purposes of tonight's operation, I think we'll reinstate your status. *Temporarily*."

"Thank you." I was surprised at how genuinely grateful I was for Fitzgerald's unofficial and temporary recognition. Nobody had honored me with the title of "Deputy" in a long time.

Fitzgerald resumed, "Anyway, meaning no disrespect, but I don't think I'd do it the way you're suggesting."

"Why?"

"Look at the map. Interstate 95 is roughly northwest of the building. The parking lot stretches around three sides of the building, west, north, and east. The southern side of the property," he pointed at the map so there was no doubt as to what he meant, "borders on the woods, where a team of Captain Garnett's men are waiting."

Fitzgerald referred to the map again, "Garnett's team are near the southwest corner of the building where the large gate and the loading dock are located.

"About a hundred, a hundred-fifty feet away, at the backside of the building, facing the woods, are the air-conditioning compressors. They are situated in a small, fenced compound of their own, which is also inside the main security-perimeter fence. High fences, both with razor wire tops."

I asked, "Are you thinking they'll make a direct attack on the AC units?"

"Why not?" Fitzgerald replied. "They're out of sight of the road. You can approach the units unseen through the woods. Cut through each of the fences, plant a small explosive packet on each of the compressors, retreat to a safe distance into the woods, and blow the units to smithereens."

I nodded, "You're right. That's the way to do it."

Heads nodded all around the table.

Garnett grabbed a walkie-talkie unit off the table,

and called "Command to Southwest."

"Go for Southwest."

"Move your team to the east to cover the AC compressors at the rear of the building. We anticipate the attack will come there."

"Copy that. Moving team to the east."

"Be careful. We anticipate that the bad guys will be *very* heavily armed."

"Copy that. That's why they pay us the big bucks."

"Big bucks. Copy that."

There were tart grins all round the table in the command center.

Garnett said to Fitzgerald, "I think I should move the Northwest team to the southwestern corner of the perimeter fence, position them to reinforce the Southwest team."

"Yes. Please do that."

Garnett spoke into his walkie-talkie again, "Command to Northwest."

"Go for Northwest."

"Move to the southwestern corner of the perimeter fence to form a reserve for the Southwest team."

"Copy that. Moving to southwestern corner."

Those of us in the mobile command center sat and downed coffee in silence, waiting to hear from the southwest STOP team.

Garnett's walkie-talkie crackled, "Southwest to Command."

"Go for Command."

"Southwest in position."

"Copy that. Report any movement."

"Copy."

There was enough time between radio communications for me to drink more coffee. To paraphrase John Milton: They also serve who wait. But I would much rather have been out in the field wearing body armor and carrying an assault rifle than sitting in the safety of the command center. Being an observer was for the birds as far as I was concerned.

The walkie-talkie came to life, "Northwest for Command."

"Go for Command."

"We're in position."

"Copy. Stand by."

"Copy. Standing by."

The waiting and coffee drinking resumed. When I was with the Marshals, the thing I probably hated most was waiting to grab a fugitive on a warrant. Making the arrest itself could be anything from funny—some fugitives are so stupid they make you laugh out loud—to dry-eyeball scary. But there was almost always an adrenalin rush, especially if you had to go through a door into the unknown: a fugitive with a gun? With a knife? With a captive? One time, I was part of a warrant squad, and the guy waiting for us on the other side of a door attempted to fend us off with a chain saw. For a second, we all thought we had rushed into *The*

Texas Chainsaw Massacre. I'm sure I wasn't the only one who had been terrified that I was about to be sawn into little pieces. We began laughing when we realized that this jackass had no power for the chainsaw. It was just an awkward, heavy piece of hardware. One of my squad mates had told the jackass to drop the saw, gave him a few seconds to comply, then tasered him when he didn't. The poor guy had quivered as people do when they are hit with a taser, then dropped the chainsaw on his own foot, breaking it. I had to admit it: I missed the action of the arrest itself. But waiting for suspects to show up was no fun at all.

I finished my coffee and asked Joanne, "Where's the head?"

She pointed to a narrow door located midway along the length of the command center. I gave a polite, soft knock on the door, received no answer, and proceeded through a door so short and narrow that I had to duck and twist to accommodate my six-feet-two frame. An airplane bathroom was deluxe—and *huge*—compared to this toilet. I urinated and then washed my hands in a sink so tiny that I could only put one hand at a time under the faucet.

After prying myself through the bathroom door, I stepped over to the table, leaned close to Joanne, and asked, "Would it be all right if I wait outside?"

"I'll join you." To the others she said, "I'm going outside for a smoke. I'm on walkie."

It was a beautiful summer night. Quiet except for

the steady white-noise of traffic on Interstate 95.

"I hate the waiting," Joanne said.

"Nobody likes it."

We walked a few yards away from the trailer.

"How long have you been married?"

"Since 2013. We got married in Maryland just a few months after same-sex marriages became legal there."

"How do you like married life?"

"I like it. I like it a lot."

"Are you going to have kids?"

"We're not sure. We both want to, but . . . I don't know . . . it's a big step."

"Yes, it is. Maggie and I wanted to but never made the decision, and . . . well . . . you know how that turned out."

"Are you sorry you didn't seize the day and have a kid?"

"Oh geez, that's complex. I don't know how to answer that. I don't have a clue how things would have been different if we'd had a child. Maybe I would have gotten my head out of my ass a lot sooner. Or maybe . . ." I had to take a deep breath to continue, "maybe I would have been a drunken shit, anyway. Maybe Maggie would have still been killed, and our child would have had a drunken loser for a father."

After a long pause, Joanne said, "For crying out loud, lighten up, Jack."

We both laughed, the bittersweet laugh of

survivors.

"You know what?" I asked. "You should go for it. You and your wife should be parents. I hear it's the greatest thing ever."

"Just not for you."

"No, I don't know, maybe sometime."

"Sometime when, Jack? You're in your forties. What the hell are you waiting for?"

"Don't you think maybe I should get married first? I know it's hopelessly square to think marriage is a requirement for raising kids, but I'm hopelessly square."

"Yes, you are, but it's one of your charms. Listen, you just told me to go for it. Well, now I'm telling you: Go for it."

"Was that an all-inclusive 'go for it'?"

"You told me that Kim's really special. What are you waiting for? Go for it. Get married. Have a kid."

My mouth gaped open as I searched through the vast, empty reaches of my brain for an appropriate response. Before I found one, Joanne's walkie-talkie came to life.

"Southwest to Command."

"Go for Command."

"We have movement back here."

"Let the suspects cut through the perimeter fence. Apprehend them the second they approach the inner fence surrounding the AC units."

"Copy. Apprehend at the inner fence."

Joanne looked at me, "I need to get inside. You coming?"

"In a moment."

"Don't get any bright ideas."

"Me? I never get bright ideas."

She shook her head and climbed the steps into the command center. I walked another ten yards farther away from the command center.

"Harry," I whispered.

"Yes."

"Aren't you a little overdressed for this occasion?"

As usual, Harry was wearing a suit and tie. He said, "Do you really want to review my sartorial habits at this moment?"

"Actually, no."

"What do you want?"

"I was hoping you'd whoosh me to the action at the back of the building."

"Didn't you just tell Special Agent Agar that you wouldn't have any bright ideas?"

"Do you call this a bright idea?"

He sighed. "I presume you want to be close to the action but not in the middle of the fray."

"Sounds perfect. I'd prefer not to be shot."

"I really think you should wait here as you told Ms. Agar you would."

"I didn't tell her that. I said I wouldn't get any bright ideas. It's not my fault if she misunderstood me."

"Why are you doing this?"

"Because I need to capture Daryl Hawkins."

"Why? Because he's a version of you?"

"What?"

Harry stared at me, waiting for me to figure it out.

"Do you think I'm trying to resolve something with him?"

"I don't know. Are you?"

"No. Of course not." Methinks thou doth protest too much, Tyrrell. I knew that was a misquote from *Hamlet*, but it was accurate for me. Was Harry right? Did I need to prove something about myself by triumphing over Hawkins?

"Do you think I need the good version of me to be victorious over my evil twin?" I asked.

"You are the one with the answer to that question," Harry replied. "Do you?"

"I hate to say this, because it pains me to admit you could be on to something, but maybe. Yes. But, I also think we need to capture Hawkins if we're going to tear apart Privatus and get George Morita some semblance of a normal life. That was the initial mission, wasn't it?"

"What a singular occurrence—you're actually making sense."

"Ou—" I was in the middle of that tiny, single-syllable word when Harry whooshed me to the back side of the Doberman building, "—ch." Fortunately, I was whispering.

Harry had deposited me onto the branch of a maple tree at the edge of woods on the southern side of the building. I swayed for a moment, grabbed another branch at chest height, and steadied myself. The branch I stood on was eight- or nine-inches thick and about ten feet off the ground. My position had good sight lines in almost every direction. From the tree to the perimeter fence was a well-mown lawn about twenty-feet wide. Another forty or fifty feet inside of the fence was the rear of the building, including the AC units inside their own fenced-in enclosure. The rear of the building was flood-lit, the same as the other three sides.

The woods spread out in every other direction. I doubted this mini-forest was more than a quarter-mile deep to the south, and it stretched out of my sight to the east and west, but that didn't exactly make it Tolkien's Mirkwood Forest. It did allow for plenty of cover for a small band of orcs or a group of criminals about to sabotage the Doberman Cyber facilities.

I pivoted slowly on my branch, peering through the dark woods—the flood lights on the building intensified the darkness under the trees. I spotted the STOP team, their rifles at the ready. They all wore helmets and peered through night-vision goggles. The combination of helmets and goggles made them look like gigantic insects. Deadly, gigantic insects.

Twisting to the east, my left, I continued to scan the woods and finally found the Privatus team. There were six of them, all dressed in black, wearing balaclavas, and carrying assault rifles or Uzis. The bad guys crept forward. The guy taking the point looked like he was pretty big. Given that it was dark and that they were hunched over to present small targets, it was hard to tell for sure, but I would have bet the leader was Hawkins. My evil twin. My personal target for this mission. Stay focused, Tyrrell. Focus on your mission, which is to stop Privatus and help George Morita—not to beat your personal demons.

The Privatus team had crept to the edge of the woods. The leader used a small pair of binoculars to check the Doberman building from one side to the other. After he was satisfied, he stood up and took a step out of the trees onto the lawn.

And froze. Statues showed more life than this guy.

My internal radar was pinging like mad. Something was wrong; the situation had changed. I had a sinking feeling the Privatus leader's internal radar was also pinging loudly in his head. Somehow he knew that his plan was going sour, knew that he needed to abort.

He took a step backward, moving in slow motion until he was under the trees. His team rose from their hiding places and began to creep slowly away.

"Freeze, police! Drop your weapons!"

The STOP team had all risen to their feet and were aiming their weapons at the Privatus group.

"Drop your weapons and put your hands up," a state trooper sergeant said. "Now!"

The Privatus group dropped in unison to the forest floor and began firing. Two state troopers spun around as bullets slammed into them. I hoped they'd both been shot in their vests. The remaining troopers returned fire. The noise was a horrific combination of the harsh burping reports of the guns, the whine of bullets, and the tearing and thudding as shots clipped leaves and branches and tore into tree trunks.

I was extremely grateful to Harry for having whooshed me to a place of safety. The ground below was a kill zone. Especially for a non-vest wearing, unarmed man like me.

The troopers were firing tear-gas canisters. A couple of canisters bounced off of trees, but a couple landed among the Privatus team. One of the gas canisters landed near the base of my tree, and the *phffft* of gas followed. I hoped it wouldn't rise to my level, but that was a ridiculous hope. I yanked on my balaclava and was thankful the mask covered my nose and mouth. That wouldn't protect me from the tear gas, but it might help a tiny bit.

Grenades were tossed by the Privatus team. Flash-bangs. Lots of noise and bright light. Nothing too close to me, but I was not enjoying this fracas at all.

The Privatus team was aggressive as hell. After the flash-bangs, they laid down a storm of automatic weapons fire. The troopers were returning fire, but they were outgunned and outmanned, an unenviable position to find yourself in. I considered what I could do: Let's see Tyrrell, you're up a tree, literally, without a gun or body armor. Just what do you think you can contribute to the law-and-order side of this fight?

Fortunately, as I realized I was useless in this situation, the backup STOP team arrived, running across the lawn, guns blazing in support of their fellow troopers. The Privatus team had no choice but to fall back and maneuver deeper into the woods. One of them went down, but two team members grabbed him by the shoulder straps of his body armor and dragged him behind them. The rest of the Privatus team fired quick bursts to slow down any pursuit.

But the cavalry arrived at that moment. The two FBI Ford Explorers swung around the far, eastern corner of the building and raced across the lawn, the passenger-side spotlights blazing into the woods. They screeched to a stop near the edge of the trees, with their headlights and spotlights casting a glare into the forest. There was a lot of light now, but the shadows were as black as the Earl of Hell's waistcoat. Federal agents hopped out of the Explorers with shotguns.

With state troopers to the west and Feds to the east, the Privatus team clustered around their wounded member, dropped their weapons and put their hands in the air. I counted: There were only five. I scanned the shadows, hoping to find the hiding place of the last man.

And there he was. As the troopers and Feds walked

toward the surrendering Privatus team, they walked right past the sixth Privatus man. I watched as he waited for the troopers and agents to close in on his team, then he slowly backed away from them, coming past the tree where I was positioned.

I wished he were going to pass a lot closer. I could drop out of the tree, slam him to the ground, and hand him over to law enforcement. But he was probably twenty feet south of me. If I attempted a vertical drop of ten feet while leaping sideways for twenty feet, I'd probably break all kinds of bones. And fall short of the Privatus guy by ten feet. He would still end up shooting me and moving on.

Any second now, the troopers and agents would realize they were a suspect short and throw out an expansive net to find the last Privatus player. At which point, he'd bolt.

The branch I was standing on was in the deep shadow caused by the headlights and spotlights. I swung down, holding onto the branch with my hands, my feet dangling below. I held in that position for a few seconds. No one—neither good guys nor bad—noticed me. I dropped the last few feet and landed softly on the ground. When it came to being quiet, all that government training and crepe-soled shoes were very handy. No way I could have been heard over the shouting of law enforcement rounding up their suspects.

I glanced at the Privatus leader's last position and spotted him. He had turned south, going deeper into the woods. As I mentioned, this mini-forest was only about a quarter-mile deep. The Privatus man was probably headed for the shopping mall parking lot on the southern edge of the trees where I assumed he had left a car.

I pursued him through the trees and brush, moving as fast as I could while remaining silent. When you're pursuing a large, dangerous, armed man, and you're unarmed, it's a good idea to catch him by surprise. It reduces the possibilities that he'll shoot you full of holes.

He was relying on his ears now; no more turning around to see if anyone had spotted him. His pace had increased but probably not to top speed. I also ran faster, until the distance between us was about fifteen feet. A couple of quick, long steps by me and a diving tackle, and I would have him. I took a deep breath and readied myself to lunge after him—

And then all hell broke out behind us. The headlights and spotlights shifted their beams, pointing deeper into the woods very near Mr. Privatus and me. Shouts from the troopers and agents filled the night: "Freeze! Police! FBI! Freeze. Hands up!"

The Privatus guy was having none of it. He took off at a dead run. I cursed under my breath and chased him at full speed. If our law-enforcement pursuers didn't mistake me for him and shoot me, I had a pretty good chance of catching this guy. He was wearing body armor and carrying an assault rifle, not to mention a pistol or two and a couple of grenades—less than optimal for a foot race.

He wasted no time turning around, didn't bother to snap off a few bursts of fire with the assault rifle in an attempt to slow down his pursuers. He knew it wouldn't have stopped the law-enforcement teams. What he didn't know was that I was much closer to him and that a quick burst from his assault rifle would have cut me in two. The guy was in great shape, and it took me the entirety of the quarter-mile of woods to catch up with him.

He charged out of the woods onto a narrow grass strip that bordered the shopping mall parking lot. He stopped for a half-second, got his bearings, spotted his vehicle, and headed in that direction. He'd barely started when I hit him with a flying tackle that would have made Bronko Nagurski proud. His feet left the ground; we flew through the air and crashed hard onto the asphalt with me on top. His assault rifle skidded several yards away with a metallic clacking sound.

The force of the tackle and the crash landing would have put most people into a coma. "Most people" meant 99 percent, but this guy was not most people. He groaned in pain but instantly rolled with the force of my tackle. I tried to maintain my grip, but he was too quick and strong. He broke free of my hands and scrambled to his feet. I did the same.

We stood, panting, face to face, for a long moment.

"You think you're fast enough to get to me before I can pull a weapon." He didn't sound totally convinced.

"Hey, please feel free to go for your gun," I said.

"But I'll feel free to break your arm when you do."

Instead of going for his gun, he reached up and pulled off his balaclava. It was Hawkins. I declined to follow suit with my balaclava. Having a secret identity is a handy thing.

"You're the fucking Magic Warrior, aren't you?" he grunted.

"Yup," I replied. As responses go, what it lacked in elegance it made up for with pithiness.

The sounds of the pursuing troopers and agents came from the woods he and I had just exited.

"I don't think you have much time," I observed.

"Gotta make a move, I guess."

"I would if I were you."

Hawkins lunged at me. I didn't understand why he would choose that action. Too easy to defend against. I stepped sideways, extending my left leg. He tripped over my leg and fell forward, assisted by a booming backhand from my left fist in the middle of his back. He hit the ground and rolled, and then his plan became obvious: he'd plucked his gun from its holster and was bringing it to bear in his right hand.

I rushed to his side and kicked the gun loose. He used his left arm to sweep my legs out from under me, and I crashed to the ground with my head near his feet. I know this because he immediately tried to kick my head off. Literally. I blocked a couple of kicks with my arms, which hurt like hell, and rolled away from him. I scrambled to my feet as fast as I could, and Hawkins did the same. He slammed me with a full-body block, sending us both to the ground.

I staggered to my feet, but Hawkins was faster and stepped in close to me, pummeling my ribs and making it hard to breathe. I threw a quick jab with my left, which he couldn't block since his fists were hitting my mid-section. My jab caught his jaw, jerked his head upright, and stopped his punches. I followed with a right-handed uppercut that stunned him. I have to admit I was disappointed: It was a solid uppercut, and it should have knocked him out. It hadn't even knocked him off his feet.

We both stood where we were, hands on our knees, gasping for breath, considering next moves. The noise of his pursuit was much louder, much closer.

"I really have to leave. Sorry," he said without a hint of the regret that the word "sorry" might have conveyed.

"Can't let you do that," I muttered. "Sorry."

He grinned, stood straight up, and stuck his hands out in front of him. His left hand held a flash-bang grenade. His right hand reached for the pin and pulled it.

"Sorry," he repeated and tossed the grenade at me.

I turned and ran a few steps before the grenade exploded with noise and light. I lurched forward, head aching and ears ringing. After a few more steps, I stumbled to a stop, turned, and searched for Hawkins.

He had disappeared.

There was a screeching of tires as a dark SUV roared out of the shopping mall parking lot. Too far away for me to see the make, model, color, or license plate. Despite the best efforts of the FBI, the Massachusetts State Police STOP team, and my humble self, Hawkins had made a clean getaway.

"Looks like you're the winner tonight," I said to the disappearing SUV.

10

It occurred to me that if I headed back to the mobile command center, I might get mistaken for a bad guy and shot. Instead, I sat on the grass and waited for the assorted law-enforcement teams to arrive.

Maybe two minutes later, I was surrounded by troopers and agents, all of whom felt compelled to point each and everyone of their weapons at poor little old me. I was instructed to lie down, put my hands on the back of my head, and hold still. I did as I was told.

As one of the FBI agents was slapping cuffs on my right wrist, Joanne's voice rang out, "I should let him finish cuffing you and have you arrested."

"That's one way to handle this situation," I responded. It didn't sound as clever as I had intended, but it's not easy to sound clever when you're lying face down with a sizable FBI agent's knee in your back, cuffing you with your arms bent around behind you.

"He's with us," Joanne said, relenting. "You can take the cuffs off."

Not only did the agent release me, he grabbed me by the arm and helped me up. Very gentlemanly of him.

"You're an idiot," Joanne said. "You were supposed to be observing only."

"I was observing only. And then the Privatus team leader made a break for it."

"And you went after him."

"I did."

"Where is he now?"

"Uhhhhhh," I shrugged and held up my empty hands, "he got away."

"He got away."

"Hey, come on, he had a gun and a grenade."

"And all you had was your stupidity."

"I almost caught him."

"Almost only counts with horseshoes and hand grenades."

"Like I said, he had a grenade—"

"Stop," she held up her hand to make sure I understood that I'd better shut up. "You're an idiot."

"Is that how you'll describe me in your report?"

"How the hell did you get back here?"

I shrugged and smiled and said, "Years of government training and experience?"

"You are so full of shit."

"I've been told that."

Joanne shook her head, called to an agent nearby, and handed him some car keys. "We took these off of one of the bad guys now under arrest." She waved at the mall parking lot, "Could you please see if there's a car to match these."

"Sure."

"The state troopers forensics team is on the way, should be here soon. Please lend a hand anyway you can."

"Copy."

Joanne returned her attention to me, "Okay, back to the command center."

"You expect me to walk? After tussling with Hawkins, I need first aid."

"You keep talking, and I might just shoot you and save everyone lots of time."

"If I put my hands up and go quietly, will you promise not to shoot?"

"Just go quietly. I'm not promising anything."

She accompanied me through the woods on the return journey to the command center. We talked as we walked.

"No serial numbers on any of the weapons we confiscated from the five Privatus team members we arrested. No identification on any of them."

"What a surprise. I wonder if their mothers are looking for them."

"Unlikely. We're waiting on fingerprints and DNA, and we took pictures and uploaded for facial recognition."

"But that will take hours or even days. You're cross-checking with CIA, Interpol, etc.?"

"Yes, indeed."

"In the meantime, the five you caught aren't talking."

"Lips sealed. Except to ask for their lawyer."

"I'm going to make a wild guess that you won't be able to establish that they work for Privatus. The five you've arrested, even their lawyer, will all be paid by some company that's part of another company that's part of *yet another* company and on and on. Shell corporations, payments from off-shore bank accounts. You'll probably never connect them to Privatus."

"I wish I could disagree with you, but I think you're right. Absolutely and completely correct."

"So, you'll charge these guys with criminal trespass, illegal possession of firearms, resisting arrest, whatever applies in Massachusetts law. Right?"

"That's about it. We'll hope that the fingerprints, DNA, and/or facial recognition pop and let us establish some prior bad acts. Maybe even some outstanding warrants. But I bet these guys don't even know that Privatus was their ultimate employer."

"I bet Hawkins knows his employer is Privatus," I said. "A guy with his experience would never be content to work for an unknown employer."

"Was Hawkins tonight's team leader?"

"He was."

"And you let him get away."

"Hey, I did my best. Did I happen to mention that he had a gun and a grenade? And that he was willing to use them? On me!"

"And you let a few little things like a gun and grenade stop you? I thought you were the best."

"Mr. Hawkins would dispute that. And he has some powerful reasons to believe that he is the best."

We had emerged from the mini-forest, crossed the lawn, and stepped over the curb into the parking lot where the command center was about two hundred feet away. Joanne gave me a long look.

"Something's bugging you about Hawkins. Does he remind you of you?"

"Are you psychoanalyzing me?"

"Somebody should. So, what's with you and Hawkins?"

"I don't know . . . he's my road not taken."

"Exactly, Jack," she patted me on the shoulder. "You didn't take his road. Let it go."

"You're right. I know you're right. But . . ." I stopped about midway between the woods behind us and the command center in front of us. "What . . . what makes me different than Hawkins? Why did he become a professional—"

"—Psychopath?"

"I think his diagnosis might be that he's a sociopath?"

"No. He has no conscience. That's why he's a psychopath and *not* a sociopath."

"Is that the difference between the two of us? That I have a conscience?"

"It's a big difference."

"Really? We're alike in so many other ways."

"I think 'so many' is overstating your case. You guys are similar physically—"

"We're damn near the *same* physically."

"Fine. You're the same—physically. And your military history is very similar up to and including your work with the CIA on special ops in Afghanistan and your medals. But after that—"

"He went on to become a successful CIA agent, and I became a drunken bum who got his wife killed. I may have a conscience, but it hasn't always worked very well."

Joanne shook her head and smiled bitterly, "You have an interesting way of judging yourself. While Hawkins was doing all kinds of dirty deeds for the CIA, you were a Deputy Marshal, twice commended if I remember correctly, and you fell in love with a wonderful woman and got married."

"And got her killed."

"Jack, not everything comes back to the one, awful mistake you made that ended with Maggie's death. That mistake is not the sum total of your life. It doesn't mean you don't have a conscience."

"It feels that way."

"What about all the good you've done since then? You've been very cagey about what you've been up to these last couple of years, but I'm pretty damn sure you've saved a bunch of lives. And I *know* you saved my life in Afghanistan. I doubt Hawkins has ever saved *anyone's* life."

"You're probably right about that." We sat for a moment, then I asked, "Why did he turn to the dark side?"

"He probably enjoys the money, the action, the violence. Who knows?" Joanne patted my arm. "What I know is that you're the good guy. Hawkins is the bad guy. Okay?"

"That simple?"

"It is for me."

"I'm the good guy."

"Yes, you are."

"Wow. If I had known you were going to give me so much free advice, I would have made it a point to visit you years ago."

"*So much* free advice?"

"Within a very short period of time, you've told me to marry Kim, have kids, and let go of Hawkins and what he represents. If I hang around you for another day or so, you'll fix everything in my life."

"In that case, I should be charging you."

"How 'bout I buy you a cup of coffee at the command center?"

"What a sport."

I sat in the mobile command center with a couple of ice packs on the parts of my body that ached the most. Joanne poured me a cup of coffee, gave me some ibuprofen, and asked me all kinds of questions, making me tell my story twice about my pursuit of and fight with Hawkins. The Massachusetts State Police listened, taking notes, which saved me from having to do it all over again with them. I was totally forthcoming, except about how Harry had whooshed me to the command center in the first place. And how he whooshed me into the woods, almost over the heads of the Privatus team. And how he was going to whoosh me out of there as soon as they stopped questioning me.

Finally, a couple of minutes after three o'clock, Joanne said, "Okay, that's enough. We know how to contact you if we have any more questions."

"May I go?"

"Sure. You need a lift somewhere?"

"No. I'm fine."

"You don't look fine."

"Well, I can't say the other guy looks worse, but he doesn't look better."

"Even if he got away."

"Even if."

"Take care, Jack," Joanne said. "I'll update you as soon as any identifications come through. And thanks for the tip on this."

"For whatever it was worth."

"At the very least, we caught some little fish. That usually leads the way to catching bigger fish."

I nodded, "As long as you're happy."

"I am. Get out of here and head home to your lady. And don't forget what I said about going for it."

"Can I wait till morning to propose?"

She grinned. "Probably a good idea."

I walked outside the command center, heading out into the parking lot so the lights from the vehicle wouldn't make my sudden disappearance from the vicinity too obvious.

"Harry, whenever you're ready."

And . . . *zip*! Harry materialized me in Kim's living room at 3:07 A.M. Except for Hawkins getting away, it had been one hell of a night. No one killed. Five bad guys arrested. Doberman Cyber undamaged. And all for the price of a few new bumps and bruises on me. No major wounds. No need to see the doctor or head to the ER.

In the guest bathroom, I took more ibuprofen, rolled more lidocaine on my sore parts, and brushed my teeth. Using all my taxpayer-funded training, I stealthily crept into Kim's room and changed into a fresh T-shirt and underwear from my overnight case. I slid into bed as light as a feather, hoping not to disturb Kim.

She rolled over to face me and spoke in a low whisper, "We have to stop meeting like this."

"You are so right," I whispered in reply. "Go back to sleep."

"Everything okay? Are you all right?"

"Everything's fine. Let's talk in the morning."

She gently kissed my lips. "I like sleeping with you."

"Me, too. Sleeping with you, I mean."

"I would really like it if you didn't show up in the

middle of the night after one of your dangerous escapades."

"Are Dangerous Escapades like the Ice Capades?"

"Exactly the same," she whispered. "Except for the guns and knives."

"For what it's worth, the guns and knives are not my favorite part of these outings."

"Then stop doing them."

"But I can't skate."

"I'm sorry to be a nag about this, but I don't know how much more of this I can take."

"Don't worry. I'm fine."

"Tonight. You're fine, tonight."

"Let's take this a night at a time, then."

She thought that over, brushed her lips on mine, and said, "I love you."

"I love you, too."

The next morning was just like yesterday morning had been: Kim woke me with a kiss on the cheek and handed me a mug full of steaming coffee. It was a little after 10:00 A.M.

"Hey there," she said.

"Hey there, yourself."

"Is it my imagination, or do you look relatively unscathed from last night's activities?"

"No, I'm relatively unscathed. Not sure I've ever been unscathed before, but I have to say I prefer it to scathed."

"How 'bout the other guy? Yesterday you said he

didn't look worse than you. What about today?"

"Uh . . . we're still pretty much even."

"Even? He must be pretty tough."

"He's as tough as I am."

"Are you sure you can handle him?"

"No. Not at all."

Kim looked away from me but stroked my arm. "Is this you trying to be disarmingly honest and modest with me? 'Cause that's not what I want."

"What do you want?"

"I want you to tell me that you can absolutely handle this guy. That I have nothing to worry about."

I wasn't sure how to respond to that, so I said nothing at all.

"Can't you handle him? Won't Harry make sure you win in the end?"

"Maybe."

"I thought you and Harry worked for the Chairman. That you make things right for people."

"Yes, we do."

"But Harry won't protect you?"

"If the Chairman wants to protect me, I'm protected. But there are no guarantees. The Chairman calls me to help people, but He doesn't guarantee results. He doesn't promise me success or safety. He wants me to make a best effort to help, regardless of how things turn out for anyone."

"I thought Harry helps you."

"He does. The Chairman gives me what I need—although sometimes my definition of need and His are very different—and Harry often . . . delivers what I need."

"Isn't your safety a *need*?"

"Uh . . . how shall I put this gently? Uh . . . no."

"What about Harry? Doesn't he know what's going to happen? Couldn't he warn you?"

"As he has informed me on multiple occasions, he's an angel, not a prophet."

She stood up from the bed. Her eyes were wide with anger. Or fear. Or both. "You could get killed as a result of trying to help others? And Harry can't or won't warn you or help you?"

"Harry will help me if I need it and if that's part of the Chairman's plan for me."

"If that's the plan? Are you okay with that? Are you crazy?"

"Yes, I'm okay with that. Sometimes. It kind of depends on how close I think I am to dying at any given moment."

Kim closed her eyes, held her hands up in front of her as if warding off an annoying person, took a deep breath, and exhaled very slowly. "Do you want breakfast?"

Before I could answer, she continued, "The menu includes scrambled eggs, bacon, and English muffins." She walked out of the bedroom without awaiting a response.

I finished the coffee, hopped out of bed, went to

the guest bathroom, and took a very short, very hot shower. Dressed in tan cargo shorts and a maroon Fordham T-shirt, I arrived in the dining room just as Kim was placing two plates on the table. I refilled my coffee mug then sat next to her.

"Are we still friends?" I asked.

"Ask me later."

"Are you still coming to Paris with me?"

"But of course!" she said in a cheesy French accent. "I'm upset with you, but I'm not crazy. Of course I'm going to Paris."

"With me?"

"Well . . . if I have to." The tiniest smile appeared.

"You have to."

"Don't forget the business-class airline tickets."

"Already done."

"Where are we staying?"

"The George V."

"Whoa. You're not messing around."

"Messing around? *Moi*? I'm taking the woman I love to Paris."

She grinned. "We're still friends."

We kissed. And kissed some more. Then she took my hands and led me to the bedroom.

"But . . . breakfast," I protested feebly.

"I'll make more."

*   *   *

214

PRIVATUS HEADQUARTERS

HAWKINS ALL BUT COLLAPSED into a chair in the black room at Privatus's headquarters.

"Do you want something to drink?" Desjardins asked.

"Scotch, neat. A double."

Desjardins nodded at a young man who hovered in the open doorway.

Freund watched the young man depart to fetch the drink, shifted in his chair, and asked, "How did things go so wrong?"

"Who the fuck knows?" replied Hawkins.

Freund leaned over the table to follow up, but Desjardins put her hand on his arm and shook her head.

The young man reappeared with a tray bearing an Old-Fashioned glass holding an inch of amber liquid. Hawkins plucked the glass off the tray and took a long pull at the whiskey.

He gasped, "That's what the doctor ordered." He finished the rest and said to the young man, "I'll have another, please."

The young man looked to Desjardins who nodded and waved him out to fetch another drink.

Freund impatiently asked, "What went wrong?"

"Everything," Hawkins said.

"That's not very useful," the German observed.

The young man reappeared with the tray. Hawkins took the whiskey, drinking more slowly this time around.

As the door closed behind the young man, Hawkins sat back, swirled the Scotch in his glass, and stared as the liquid spiraled and cast light reflections around the room.

Hawkins said in a low, slow voice, "They knew we were coming. Looked like a massive team of FBI and state police SWAT types. They outnumbered us and were as heavily armed as us. From a tactical standpoint, when you lack the element of surprise, and you don't have an edge in manpower or firepower, you lose. But how did they know? Where the hell is Morita? Have you found him yet?"

"No, unfortunately," Desjardins said. "But we've double-checked, and Morita didn't have access to anything regarding our operations for Waronov-Tybalt. He may have managed to steal some information regarding the targets of the operation, but there's no way he could know when and where we were moving. Someone else is spying on us."

"I don't suppose you have a clue as to the identity of the spies, huh?" Hawkins grunted.

"No, nothing." Freund said. "Was your so-called Magic Warrior there?"

"Oh yeah. In the flesh."

"You didn't manage to kill him, did you?"

"Nope."

"But you will next time, won't you?" Desjardins asked. "He seems to be the central figure in our problems."

"Are you re-prioritizing my missions?"

"No," Desjardins shook her head. "Paris will still be the next op. It's the most important."

"Got it. Onto Paris. And if I get the chance to kill the Magic Warrior, I should take it."

"Exactly. We've already assembled the team you requested. You'll meet them on site."

"Have we recruited our pet terrorists?"

Freund said, "A bunch of neo-Nazi youth, mostly unemployed, no college degrees—calling themselves the *Europäische Weisse Ordnung.* The European White Order."

"Well, if anyone knows how to manage a bunch of neo-Nazis, it'd be you, eh, Freund?"

"*Fick dich.*"

"After you," Hawkins chuckled mirthlessly. "Will you be in Paris to handle the Hitler Youth?"

"*Nein.*" Freund grinned, also without mirth.

"Aww," Hawkins responded, "I'll miss you."

Desjardins quietly drummed her fingers on the conference table. "The important thing is that the White Order has been convinced that the best way to force the European Union into tightening its immigration policies is to attack the EU's markets.

"They believe they are operating on their own, when in reality, we're using them for cover. Your team, Hawkins, will make sure their security is tight and back them up. If need be, you'll handle the operation itself, leaving behind the *Europäische Weisse Ordnung* as evidence."

"When you say 'leaving behind,' I assume you

mean dead."

"Whatever is necessary," she said. "The operation needs to go off without a trace that leads back to us and/or Waronov-Tybalt." She stopped drumming her fingers. "However, assuming the Magic Warrior makes an appearance, please capture him if you can."

"And if I can't?"

"Kill him."

*   *   *

After lovemaking, Kim and I had breakfast. Then she changed and headed out for a meeting with one of her clients. Working from home has its scheduling benefits (like fitting in a bit of morning sex), but sooner or later, the bills have got to be paid.

I made a cappuccino and went upstairs to the roof patio. I sat under an umbrella and admired the view to the west: the Hudson River and the southern cliffs of the New Jersey Palisades, marred only by the apartment buildings at their tops and their base.

Since I was alone, I thought I would make the most of this time. "Harry?"

"Yes."

He was standing in the sunlight just beyond the rim of the umbrella.

"Would you like me to make a cappuccino for you?"

"No thanks. Did you have something in mind

besides sharing caffeinated beverages with me?"

"Can't I be hospitable and strategic?"

"Strategic?"

"About our case."

Harry pursed his lips but said nothing. He sat down in the chair next to mine.

"How is George Morita?"

"He's safe. His whole family is safe."

"Are they happily ensconced someplace nice?"

"Very nice."

"And Privatus isn't going to be able to find them?"

"Of course not. When I hide someone, he stays hidden. And safe."

"That's very comforting," I said approvingly. "In that case, let's discuss Paris."

"Let's."

"Does George know anything more about what Privatus is up to there?"

"No, he does not."

"In that case, could you brief me, please?"

Harry glanced skyward then returned to me. "Yes. Privatus has recruited a small terrorist group, the *Europäische Weisse Ordnung*, in English: the European White Order."

"Neo-Nazis? Let me guess, pissed about the state of immigration in their native Germany? Looking for a way to square things with the EU?"

"Yes to all of the above."

"You said Privatus recruited them—how?"

"They staked out unemployment agencies in Germany, then followed some of the more obviously disgruntled men to coffee houses or tiny little bars."

"Throw around a few Euros, buy a few lagers, and then next thing you know," I said, "you have your very own terrorist group."

"Exactly."

"Will Privatus provide them with weapons and explosives to attack the EU market operations in Paris?"

"Yes."

"Why not recruit French terrorists?"

"German terrorists attacking the EU in France will sow more confusion."

"And the more confusion, the easier for Privatus to hide its involvement." I pondered the possibilities of well-armed, overwrought neo-Nazis on the loose in Paris. It was not a pretty picture. "How many?" I asked. "Will they directly attack the EU's decentralized agency for the markets? The one George described to us?"

"Yes, they are going to attack the European Securities and Markets Authority offices. Gunfire and explosions to kill as many as possible. Commit suicide if escape isn't an option."

"They should save us all the trouble and start with the suicide part."

"I understand your sentiment, but practically speaking—"

"There's *no* practically speaking. I was making a bad but bitter joke." I was picturing Paris even as I was staring at the Hudson River. I exhaled, attempting to blow the fog out of my brain. "The European Securities and Markets Authority will have a secure facility. A direct assault means overcoming some kind of reinforced entryway, private guards, maybe even police units. That means very heavy weapons. Something like rocket-propelled grenades, the kind of thing you use against tanks."

"You're the expert on that," Harry said.

"Yeah. We're looking at mass casualties, I mean dozens of people hurt and killed, if the White Order pulls this off."

"If? We can't let them attack. We must stop them."

"Yes, we have to cut them off." I stood up and walked to the rooftop railing. Yes, being fifteen feet closer to the Hudson River and the Jersey cliffs made everything much more clear. "Do you know how many little neo-Nazis we'll be dealing with?"

"There are eight of them." Harry walked over to join me at the railing.

"And the Privatus team? How many?"

"Another eight."

"Will Hawkins be leading?"

"Yes. Is that a problem?"

"Absolutely not."

"You answered that very quickly. Very

221

affirmatively."

"What are you saying?"

"I think Hawkins is—to borrow a phrase you would use—in your head. You've developed a need to settle things with him."

"I need to get the job done. Save lives. Free George Morita from the evil clutches of Privatus. Settling things with Hawkins will probably be a necessary component of achieving those results."

Harry shook his head, "Very nice rationalization, but this has become personal for you. You're worried that you might still turn out to be exactly like Hawkins."

"No, Obi Wan, I'm not going over to the Dark Side of the Force."

Harry responded with a blank look.

"Obi Wan? The Force? *Star Wars*?"

His Mona Lisa smile flitted across his face. "I am not the one who's worried about your turning to the Dark Side. You are."

I finished the last of the cappuccino. "You think I'm invulnerable to the pull of the Dark Side?"

"No, I said I'm not the one who's worried about it."

"You are soooooo reassuring." I stretched the word "so" out for sarcastic emphasis.

Harry didn't bother to react.

"Do you know where the neo-Nazis and the Privati will assemble for a final briefing?"

"The *Privati*?"

"I'm treating 'privatus' as a Latin noun, *privatus*, *privati*. Privati being the plural. Do you know, or will you know when and where they'll meet for a final briefing? Will we have enough time to adjust our plans if necessary?"

Harry again turned to the sky for guidance then back to me. "Yes, I'll know, and yes, you'll have time."

"Could you whoosh me into their meeting? Keeping me invisible?"

"Of course."

"Speaking of whooshing, could you whoosh my weapons to my hotel room at the George V? There's no way I could take that stuff on a plane."

"Yes, I will transport your weapons. Select and pack what you need into one of your backpacks then leave it on your bed. I'll take care of it."

"How do I let you know what room we're in? Can you hear me in Paris when you're in my bedroom in New York?"

"Are you trying to insult me?"

"I'm still learning how this angel stuff works."

Harry took a deep, centering breath and said, "I am convinced that the Chairman assigned you to me to give me the opportunity to work on my patience."

"You guys have to work at bettering yourselves spiritually and psychologically?"

"Everyone does."

"So, I'm helping you at the same time you're

helping me."

"That is one perspective, yes."

"You're welcome."

Harry took another deep, centering breath. I wondered if he practiced yoga. Until sixty seconds ago, I didn't realize he needed to work on things like patience. God only knew what else he was up to. Maybe yoga was the tip of the iceberg.

"Is there something else you need to discuss with me?" he asked.

"Geez, Harry, you're such a know it all."

"I have told you before I am *not* all-knowing." He paused, waiting for me to respond. When my only reply was to smile at his admission, he continued, "However, I am exceedingly familiar with your character. I know when you are trying to be clever by withholding information. Or when you're embarrassed to admit you've done something that you should have asked about before hand."

The smile was wiped right off my face. "Serves me right for getting smug with you. Sorry."

"I know you enjoy this verbal sparring, but I don't. Please get to the point, Jack."

"Come on, you enjoy the sparring a little, don't you? Especially when you get the better of me as you just did."

"Jack. . . ."

"Okay. Sorry. I should have discussed this with you first, but I invited Kim to go to Paris with me, and I already purchased tickets and made hotel reservations. Kim and I will be leaving tonight, enjoy a long weekend, and then on Monday, she'll head home while I remain in Paris to deal with the boys from White Order and Privatus. Is that okay?"

"Why wouldn't it be?"

"I want to make sure Kim will be safe."

"Didn't I tell you she would be safe?"

"Yes."

"Don't you believe me when I promise something?"

"Yes, of course But I don't expect the promise to be kept if I do something stupid."

"What constitutes something stupid?"

"Let's say the bad guy is pointing a gun at me, and I hide behind Kim, 'cause you promised she's always going to be safe. That's stupid."

"No, that is moronic."

"So . . . my thesis that stupid behavior on my part negates the promise is correct, right?"

"Yes, it's correct."

"And what I'm really asking about Paris is, is this stupid? Will Kim be safe? After all, Privatus doesn't know who I am, do they?"

"No."

"Paris will be safe for her, won't it?"

Harry did his upward-glance move then said, "Yes. Are you planning something romantic?"

"Excuse me?"

"Paris is generally considered to be one of the romantic cities in the world, isn't it?"

"That's what I've heard."

"And you're planning to take advantage of it."

"Are you sure you're not all-knowing?"

He allowed himself a Mona Lisa smile. "You're not that hard to read, Jack."

"You've got me there." I swallowed. "Listen, I know you help me get what I need and not just what I want, but could you help me with one or two things for Paris?"

Harry's eyebrows went up.

"This trip is happening on short notice. I'd like to take Kim somewhere special for dinner, but I'm pretty sure it'll be impossible for me to get a reservation at this late date."

"You expect me to be your personal concierge?"

"I don't expect anything. I hope that yes, you will use your magic to help me. I'm requesting your assistance, not expecting it."

"Since it's for Kim, I'll do what I can."

"You're an angel," I deadpanned.

"Yes, I am."

11

After Harry disappeared, I went downstairs, made another cappuccino, returned to the rooftop patio, and called Joanne Agar.

"Are you calling for advice or to alert me to more trouble?" Joanne asked.

"Hello to you, too."

"Advice or alert?"

"Alert. From the same source that warned me about the attacks on GraySecurFirm, Intimidation, and Doberman."

"I get it, Jack. Your source is gold. Solid gold. What's the latest?"

"Fancy a trip to Paris?"

"Oh my," she laughed. "Really? I'd have to work on some kind of international team. Probably involved with Interpol and local police in Paris. Your info had better be really good."

"It is. Privatus has hoodwinked a neo-Nazi outfit called the *Europäische Weisse Ordnung* or the European White Order into thinking that the best way to go after the EU's immigration policies is to attack the financial markets. Privatus is going to use this brotherhood of Hitler morons to blitzkrieg the ultra-secure offices of the EU's European

Securities and Markets Authority."

"Let me guess: The resulting market disruption will help Privatus sell their security services."

"Bingo," I said.

"What do you know about the attack?"

"Next Tuesday."

"Maximum casualties. Do you have any details?"

"I don't know the specific time, but I do know you've got eight people from the White Order and another eight from Privatus. And . . ."

"'And . . .' sounds worrisome. What are you afraid of?"

"Well, if I were crazy enough to do something like this in the middle of the day in the middle of Paris, I'd go in very heavy. Like an RPG. Or two. Followed by tear gas and flash-bangs."

"Even if we catch them in the act, there could be a lot of wounded and fatalities."

"So you need to get them before they attack. And by you, I mean you, Interpol, the CIA, the Paris SWAT team, the Sûreté--"

"That's not the official name, you know."

"I know. Bring 'em anyway."

"Jack, please leave the international cooperation to me," Joanne said. "How do you propose that this massive, international law-enforcement team preempt this attack?"

"My source is going to let me know where and when Privatus and the White Order are getting together for a final briefing and weapons distribution. As soon as I know, you'll know."

"The team will have to stand by in ready mode."

"Yup. The kind of readiness when you take naps in your body armor with your weapon in your hand."

There was silence on the line. I took the opportunity to swallow more cappuccino.

"Jack, are you absolutely sure about this? I'm going to have to do a lot of convincing and call in a lot of favors to make this happen."

"I'm sure." I glanced skyward as I had seen Harry do hundreds of times. "My source is never wrong."

"Never?"

"Never. You can bet your life on this information."

"I think that's what I'm doing."

There was another pause on her end, and I took that moment to finish my cappuccino. I watched a white-hulled sloop glide down river. No sails. It would have made a much prettier picture if she'd been running with full sails, but I would have to be content with the white hull on the surface of the blue-gray river.

Joanne interrupted my appreciation of the sloop, "Are you, by chance, going to be in Paris?"

"I thought I'd stop by."

"You're not going to go after these guys by yourself, are you?"

"Would I be calling you if I were?"

"No, you wouldn't. Are you planning to observe

like you did at Doberman?"

"Yes, I'm planning to observe."

"Will you behave this time?"

"I always behave."

"In some fashion or another."

"Hey, I'm bringing Kim with me. We're leaving tonight. We'll enjoy the scenery and the great food, and once my source tips me to the place and time of the final briefing, I'll let you know. Would I bring my girlfriend along if I weren't planning to behave?"

"Jack, you always start with good intentions, but somehow things always get out of hand."

"Not this time. Did I mention that I'm bringing my girlfriend?"

Joanne chuckled. "You might have. Sorry to be a spoil sport, but she's not invited to observe."

"You should reconsider—she's guaranteed to behave better than I."

"That's pathetic. But true."

"Much as I enjoy giving you opportunities to insult me, I have packing to do. I need to end this conversation."

"Okay. Thanks for the alert. And, Jack?"

"Yes."

"I hope you know what you're doing."

"Me, too."

* * *

I walked the few blocks to my apartment, stopping

at the foot of the steps outside. This was the spot where Maggie had died. The place where my wife had been shot and bled to death because I'd been drunk and stupid and cheated a Mafia boss. A vision of her lying sprawled with her upper body on the steps and her legs on the sidewalk, her eyes wide open and staring lifelessly came to me. I quickly turned away and took the steps two at a time, rushing away from memories of Maggie.

Inside my apartment, I did the kind of packing you do when you're going to Paris and staying and eating at some wonderful places. I was aware that at the very moment I was packing, so was Kim. And there was no way she wouldn't look fabulous. So I had to do a good job with my things. Clothes, shoes, toiletries, all went into a medium-sized duffle on rollers. Then I packed my navy-blue, carry-on backpack. (Please, don't hate me 'cause I have an affinity for backpacks—I admit to owning six of them. No, wait, seven.) I always carried some paperbacks so I didn't have to worry about whether my phone would violate any airline protocols. I took a bunch by Ross Macdonald: *The Far Side of the Dollar*, *The Goodbye Look,* and *The Underground Man*. Nothing like books full of murder and tangled family histories in southern California to entertain a man on his way to Paris. Also packed in my carry-on backpack: a charger for my phone, a couple of electrical adapters for France, my passport, and fresh underwear, socks, and a polo shirt in case my checked bag got lost in transit.

Then it was time to prepare the backpack that was going to Paris via Harry's Transport. This pack—black—was double the size of my carry on so it would easily hold both Ruger pistols, shoulder holsters, extra magazines, three each of smoke and flash-bang grenades, and my stealth outfit: cargo pants, T-shirt, windbreaker, balaclava, and crepe-soled shoes. I'd be hot under the windbreaker and the balaclava, but I'd also be damn-near invisible. I hoped.

The idea of taking even more weapons was sorely tempting. But Parisians were definitely going to be upset at the sight of a man wearing black and carrying uzis and shotguns. Law-abiding citizens and dreamy tourists just don't see the charm of heavily armed men.

"Oh well," I said to myself. I left the black pack on my bed as Harry had instructed me to do. He could be very particular about my following his instructions.

I shrugged into the straps of my blue pack, grabbed the handle of my duffle, and left. As I exited the building, I kept my eyes up and walked past the spot of Maggie's death without even a quick look. Why was I so sensitive to that spot now? I had passed the bottom of the stoop hundreds of times since the summer evening she had died there and not been grief-stricken. Actually. . . .

Every single time I passed that spot, I suffered a flash of grief and guilt. Every single time. But it had always been a fleeting sensation. A searing pain that disappeared almost instantly. So why was it so intense now? Because I was headed to Paris with another woman?

Because I was contemplating a future with another woman?

You can't mourn forever, Tyrrell. That doesn't mean you'll forget. But you . . . you, what? Gotta move on? Let go? Build a new life? I knew I was entitled to do those things, to feel those things, but . . . it was a lot harder to do than to feel. It was hard to move on. I felt guilty—as if I were betraying Maggie's memory, even though that was not my intention. At the same time, I was capable of loving someone new. And I believed that it was okay to do that. So go ahead, Tyrrell. Love Kim. Take her to Paris. Enjoy.

During my ruminations, I had walked half the distance to Kim's place. The duffle was heavy, even on wheels. I switched hands and kept going. Move on, Tyrrell. Move on.

* * *

The Air France Business Class cabin was everything I had hoped. Kim appeared to be very happy at the thought of a trans-Atlantic journey under these conditions. Our plane did not have seats that were like mini-cabins with their half walls and tray tables. Side-by-side seating was fine for us, we wanted to whisper and hold hands, and the new mini-cabins, while very comfortable, made it harder to fly as a couple. Our seats were huge, comfy, and converted to beds.

Most of the business-class cabin was full. The last passengers, a man and woman, were seated in the row in front of us. They were a real-life cliché: the man was mid-fifties, not bad looking, with slicked-back salt-and-pepper hair and a goatee to match, and a tiny bit of a paunch. The woman was a good thirty years younger, a smoldering brunette with astounding curves. Thanks to her high heels, she was taller than he.

"Do you think they're headed for the Mile High Club?" Kim whispered. The dull roar of jet engines that came through the aircraft fuselage was more than enough to drown out normal conversation, but Kim was enjoying being conspiratorial.

"If that guy goes to the Mile High Club," I retorted, "he'll throw his back out."

"Isn't the bathroom bigger in business class?"

I grinned, "I don't know. But it won't be big enough for that guy."

"Do you think the flight attendants have ways to assist passengers with those kinds of problems?"

"They're going to need the Jaws of Life if that guy gets stuck in the bathroom."

Kim laughed and protested, "He's not that bad."

"Not that bad? Goatee, pot belly, and a bad back. He's terrible."

"How do you know he has a bad back?"

"Expensive clothes, expensive grooming, and orthopedic shoes."

"Those are Mephistos, and they're not exactly discount shoes."

"They are, however, a fave of people with bad

lower backs and hips."

"Maybe. On the other hand," Kim smiled, "we've established that he has money."

"For all we know, he might be wearing every last stitch of his nice clothes."

"Oh?" Kim's eyes went wide. "Do you think she's paying for the airfare? If she were, the guy would be much younger and have a strong back."

"You may have a point . . ."

The flight attendant came by for our pre-flight drink orders. Kim couldn't resist champagne. When in France. In keeping with the theme of French sparkling drinks, I ordered Perrier. We watched the couple in front of us. The man made it a point to stroke her arm whenever he could.

"Affectionate or possessive?" I pointed out the behavior to Kim.

"Let's give him the benefit of the doubt. It's both."

The flight attendant returned with our drinks. Kim raised her champagne glass, and I raised my Perrier. We softly clinked our glasses.

"To us," I whispered.

"To us," she repeated, kissing me lightly on the lips.

Kim watched as I took a couple of swallows of Perrier.

"Could I ask you a personal question?"

"Hasn't our relationship passed the point where we

need permission to ask each other personal questions?"

"I guess so. I hope so."

"Okay. Ask."

"Are you an alcoholic?"

I didn't have an intelligent, precise response to that, so I replied by saying, "Uhhh. . ."

"I'm sorry. I didn't mean to hurt your feelings—"

"I know that."

"But you never drink," she pointed at my Perrier, "and you've told me you used to drink."

"Used to drink is a massive understatement."

"Well . . . you can see why I wondered."

"I wonder, too. I tried to drink myself into oblivion after Maggie was murdered. Then, when she first appeared to me, she asked me not to drink for twenty-four hours. I didn't and she reappeared."

"And introduced you to Harry."

"Yes. Well, not right then and there, but she set us up like a blind date."

Kim looked at me quizzically.

"Okay, never mind the blind date, you get what I mean."

"Yes, I do."

"Anyway, I haven't had a drink since the night Maggie asked me not to. I've felt much better so . . . I don't drink."

"And it doesn't bother you when I drink?"

"Not at all."

"Have you ever thought of going to AA? Wouldn't you feel, I don't know . . . reinforced by going? Supported?"

"Part of a team instead of a lone wolf?"

"You're romanticizing it when you say 'lone wolf'. There's nothing romantic about being the lone wolf."

I did what any normal person (or alcoholic) would do in that situation. I gulped more of the bubbling, non-alcoholic beverage.

"Do you think I should go to AA?"

"I honestly don't know. I just think that maybe you'd get something out of it, if you went."

The thought of attending AA meetings had crossed my mind on more than one occasion. I couldn't give you an honest answer as to why I hadn't already gone. I knew that lots of cool people were in recovery. Rock stars, movie stars, and athletes. Even uncool people like politicians. I supposed I thought there was no way to explain my relationships with Harry and the Chairman—so what good would it do to go to AA? But I had always thought that maybe I should. I'd clearly had a problem with drinking in the past. And getting support for sobriety was a good idea.

"I'll give it a shot when we get back to New York." I leaned over and kissed her. As I resettled into my chair, I noticed the rich guy and his younger woman were not in their seats.

Pointing, I said, "You don't think . . .?"

Kim laughed and shook her head, "Oh my God, I

hope not."

"Have you ever?"

"No way! You?"

"No. But . . ."

"But what?"

"Well . . . I'm sure that the contortions necessary to accomplish the feat would make for terrible sex. On the other hand, knowing that you're doing it in an airplane, with all your fellow passengers on the other side of the door, the sneaking in and out—it must be pretty exciting."

"Sounds awful to me. Awful."

"Okay, I get it. Not a fan of bathroom sex."

"Not a fan of *airplane*-bathroom sex." She arched her right eyebrow. "We've had a shower encounter or two. And, if our bathroom at the George V has a nice, big tub . . . *Voila!*"

"Hmm. I'll keep that in mind. I may have to upgrade our room when we check in—just to be sure we have a super-deluxe bathtub. Should I get bath salts with that?"

"Maybe just some candles."

Gee, if I had only known how much fun Paris could be, I would have gone a long time ago.

Kim interrupted my daydream, "I don't mean to dampen the mood, but can you really afford such a high-class trip?"

"What's going on here?" I asked in an exasperated whisper. "Are you trying to straighten out my life? First it's

AA, then it's what kind of sex gets the stamp of approval—"

"What kind of *bathroom* sex gets the stamp of approval—"

"And now you're onto me about money." I glanced around the cabin to be sure no one could overhear us. No one else indicated the slightest interest in what we were discussing. I continued, "Will there be additional sensitive topics under discussion on this flight?"

"No. I'm saving some highly sensitive and embarrassing topics to discuss later in our weekend."

"Oh goody. Something to look forward to."

She smiled. "Now, seriously, and I only ask out of concern, but can you afford this trip?"

"Well . . . maybe I could ask you to split the Amex bill with me when we get home?"

"Depends how nice this trip turns out to be."

"Wow, how quickly you turned from concerned to cheap."

"I didn't say 'no.' I said it 'depends.'"

"This trip is going to be very nice. Very. And yes, I can afford it. My security consulting business does quite well, thank you."

"Aren't your clients pro bono?"

"Only the special ones that Harry brings to me. My regular clients sign contracts, pay annual retainers up front—fat, juicy retainers—and then fees as the year progresses. I just landed two new accounts last month, so yes, I can afford this trip."

"You're amazing," she deadpanned. "All that government training and business acumen all rolled into one decent-looking package."

"Yup."

"What do you do for your clients?"

"Well, as I've told you before, I walk around, looking things over. I squint a lot and talk through clenched teeth like Clint Eastwood."

"And that works for you?"

"Pretty much. Occasionally I have to layout a new defensive plan: fences, locks, alarms, guards, all that jazz. Harry's put me in touch with a few specialists whom I use to test the hackability of my clients' computer networks and communications."

"I had no idea that you were so much more than a pretty face and a bad Eastwood impersonation."

"Now you know."

"Yes, I do."

"Will you be able to sleep tight on the rest of the flight, knowing that your French vacation is financially secure?"

"*Oui.*"

The rich guy and his younger girlfriend emerged from the restroom. She gave her ultra-short skirt a tug to smooth it out and gave him a shy grin.

"Look," I whispered urgently to Kim, "the bathroom is free!"

She slapped my arm and laughed. Within minutes, the business-class flight attendant asked for our dinner orders. We both ordered salmon.

"In the movie *Airplane!*, everyone who eats the fish ends up getting sick," I mentioned casually.

"Thanks for telling me," she replied.

We enjoyed our meals and had sorbet after dinner. As soon as the plates were cleared Kim finished her champagne, sipped some water, kissed me, adjusted her seat into a bed, stretched out, and fell asleep.

I was awake for a little while longer. Thinking about the Mile High Club and how I was not destined for membership. Thinking that I was on the brink of a romantic adventure in Paris with Kim. And on the brink of tangling with neo-Nazis and spies for hire. I really knew how to put together a great time, didn't I?

The George V was only too happy to provide a limo from Charles de Gaulle Airport to the hotel—too happy as I was paying for it, of course. But, unlike my girlfriend, I was not worried about the cost. As far as I was concerned, this was a once in a lifetime experience. At least I hoped it was once in a lifetime—if I never again mixed it up with neo-Nazis, that would be a good thing.

Our flight had been about seven hours, and we'd both managed to sleep for about three hours. Three hours doesn't usually constitute a good night's sleep. But, by redeye standards, it was great. We both had enough energy to enjoy the sights on the trip into Paris. The first part of the journey isn't much to tell about: the A1 highway is pretty much like any highway between a major airport and a city. Then our driver exited to the A86, which circled to the west side of Paris. Guess what? A86 was no more scenic than the A1. But . . . once onto the A14, we headed east into Paris itself. At first we passed through an area with modern buildings that had a tiny bit more charm than the Van Wyck Expressway (the major route to JFK airport) in New York had. But, in a very short time, we could see the Eiffel Tower to our right.

"Wow," Kim murmured, admiring the tower. She turned to me and gestured with both hands, encompassing the opulence of the hotel's limousine. "You really know how to take someone to Paris."

"I do this for all the women I'm madly in love with."

"All of them?"

"Every . . . single . . . last one."

"I guess I'm lucky to be included."

"I think I'm the lucky one."

Before we knew it, we were circling the Arc de Triomphe and heading down the Champs-Élysées. The limousine made a right turn onto the Avenue George V, and two minutes later, the car pulled to a stop in front of the hotel, and we went inside.

The lobby of the George V is collection of 18th century French antiques and intricate reproductions. A gorgeous chandelier (from Florence, I was told by the bellman) hangs above original tapestries and bronze sculptures.

At registration, I had to catch my breath after walking across the splendor of the lobby. Then I said, "*Bonjour, Madame.*"

The woman behind the desk said, "*Bonjour, Monsieur,*" in return, then asked, "Do you have a reservation?"

"Yes, for Tyrrell."

"*Oui, monsieur.*" She delicately clicked away at a computer and said, "Yes, here it is."

We signed in, and she signaled to a bellman, handed him the key, and gave him our room number. I assume she gave him our room number; her French was way too rapid for me to follow.

The bellman loaded our luggage onto a small cart and said, "This way, *s'il vous plaît.*"

Kim and I followed him to the elevator. I leaned close to Kim and whispered, "My command of French is so pathetic, for all I know, the woman at reception told this guy to go dump us in the Seine."

"My French is not pathetic," Kim replied. "And the woman at the desk said no such thing."

"You speak French? No wonder I brought you along."

"I thought you loved me madly."

"That, too."

Once in our room the bellman did the usual routine

of giving us a quick tour of the closet and bathroom. Our room was very spacious with Louis XVI-style furniture and a view of the hotel courtyard. The bellman tucked our bags into the closet, while I made a mental note that the tub in the bathroom was quite deep.

I gave the bellman a ten-euro note.

"*Merci, Monsieur*," he said with a slight bow and departed.

As soon as the door shut behind him, Kim said, "I think we should take a nap and sleep off our jet lag. And . . ."

"And . . .?"

"And . . . I'll show you just how grateful I am that you've brought me to Paris."

"*Mon Dieu*!" I uttered.

She grabbed my hand, pulled me close to her, and gave me a long kiss. She leaned back in my arms and undid my belt buckle and unzipped my pants.

"Talk about room service," I said.

"You ain't seen nothing, yet."

It was hard to say if our lovemaking was fabulous because we were in a foreign country or in a luxury hotel with high-thread-count sheets or happy to be alone after hours of travel. Maybe it was true love. Whatever the reason, the sex was tender yet intense. Our kisses were soft and lingering. One moment we drowsily caressed, and the next found us clutching each other as if we would never let go. Wonderful. Amazing. Romantic. Perfect.

Then, like the weary travelers we were, we fell fast asleep.

Welcome to Paris.

12

Hours later, we took the exclusive elevator to Le Jules Verne, the restaurant built inside the Eiffel Tower. The restaurant was on its second floor, a bit more than four hundred feet high. As you might imagine, the view of the City of Lights at night was breathtaking. I had heard conflicting views regarding the food, but I was counting on the spectacular nature of the restaurant's location to help make this a special evening.

We were dressed to kill. Sorry, poor choice of words. Kim was in a cobalt-blue, knee-length sheath that fit her like a glove and contrasted beautifully with her red hair. I did not try to compete with her, since that was beyond the ability of a mere mortal. I was dressed in a dark-gray Hugo Boss suit, white shirt, and a deep-red, Italian silk tie.

As the maître d' was leading us across the restaurant to a table for two by the window, I looked up and whispered, "Thank you, Harry."

"What?" Kim said.

"Nothing."

The maître d' seated us, and we immediately turned to take in the sights. The Seine River was directly below us. Long river boats with their softly lit, glass-enclosed dining rooms on their decks glided silently below us.

"This is amazing. Absolutely amazing. How did you arrange this?" she asked, beaming.

"I have friends in high places. The highest place, actually."

"Thank you," she said and reached her hand across the table and grasped mine. "This is so . . . this whole trip has been amazing. Oh, I said 'amazing' before. I need more words to describe this. Thank you."

"I guess you know I'm not kidding when I say I love you."

The restaurant's service was smooth and graceful, and Kim, speaking in fluent French, ordered drinks for us. (Well, she sounded fluent *to* me.) I recognized "Perrier" for me and "champagne" for her. We sat quietly, enjoying the view, until our drinks arrived.

We gently clinked glasses, and she said, "To us."

"To us," I echoed.

Kim looked at me across the table, her eyes narrowed, her lips pursed. "Okay, this is lovely, it truly is, but I can't help thinking you have something . . . ominous on your mind. If you're breaking up with me, this is the worst idea, ever. Ever."

I chuckled, "Why on earth would I bring you to Paris to dump you? A short drive to Bayonne would have done the trick. I'm not breaking up with you. I love you."

"Stop stalling. What's going on with you?"

"Remember a few days ago, when you asked me

about my therapy with Dr. Hoffman?"

"Yes," she shifted in her chair. I've interrogated enough suspects and persons of interest to know when someone is tense and uncomfortable. Kim was very tense.

"Relax," I smiled as charming a smile as I could and stroked the back of her hand. "I think I told you that I was feeling kind of lost."

"After you caught Maggie's killers, you thought you should be finished. But there were still people to be helped, but you weren't feeling highly motivated to help them."

"Man, when you say it, it sounds so simple. Why the hell was I so confused?"

"Well . . . because you're you. You're an emotionally challenged Irish Catholic boy."

"Hey, you're Irish Catholic."

"Yes, but I'm an enlightened Irish Catholic. I don't carry around a deluxe load of guilt and shame."

"Wait. Are those bad things?"

She chuckled. "Yes, they are. Anyway, you were a lost soul in search of a purpose, a mission. And now you've found them, right?"

"I did. As part of finding a renewed sense of purpose, I realized that I also needed to find me in my personal life. I believe the Chairman calls me to help others. And I came to believe that He called me to be with you."

"Oh," Kim said in a husky voice barely above a

whisper. "Oh."

"So . . .," I reached into my suit-coat pocket and knelt by the side of our table. "Will you marry me?"

Kim was smiling broadly but her eyes were wide with a panicked gleam. "I think you should get up."

"I think you should answer me," I pulled my right hand from my pocket and held it out to her, palm up. A ring box sat in the middle of my palm. I flipped the box open to display a small coil of purple wool yarn on white satin. "Will you marry me?"

"I think someone stole your ring."

"No, you tie the yarn, around your finger to remind you of something."

"And what's the something?"

"That you have to choose an engagement ring." I paused for emphasis. "If you say 'yes.'"

A number of our fellow patrons at were staring at us. Since they couldn't see the yarn inside the ring box, they were all smiles instead of bewildered. But I couldn't say for sure what their reactions were since 99.9 percent of my attention was focused on Kim.

"This is such a cliché," she whispered.

I was wondering if I had made a gross miscalculation regarding our relationship and the best way to move it forward. But what the hell? I was on one knee on the floor of a glamorous restaurant with all of Paris sparkling in the night below us, proposing to the woman of my dreams. Too late now for Plan B. Whatever the hell

Plan B would have been.

"A cliché? With a purple yarn ring?" I summoned my courage by taking a deep breath and asked, "Will you—*please*—marry me?"

Tears were running down her face. "Yes."

I tied the yarn in a bow around her left ring finger.

"Don't forget, now. You have to choose the ring you want to wear for the rest of your life."

"The purple yarn is growing on me."

I kissed her. Everyone in the restaurant applauded.

* * *

The next day, Friday, was spent doing absolutely nothing, but doing it Parisian style. We slept in, then had café au lait, juice, croissants, and omelettes in our room. We ate breakfast in bed, but we were very careful to make sure there were no crumbs or spills. After all, we didn't want to make a bad impression on the hotel staff.

A couple of hours later, we emerged from the hotel and turned right on the Avenue George V to the Seine River. We crossed the river on the Pont de l'Alma, which is not, in my opinion, one of the glorious river crossings of Paris, but it was the most direct way for us to walk to the Left Bank. Once on the southern side of the river, we turned left and strolled along the Quai d'Orsay past the Esplanade des Invalides. Across the river was the domed-glass roof of the Grand Palais. We both felt overwhelmed by the beauty of Paris. Overwhelmed at every single step.

We turned right on the Rue Robert Esnault-Pelterier and walked along the eastern side of Invalides and its park with trees in full summer bloom. We continued walking on the Rue but it changed names to the Rue de Constantine. At the southern end of the Esplanade des Invalides, we turned left on Rue de Grenelle.

"Is there a purpose to these wanderings?" Kim asked.

"Yes, just trying to soak in every inch of Paris." I'm sorry to say that was a lie. As scenic as walking along the Esplanade des Invalides was, my real purpose was to get to the Rue de Grenelle where the offices of the European Securities and Markets Authority were located. Even though my plan was to catch the lovely folks at Privatus and the *Europäische Weisse Ordnung* at their planning meeting, I wanted to do a quick reconnoitering of the EU agency they had targeted. Just in case.

The agency was house in what, to my untrained eye, looked like a classically elegant French government building. Not quite a Renaissance palace, but not too far from that. There were iron gates in front that looked as if they had been part of the original design of the building. And there were camo-wearing soldiers carrying assault weapons—a 21st century display of security.

"Nice building," I said, pointing.

"Not bad. A blend of French style and government grim."

"Let's head to the Boulevard Saint-Germain," I

pointed north.

"Now you're talking."

Boulevard Saint-Germain was an elegant sampler of Paris with cafés, art galleries, bookshops, and boutiques. We discovered a charming little creperie with outdoor seating, and sat down to lunch at a bistro table. We both ordered crepes with a mix of mushroom, spinach, and cheese. The crepe maker was stationed inside the restaurant's large plate-glass window so the passersby could be tantalized by her artistry. She made her crepes by coating the bottom of her cast iron pans with crepe batter, then placing the pans—bottoms up—on a rack over the flame. I almost signaled our waiter to bring me a bucket for my drool. Instead, I dabbed my mouth with my napkin and and enjoyed the warm air, blue skies, and the trees shading on the boulevard's sidewalks.

"I could get used to this," I said.

"Me, too. Want to relocate?"

"Right this minute, definitely. But if I'm honest with myself, I'd have to wonder just how much *fromage* can one man eat?"

"Spoilsport."

"Besides, don't you want to go back to America and announce that you're engaged?"

Kim shook her head and smiled, "It's hard to believe we're actually engaged."

"'Cause the possibility of a life with me is so terrifying?"

"Shut up," she laughed. "No, it's hard to believe because a year ago I didn't know you. I had no idea that sharing a table at Café Sabatini was going to change my entire life."

"When you put it like that, it does sound cosmically difficult to believe. One little event and your whole life turns out differently than you ever imagined."

"To paraphrase Henry Higgins: I do believe you've got it," she said.

Our food arrived at that instant. We spent the next few minutes in silence, savoring the delicious crepes. Well, silence if silence included appreciative moans of culinary delight. For dessert, we split a crepe filled with molten, dark chocolate and raspberries. Dark-roast coffee was the perfect contrast to the sweetness of the crepe.

After we finished dessert, we sat and relaxed in the July afternoon weather, which was warm but not hot. I had friends who'd spent a week in Paris in 90-degree weather, and the heat had burned off a lot of their vacation pleasure. So far, we had been very lucky: warm but not stifling.

"What's next?" Kim asked.

"I was thinking we could walk to Notre Dame, see if we can spot Quasimodo. Then cross to the Right Bank, walk back to our hotel past the Louvre and through the Jardin des Tuileries. When we get to the Obelisk at Place de la Concorde, we might make a right turn on Rue Royale and go to Fauchon's for coffee and a pastry."

"Is it all about food for you?" She sounded mildly

exasperated.

"Hey, I included a famous church, a beautiful park, and a stunning Obelisk in the itinerary before I got to the food. Sounds like a well-balanced afternoon to me."

"Okay, assuming I'm willing to accept that agenda at face value, which I'm not, what happens after Fauchon's?"

"I don't know," I said with an unconvincing shrug. "Back to the George V for a nap."

"A nap? Will there be any sleep included in this nap?"

"Maybe. Afterward."

"You are so obvious."

"Hey, I'm a newly engaged man with a gorgeous fiancée. Can you blame me?"

"You are incorrigible."

"But you love me anyway, right?"

Kim smiled, reached for my hand with her engagement-yarned left hand, and gave me a gentle squeeze. She said softly, "I do love you anyway."

"I love you, too. For always."

We stared dreamily at each other for a long enough moment that we both began to feel a tiny bit embarrassed.

Kim released my hand and said, "Okay! Off on your tour agenda. With a finale at Fauchon's."

"That's not the finale."

We stood up and kissed quickly. "No," she said with an arched eyebrow and a grin, "that's *not* the finale."

*   *   *

Saturday, we did something neither of us had done for years: we went to Mass. I can't really tell you the reason we decided to visit Sacré-Cœur, but Kim suggested it, and I thought it was a great idea. So, after having breakfast in bed, again, we showered and dressed in nice but casual clothes. We both wore button-down shirts (mine was pale blue; hers was a light yellow) and lightweight slacks. Since we're talking about Roman Catholic activities, I should make a confession and be completely honest: we had dressed better for dinner at Jules Verne than what we were wearing to church. But this was a non-Sabbath visit to church, and that had been a proposal of marriage on the Eiffel Tower.

Outside the hotel, we hailed a taxi, and the driver wound his way to the top of Montmartre to the beautiful, white, domed church, Sacré-Cœur. The Mass was in French, and as I said, it's been a long time for me, but the liturgical ceremony was beautiful and, except for the sermon, I knew what was going on most of the time. We both received Communion. I'm sure the monsignor from my childhood parish would have been disappointed that I hadn't gone to confession before receiving, but that was his problem. If he was displeased with my behavior, he could make a direct appeal to God.

After Mass, and we had gone in peace (as the priest urged us to do), we walked downhill through the winding streets of Montmartre, a neighborhood that was incredibly charming even if overwhelmed with tourists and the kinds of shops and boutiques that draw in tourists.

We reached the bottom of Montmartre and continued to walk to the 2nd Arrondissement, not very far from the Louvre. We found a café, plopped ourselves down at a table outside, and ordered *tartines tartare de thon*, which are open-faced sandwiches on toasted baguettes with tuna tartare.

"Were you able to follow the priest's sermon?" I asked.

"Do you think I'm a theological ignoramus? Of course I could follow his sermon."

"What I should have asked was: Was your French good enough that you understood what he was saying?"

Kim stretched out her hand, palm down, and rocked it in a gentle see-saw. "I was struggling a little bit, but then I realized he came back to the same themes over and over, and it all made sense to me."

"What was he talking about?"

"Love."

"Ah . . . a Frenchman talking about love. There's a shocker."

"Oh my God, you're such an idiot. God's love. God's love for us."

"I guess that would make sense."

"You think?"

"But our love is a manifestation of God's love, isn't

it?"

"Actually, that's what the priest said."

"He used the word manifestation?"

"It's the same in French as in English."

"Just pronounced differently."

"Yes." She smiled, "It sounds much better in French."

"Doesn't everything?"

"*Oui, mon amour.*"

"Show-off."

"*Je ne suis pas un . . .*" she had to search for the word, "*frimeur.*"

I grinned, "Thank you for proving my point."

"*Le point est à vous, mais le plaisir est tout à moi.*"

"I surrender."

Kim smiled. "When do you want to get married? Are you thinking of a big wedding or small? In church? Maybe have a justice of the peace? Or hadn't your devious mind gone beyond giving me my purple-yarn engagement ring?"

"Actually . . . an old friend of mine from my ill-spent youth at Fordham is now a Jesuit priest. He's up at St. Ignatius Loyola on 84th Street and Park Ave. I thought it would be nice—assuming you like the idea—that we have him preside at our wedding."

"That church is huge," she protested.

"We don't have to fill it. Our meager little crowd can take up the first pew or two."

"It would be nice to have someone we know—or one of us knows, anyway—perform the ceremony."

"Yes, it would."

"When?"

"September? Middle of the month, maybe. Assuming we can get everything arranged."

"The weather is usually very nice in September."

"That's what I was thinking."

She shook her head, grinning, "I would never have figured you for so much romantic planning."

"You doubt me? Even after the splendor of your yarn ring?"

"What was I thinking?" She sipped some after-lunch coffee. "Have you got any great ideas for our honeymoon?"

"Maybe Cape Cod?"

"You are *so* good at this!"

"Really? You like all these ideas?"

"I'm not ready to etch them in stone, but yes, they sound pretty darn good."

We sipped our coffee and enjoyed the moment.

"This is really happening," she said.

I laughed. "Yes, it is. Are you pleasantly shocked or fearfully stunned?"

"Pleasantly shocked, of course."

"Well, should I set the wheels in motion? Give my friend, Mike the Jesuit, a call when we get home and see if he can do it?"

"I guess so . . ."

"Excuse me, I am truly sorry to interrupt," Harry said and joined us at our table. He looked at Kim, "Congratulations on your engagement."

"Thank you! How did you know . . . never mind."

He gave her a smile, bigger than his usual Mona Lisa expression, but nothing close to a full-mouth, crinkle-the-corners-of-your-eyes smile. He turned to me. "I'm sorry to interrupt, but we have business to attend to."

"What?"

"The meeting we want to attend is in a few hours."

"But I thought we had a couple of days."

"Seems our acquaintances at Privatus decided to advance their schedule. They're meeting with their local team on the ground is this evening."

"Wait a minute—are you doing business here?" Kim asked. She was not happy. Not happy as in your dentist telling you he's going to pull all your teeth and replace them with ill-fitting dentures. Really, truly unhappy.

"No," I said then realized that was wrong. "Yes, but I told you that I had business here next week. I thought you and I had a couple more days."

"I didn't know your business here was with Harry. You made it sound like the business thing was just an excuse for the trip. Now I find out that *our* trip was the excuse. Or maybe I should say we were your cover. Right?"

"No, all I wanted to do was enjoy Paris with you."

"Was yesterday's walk some kind of scouting trip?"

I exhaled, "Yes, but it didn't stop us from enjoying what we wanted to do, did it?"

"When you do business with Harry it's very dangerous. Very. You know it scares the shit out of me. I don't understand why you couldn't be straight with me about this trip."

"I was straight with you. I wanted to be here in Paris with you. To propose to you here."

Kim's mouth was set in a tight line. She stared at the building opposite us, but I was pretty darn sure she wasn't interested in the architectural details. After an eternity—probably only a minute or two—she looked back at me.

"I'm going back to the hotel. Alone. Don't come back until you're done with this business of yours and Harry's."

"Kim—"

"Don't come back until then. I mean it."

I started to say "I'm sorry," but she was on her feet and walking away before I got to the first syllable of "sorry."

"I apologize," Harry said. "I didn't realize I was going to be the source of conflict."

"It's not your fault. It's mine." I stood up. "I gotta go after her."

"No time."

I froze by the side of the table. "I should call Joanne and see if the international team is in place."

"Yes, you should."

I watched Kim disappear around the corner toward our hotel. I sighed and pulled my phone out and dialed Joanne.

"I haven't really got time to talk, Jack," she said in lieu of "hello." "I'm on my way to the airport."

"Yeah, about that . . ."

"What?"

"The timetable's been advanced. The bad guys are meeting in a couple of hours."

"Are you shitting me?"

"I shit you not."

"The team is set for Monday, which you told me was the meeting time. You said it was a day in advance of the attack."

"I'm sorry. What can I say? The meeting is happening now. Well, almost now."

"Is this information from the same source who gave you—"

"The same source who gave me *everything*. This guy's info is as solid as anyone's in the universe."

"All right," Joanne groaned, "I'll get back to you in ten minutes with the contact information and names for Interpol and CIA."

"Great. Thanks."

"Jack?"

"Yes?"

"My not being there doesn't have any impact on your status as an observer."

"I know."

"I'm not kidding, Jack."

"Got it."

"You'd better."

I disconnected.

Harry said, "My apologies for pointing this out, but time is not on our side."

"Exactly when are the bad guys meeting?"

"They are arriving now. We need to be there in five minutes."

"Damn. I've gotta talk to Kim."

"Jack, we can't."

"Harry, I know we have almost no time. But I have to talk to Kim. Must. Absolutely imperative."

He shook his head, but in less than a blink of an eye, I was standing in my hotel room. Kim was at a window, looking forlornly down into the hotel courtyard.

"Kim," I said softly.

Her shoulders rose in surprise, but she got herself under control and turned to me with a stoney expression on her face. "I thought you had to go fight bad guys."

"I do. But you're too important for me not to talk with you first."

"Kind of a verbal last will and testament?" she uttered without a trace of sympathy or concern.

"No. Well, maybe. I love you. I'm sorry about the way I handled this. I should have explained things much more clearly. I'm sorry. Really and truly sorry." I walked over to her and stroked her arm. "But I did give you that lovely yarn ring and ask you to marry me."

She softened a trace, "Yes, you did." She held her left hand up and examined the yarn bow. "It *is* a lovely piece of yarn."

"I think you should go home," I said. "Harry can whoosh you. No jet lag, no problems at customs, no worry getting a car from the airport to your apartment."

"What? You mean leave now?"

"I think it might be best. I don't know what's going to happen, and I want to know you're safe and sound at home."

"I'm staying. What if you're hurt? Who'll come to the hospital? What if you're killed? Who will accompany your body home?"

"You thought you were coming to Paris for a lovely little vacation. You didn't sign on for this."

"Jack, you asked me to marry you. I said 'yes.' As far as I'm concerned, for better or worse is already an active clause of our agreement."

"That's not . . . that's not really how it works."

"It is for me."

"Really? You don't sound happy with this current situation?"

"How the hell can I be happy? How?"

"I'm sorry. I put that badly. You sound like you're trying to convince yourself about staying."

"I am. And you're not helping me. I'm scared out of my mind."

"Do you regret saying 'yes' to my proposal?"

"No, I don't know. Maybe I do regret it. I'm confused. And scared."

There was a long moment of silence. I leaned in, held her close, and kissed her.

"I'm sorry. I love you," I said.

"I love you more," she replied.

Harry appeared at that moment with my weapons backpack in his hand.

"Jack, we really must be going . . ."

I searched for the appropriate thing to say to Kim, but she spoke first, "Go! Go save the world."

"That's a wee bit much."

"Go save a little part of it."

I said to Harry, "Shall we?"

He replied, "Of course."

13

A millisecond later—maybe even less—I was behind a dull-gray van in a multilevel parking garage. The van was parked nose-in to a three-foot-high retaining wall. I was again dressed in my usual cat burglar outfit—thanks, Harry. Staying low behind the van, I crept to the wall and looked out. I was staring at the front of Gare de Lyon, the train terminal that connected Paris to points south. I recognized it by the clock tower at the southwestern corner of the terminal. Judging by my position relative to the clock tower, I guessed I was on the third level of the parking garage. I straightened up just enough to look through the windows in the van's back doors. A group of men had gathered in a couple of open parking spaces between a Mercedes SUV and a small Renault. My old buddy Daryl Hawkins was speaking, but I was too far away to make out what he was saying.

Harry was standing behind the van, too, and was holding my black backpack.

"Do you have a cell phone?" I whispered.

"Yes." He pulled a phone from the inside jacket pocket of his suit coat.

"Can you please set it to record the meeting?"

"Yes."

"Would you mind whooshing it close enough to them to get a clear recording? Please?"

Harry looked skyward—okay, in reality he looked at the cement ceiling of the parking garage, but when your guardian angel was consulting with the Chairman, it seemed better to refer to his going skyward—then he turned back to me. His phone had disappeared.

"Thank you," I whispered. I dug into the pack, grabbed my shoulder holsters, and slipped into the harness for them. The Rugers went into the holsters, extra magazines went into my pockets. Since I was on holiday, I had expected to adhere to my agreement with Joanne to be an observer only, but the realities on the ground were not going to allow me to behave.

Lastly, I put my balaclava over my head and rolled it up so it didn't cover my face. It was too damn hot to be wearing one of these, but protecting my anonymity seemed like a really good idea.

I nodded to Harry, and he obligingly made the backpack disappear. I assumed it was sent back to the hotel, but I had other things to worry about. I checked my muted phone. There was a text from Joanne with the contact information she had promised. I texted the leader of the international law-enforcement team, Senior Investigator Montesquieu at Interpol:

I am Jack Tyrrell, Joanne Agar's contact. At meeting between Privatus and White Order –

third level, parking lot opposite Gare de Lyon.
Approximately 16 men, probably heavily armed.
Need assistance soonest!!

While I waited for a response, I dropped to all fours and looked under the rear bumper at the group of men who were meeting a few parking spaces away. My view was partially obscured by the Mercedes SUV, which was parked with its rear bumper against the garage's retaining wall, but I could see a couple of young men with chopped, short hair and swastika tattoos on their necks. Their dark clothes and petulant body English proclaimed them as moronic neo-Nazis. Careful, Tyrrell, don't be dismissive or one of those morons might just kill you. Once they're dead or under arrest, you can be as disrespectful as you want. But as long as they have loaded weapons at their disposal, be careful. Give their weapons the respect the Nazis themselves so desperately crave.

The Privatus men were a hell of a lot more normal looking, although I'm sure one or two probably sported tattoos from their days in the military. And, two of the Privatus men were women. Male or female, the Privatus team was experienced, tough, and confident. The neo-Nazis were angry, belligerent, and racist. The common trait they all shared? They were dangerous. Extremely dangerous.

Hawkins was leading the meeting. I wished I were closer so I could hear what he was saying. Harry, on all fours next to me, whispered in my ear, "He's explaining the timing of the attack, the diversion at the entrance to the building, and what they will do once inside the offices of the EU agency."

"Is your phone recording all this? We'll need evidence to prove the conspiracy."

"Yes, it's recording and the words will be audible."

"Great."

"Senior Investigator Montesquieu just replied to your text."

"How do you—never mind." I checked my phone. Montesquieu had replied:

On route to your position with Response Team.
Arrive in five minutes.

I whispered to Harry. "Five minutes till the police team gets here." I pointed at Hawkins. "What's going on?"

"They're concluding the meeting."

"Can't you stall them?" I asked.

"No. But you can."

"I can? I'll get killed!"

"That remains to be seen."

"Really? Jokes at a time like this?"

Harry's face wore its usual serious expression. "I'm sorry, I can't do anything about their departure. You'll have to."

"Shit!" I hissed in an angry whisper. I crawled backward, out from under the van's bumper. I pulled the balaclava down over my face, yanked out both Rugers, stood up, and strode toward the meeting of bad guys.

A short, blond-highlighted, swastika-tattooed man spotted me, clawed under his black jacket for a weapon, and began to shout. I shot him and he dropped like a stone. A Privatus man on my left was bringing his gun to bear when I shot him in the chest. Another neo-Nazi was sweeping a sawed-off shotgun up and out of his trench coat. I barely looked at him as I pointed at him and fired, killing my third villain in three shots.

"Hold it!" I shouted. My voice echoed in the concrete space of the parking garage.

Around me, eleven people all halted as they were reaching for weapons or clutching their guns but not yet aiming them at me. Not yet. Everyone held in a weird tableau of violence.

"Oh . . . shit," Hawkins said. "The Magic Warrior, himself. Here in Paris."

"Where are your lookouts?" I asked.

"What lookouts?" Hawkins grinned.

"Don't screw with me," I said. "The two people you have making sure you don't get interrupted. Call them and tell them to come in with their hands up."

"I know you're good," Hawkins said. "But do you really think you can take us all?"

"No, but I can shoot you first if anyone tries anything."

"Given that I've seen you shoot," he gestured at the

fallen bodies, "I guess I'm going to have to do it your way." He raised his voice, "Everyone hold your position. Don't shoot . . ." His grin returned, ". . . until I tell you to."

"Funny guy," I replied. "Everyone! On the floor! Slowly."

They all looked at each other, decided that discretion was the better part of valor, and slowly went down on their knees. They put their hands out and lowered their torsos to the cement floor of the parking garage. All except one tall, thin, reddish-blond neo-Nazi. He was on his knees and decided to go for his gun instead of lying down. He and I fired at the same time. His bullet hit the Mercedes SUV behind me with a deep *thunk*. My bullet caught him in the chest and killed him.

But the split-second I had been focused on him was enough for two or three of the others to go for their guns. One of the women had an Uzi and sprayed fire in my direction. I dove onto the hood of the Mercedes and rolled across it to the far side. The windows shattered and rained glass all around the now-wrecked SUV. The tires on the woman's side were both flattened, and the vehicle was canted over to that side, making it all but impossible to fire under the SUV. I hid behind the front of the vehicle since the engine block would be the most bullet-proof part of the Mercedes.

But shells slammed into the side of the vehicle where I was crouched. I twisted around. Two men, both Privatus types and carrying assault rifles, scurried from vehicle to vehicle, laying down covering fire as they closed in on me from another part of the garage. They must have been the damn lookouts.

"Hold your fire! Hold your fire!" Hawkins shouted. "HOLD your fire, damnit!"

The two lookouts maintained cover behind two parked cars. Their respective positions pinned me down in a crossfire.

"Hey, Warrior," Hawkins called. "Come out with your hands up. I won't kill you. I promise. I just need to talk to you."

"Why wait?" I raised my voice in return. "I'm listening."

"Come out with your hands up. We'll sit down, have a drink, have some conversation. One professional to another."

"This isn't a social event, Hawkins." I glanced in every direction, taking in as much of the garage as I could see, wondering how the hell I was going to get out of this particularly sticky situation. The only possible escape route that I could imagine was to dash for the retaining wall and vault over it. Take my chances with a three-story plunge to the pavement below. Can't say I liked my chances with that plan.

"You're boxed in," Hawkins said. "You either surrender or you get shot."

"Or . . ." I replied loudly, "I surrender *and* get shot."

"I told you: I need to talk to you. I have to find out how you know so much about our operations."

"Yeah, I can see that you're in a bit of a situation."

"That's rich coming from you."

"I'd like to show you rich." I muttered. I checked the positions of the two lookouts. Each man had set his assault rifle on the hood of a car and was aiming directly at me. Their odds of hitting me if I stood up and ran from the vehicle: 99.99 percent. If I decided to make a play for them, I'd have to snap off two head shots with a handgun at a distance of about sixty feet while moving very swiftly to prevent my own death. Poor shooting conditions with a less than optimal weapon at small targets. My odds of hitting both men before they killed me: 2 percent. Maybe less. . . .

"God, I don't usually ask for your help in, well, shooting people—although I have lately—but . . . could you please help me now? I don't see another way out of here." I mumbled. I holstered one Ruger then took a few deep breaths and said, "God, however this turns out, thank you."

I dove away from the front of the Mercedes SUV, rolling as I hit the cement floor ground. Bullets pinged off the floor where I had been. I came out of the roll onto my knees, my right hand braced with my left, aimed at the lookout on my left, and fired. His head snapped back and he disappeared.

I felt something pluck at my right sleeve at my triceps. I twisted to face the lookout on my right, aimed quickly, and pulled the trigger. The bullet caught him in the eye and there was a splurt of blood as the bullet exited his skull. He, too, disappeared, dropping his rifle onto the hood of the car.

Everything was silent for a moment. My guess was that Hawkins was assessing the situation. Maybe he was considering surrender. Or not.

"Fire!" he shouted, and what was left of his team unloaded on the Mercedes. I scrambled back until I was low behind the engine block again. Suddenly, the guns were silent.

What the hell . . .? Then I knew what was happening. I lunged to the rear of the Mercedes and tucked myself close to the retaining wall. A woman leapt to the hood of the SUV and then dropped down to where I had been crouched. I fired twice as soon as her feet hit the ground, rocking her body into the center lane of the parking garage.

I was grabbing the second Ruger and reaching for fresh magazines as two neo-Nazis ran around the front end of the Mercedes. They began firing assault rifles the instant they spotted me. I brought up my left hand and fired until the weapon clicked empty. Both men were down.

Once again, silence reigned in the parking garage.

I slapped new magazines into both Rugers. "Hey, Hawkins, do you want to keep going?" I shouted. "At this rate, are you even going to have enough people to pull off your terrorist stunt against the EU?"

"Don't worry about me and my team."

"But I do worry. After all, you can't have an endless supply of neo-Nazi jerks to do your bidding."

There was no response. Was Hawkins coming up with another plan? I hoped not. I had had enough. 'Genug' as the neo-Nazis would say in German.

"I still have enough people to kill you," Hawkins said.

"All evidence to the contrary," I replied.

"You're awfully confident."

The sounds of revving engines revving and screeching tires filled the air from the lower levels of the garage. The noise echoed as it bounced off the cement of the parking structure.

"Hear that, Hawkins?" I shouted very loudly. "Those are my police pals. They came without sirens. The better to catch you and your swastika-wearing clowns."

I heard running feet running and car doors slamming nearby. I took a chance, stood up, and looked out over the wreckage of the Mercedes. Two groups of three bad guys were in two Citroen hatchbacks. The engines roared, and the cars took off with a squeal of tire rubber. They accelerated hard, racing to the ground level exit. Which, I hoped, was blocked by Parisian SWAT teams.

Another pair of feet pounded toward the far side of the garage. I spotted Hawkins and raced after him. He stopped at the retaining wall, grabbed a coil of rope from his pocket, tied it to the metal rail atop the retaining wall, and dropped the rope over the rail on the outside of the building.

Hawkins was wearing leather gloves and an Uzi slung over his shoulder. He gripped the rope, swung his legs over the rail, and dropped out of sight. There was a burst of gunfire. I reached the wall and cautiously looked down. Hawkins was descending rapidly, using his left hand as his rope-brake, his right hand firing the Uzi downward. On the ground below him, four bodies in dark fatigues lay sprawled in puddles of blood.

Hawkins reached the ground, turned, and looked up at me. He smiled, gave me a mocking salute, then sprayed the wall with bullets. I'd realized he wasn't going to let me off easily so I had ducked behind the wall as he saluted. I was safe, but I felt the shock of the bullets thudding into the other side of the cement wall. He stopped firing. I crept ten feet along the back of the wall and popped up with my guns at the ready. I scanned the ground in every direction.

Hawkins was long gone.

Harry appeared at my side and handed me his smart phone. "The recording is clearly audible and very incriminating."

"Conspiracy?"

"A rookie prosecutor could make this case."

"Listen to you with the tough-guy talk."

Sirens wailed upward, coming toward us. I stepped away from the wall and placed both Rugers on the ground.

I slipped out of my shoulder holsters and dumped them on the ground next to the pistols, then I yanked off my balaclava and dropped it, too. July in Paris was too damn warm for a balaclava.

Harry flashed his Mona Lisa expression at me and said, "It would be a shame if you were killed by friendly fire. You did very well today."

"I killed a lot of people. Not happy about that. Not at all."

"You had no choice. You did what you had to do. And you prayed before you took action, asking for help."

"Help killing?"

"If I were you, I would assume that since you prayed, what happened afterward was part of the Chairman's plan."

The police sirens were very loud, and the emergency lights were flashing off the wall above the ascending lane in the garage.

"What if I was insincere in my prayers? What if I was just scared and selfishly asking for help?"

"Don't you think the Chairman would recognize your feelings?"

Police cars roared toward us.

I raised my hands and said to Harry, "I guess He would at that."

Harry gave me his Mona Lisa again, "By the way, it might help you to feel better to know that only three of the people you shot died."

"The Chairman works in mysterious ways."

"Yes, He does." Harry disappeared.

Two police cars and two unmarked cars jerked to a stop in a rough circle surrounding me. Police officers jumped out of the cars near me, pointed their weapons, and shouted, "*Arrêt!*"

I stood stock still, my hands held high. A plainclothes policeman stepped forward, carefully staying out of the line of fire of his comrades and patted me down.

"I'm ticklish," I said.

He stopped and looked puzzled.

"Just kidding," I smiled.

He resumed patting me down, found Harry's and my phones tucked away in my pants pocket, yanked them out, and said, "*Clair.*" (For the benefit of us non-French speaking types, "Clear.")

A mid-fortyish woman with bobbed brunette hair walked over to me. "Monsieur Tyrrell?"

"*Oui. Parlez vous anglais?*" I asked.

"Yes. Special Agent Agar sent me your photo, just in case we ended up . . ." she was searching for the right word, "apprehending you."

"That was thoughtful of her."

"Yes, it was. You may put your hands down. I'm Interpol Senior Investigator Evelyn Montesquieu. I'm leading this operation, coordinating all the concerned parties."

"All concerned parties? Like the CIA and French

police? From what I saw, you did one hell of a job coordinating."

"*Merci.*" She offered me her hand.

As we shook, I said, "I'm very glad to see you."

Montesquieu glanced around. "You don't seem to have needed any assistance." She pointed at my right arm. "Although you do seem to have been shot."

"It's only a scratch."

"Really?"

"Unfortunately, I've been shot enough times to know when it's bad wound and when it's just a scratch."

An agent walked over to her, holding my guns and holster.

"We'll see to your arm at the debriefing," Montesquieu said. "Special Agent Agar told me you would be here as an observer only."

"Yeah, well, the circumstances called for direct action. Joanne—Special Agent Agar—probably told you to shoot me in the leg if I didn't strictly adhere to my observer status."

Montesquieu grinned. "Those were her exact words." She pointed at my weapons. "We will keep these until all the forensics on this scene have been completed."

"I understand." I pointed at Harry's phone. "That phone has a recording of the bad guys planning to do some horrible things to the European Securities and Markets Authority."

"You managed to record their meeting?"

"Yes."

"Very impressive."

"Can I quote you to my fiancée?"

"What about the other phone?"

"My personal phone. I'd like to have that back, please."

She handed it to me and asked, "Can I buy you a cup of coffee while we debrief you?"

"Yes, please."

*   *   *

"Jack, are you all right?" Kim sounded breathless and worried over the phone. I looked down at my right arm, which was being treated with an antiseptic cream and a bandage.

"I'm fine. Really."

"You're not just playing the tough guy, are you? You're *really* okay?"

"Really. Truly. Absolutely."

"Where are you?"

"In a conference room at the Commissariat de Police du 8ème arrondissement. It's on the Avenue du Général Eisenhower. Right next to the Grand Palais. Very nice neighborhood."

The police officer treating my arm frowned at my pronunciation. I cupped the mouthpiece and said, "*Pardon.*" To Kim, I said, "Pardon my mangled French. It's a police station. Interpol is coordinating with the CIA and the Paris police force's SWAT team, so I was brought here for a debriefing."

"Why are you being debriefed?"

"I helped arrest some neo-Nazis. No big deal."

There was a pause so long and deep that you could have launched the Titanic into it.

"Kim, I'm okay. Really. I just need to answer some questions. I'll be back at the hotel later. Don't wait up."

Her response was another long silence.

"Kim?"

"You know . . . my boyfriend asked me to marry him and gave me the nicest purple-yarn ring."

"Wow, sounds great."

"It is. He'd better make sure he comes back to me in one piece."

"He will. I promise."

"I love you."

"I love you, too."

The officer finished the first aid and handed me my shirt. I pulled it over my head and carefully put my arm into its sleeve. Didn't want to snag the sleeve on the bandage and ruin the officer's work. As I was re-buttoning my shirt, Montesquieu arrived with a cup of coffee.

She introduced me to two Paris police *capitaines* : Dantin and Vercher as well as John Smith, an American in a drab gray suit that looked like he'd been wearing it for too many hours. CIA, I guessed. Yes, he actually claimed his name was John Smith.

Montesquieu finished the introductions by saying, "We're all working together on the international task force that Special Agent Agar briefed you about."

"Tyrrell, what's your connection to this?" Mr. John Smith of the CIA asked. He stood across the table from me, while Montesquieu and the police officials had seated themselves.

"I've got a private client who wants to retire from Privatus. Retire and survive."

"And you're the guy who can pull that off? What are you, private security? You handle personal protection and shit like that?"

"Mostly shit like that." I stood up and was gratified to see that I was two, maybe three, inches taller than Smith. "Listen, maybe you and I should go out in the hall and measure our dicks there."

Montesquieu stifled a smile and spoke to Smith, "Special Agent Agar personally vouched for Mr. Tyrrell. He was in Special Forces in Afghanistan and worked with the CIA there. Awarded a Silver Star and a Purple Heart. Then worked for the U.S. Marshals Service for six years, commended twice.

"Initial analysis of the crime scene at the parking garage at Gare de Lyon indicates that Mr. Tyrrell, armed only with a pair of Ruger pistols, took out nine heavily armed hostiles all by himself, killing three."

Smith didn't have a response.

"If we're done with the . . ." Montesquieu smiled

widely now, "measuring of dicks, maybe we could proceed with the debriefing."

"Speaking of hostiles," I said to Montesquieu but looking at Smith, "what happened to the clowns who raced away in the Citroens?"

"One of the escape vehicles attempted to run the police barricade at the garage exit. Two men, both members of *Europäische Weisse Ordnung*, died from injuries sustained in the crash. The third, riding in the back seat, has a broken nose, fractured right arm, and three broken ribs. He is conscious and seems to be . . ." she considered her English slang options, "freaked out, I think you would say."

"Why do you say he's freaked out?" Smith asked.

"We explained his rights to him, but he insisted on babbling away, answering all the questions of the police officers at the hospital."

Capitaine Dantin said, "We've been in touch with Interpol in Germany and the local police in Cologne and Frankfurt. They will be arresting members of *Europäische Weisse Ordnung* in both cities. In twenty-four hours, these neo-Nazi groups will be, to use a German word, *kaput*."

"Which doesn't mean," I interjected, "that Privatus can't find another group of young, dumb, angry terrorists and make another attempt."

"As you might imagine, security around all EU offices is very effective," Montesquieu responded. "However, we are looking at additional measures that can be taken to harden these targets. Extend the security zone around the buildings, use dump trucks to form a barricade for motor vehicles, and a number of longer-term solutions as well."

"Mostly shit like that," I nodded. Was it my imagination, or did Smith's mouth go very tight? It definitely wasn't my imagination that he loosened his tie, pulling at its knot as if he hated it.

Capitaine Vercher pointed out, "All of these security measures will make it harder to attack an EU office, but they don't make it impossible."

"If you get a big enough hammer, you can drive any nail," I said.

"I'm not sure I understand," replied Vercher, "but I think so."

"Anything that can be done, will be done to secure the facilities," Montesquieu said. "But what we really need to do is shut down Privatus. They are the true bad guys here."

"Which reminds me, what happened to the second car that drove away? Was it full of Privatus people?"

"It pulled to a stop when the *Weisse Ordnung* car crashed into the barrier. We arrested all three people, two men and a woman. As for whether they work for Privatus . . ."

"They're not talking."

"No. They're all known to various law-enforcement agencies. The two men are British, former SAS. The woman is American, former CIA."

"But none of them has any obvious connections to Privatus," I said.

"No."

"They probably work for some kind of shell company. Paid through some completely legitimate bank account in the Caymans or Panama."

"That is our working theory," she nodded. "We'll track it down eventually, but that is our theory: There is no direct connection between these people and Privatus."

"You can send them all to prison, right?"

"With your recording and your testimony, and all the weapons seized, as well as the testimony of the young neo-Nazi, we will be able to send them all to prison for a long time. I don't know what the exact charges would be in America—but we should be able to send them all to prison for conspiracy, possession of illegal weapons, assault—"

"Assault? On lil' ole me?" I asked.

"*Oui*," she agreed, smiling broadly.

"Will these be long sentences?"

"I think you'll be pleased."

I drank most of my coffee, thinking as I swallowed. "What about Hawkins? I'm pretty damn sure he can lead you right back to Privatus. Any word on him? I'm guessing you've got all the airports, train stations, ports, etc. locked down, and you're hoping to catch him?"

"We do."

"But you don't expect to catch him, do you?"

"We do not."

Tyrrell, your doppelganger is one hell of a slippery guy. The next time you have the opportunity to catch that guy, you'd better do it. Or kill him.

No matter what.

14

I strolled out of the Commissariat de Police du 8ème arrondissement at 10:23 P.M. I felt as if Harry and I had gone to the Gare de Lyon a few weeks earlier, not a few hours earlier. The police had offered to drive me back to George V, but I declined. I was exhausted yet completely wired, as if I'd had one too many double espressos. Much as I hoped to find Kim awake when I returned to the hotel, I needed to relax a bit. A walk in Paris was the perfect prescription for my wired state.

I went left on the Avenue du Général Eisenhower, which curved around the northern side of the grounds of the Grand Palais. I turned right on Avenue de Selves and walked north to the Avenue des Champs-Élysées. I crossed the Champs-Élysées and stood on the sidewalk under the trees of the Jardins des Champs-Élysées. I closed my eyes and inhaled deeply. The night air was soothing.

After several blissful moments of thinking about nothing, I headed northwest along the Champs-Élysées.

The Arc de Triomphe, about a half-mile away, was bathed in light, beautiful and strong. It was a late July evening, ten days after Bastille Day, and I was strolling along the main boulevard of Paris, enjoying the night air and the glamour of the City of Light. I wished that I were the title character of Joni Mitchell's song "Free Man in Paris." That guy felt "unfettered and alive" with "nobody calling [him] up for favors and no one's future to decide." I was far from unfettered, and there were people's futures to save. I'm not saying that saving is the same as deciding, but saving felt like one hell of a heavy responsibility to me.

While I was yearning for this unfettered existence, my internal radar pinged. A loud, insistent pinging. Two men, without a good intention between them, were following me in Paris. I walked a couple of more blocks toward the Arc, then crossed the street in a leisurely, tourist-like fashion. I gazed in some store windows but had no clue what goods I was looking at. In the reflection of the store windows, I saw the two men cross the Champs-Élysées, coming in my direction. I headed southeast, away from the Arc and more importantly, away from the Avenue George V and our hotel. I picked up my pace.

In less time than it takes to tie your shoes, I had gone from savoring the beauty of the tree-lined Champs-Élysées to anxiously twisting around to look behind me at the Arc de Triomphe.

The two guys were tailing me. My internal radar was pinging madly. If these guys weren't ex-CIA and/or former SEALS or Delta—exactly the paragons of security that the nefarious people at Privatus employed—I was sadly mistaken. I would have gladly admitted to such a mistake. But my damn radar wouldn't go silent. These guys were bad news. Lethally bad news. And my Ruger pistols were, at that exact moment, in the possession of the Paris police.

Picking up my pace, I continued walking, not pausing to twist this way and that to take in the sights. A few blocks ahead of me was the traffic roundabout where the Champs-Élysées met Avenue Franklin Delano Roosevelt. On the far side of the roundabout there was a park, the Jardin des Champs-Élysées, the same place where I had stopped to take a deep breath of night air. More parks to the south included the Theatre du Rond-Point, the huge glass-vaulted-and-domed Grand Palais, and the Petit Palais. If I was going to lose my tails, I would have my best chance in the *jardin*, although I knew there was a lot of open space among the trees.

When I reached the rotary, I saw a tiny break in the swirl of traffic and dashed for it. Parisian roundabouts can be terrifying—all the drivers are playing traffic-circle chicken—and I *was* terrified, but my adrenaline rush gave me speed. I plunged across the four lanes of traffic, dodged a couple of scooters, jumped back to avoid being crushed by a small panel van, immediately resumed my rush forward, and felt the sideview mirror of a Citroen pluck at my sleeve. Brakes screeched, car and scooter horns honked, and the air was filled with Gallic cursing.

I made it to the small center of the rotary, a veritable island of safety in the midst of vehicular mayhem. I took a deep breath and plunged into the 4 lanes of traffic on the far side of the traffic circle. More honking, more cursing, and a helmeted scooter driver whacked my shoulder with his hand and shouted something that sounded like "*Piqûre stupide*!" I didn't ask him to translate.

As I reached the sidewalk, I heard a fresh burst of screeching, honking and cursing that I guessed was due to my pursuers, but I wasn't going to waste a second checking on their progress. I ran under the trees into the *jardin*, continued running across the walkways into a thick clump of shrubs, and ducked into them, hiding in the nighttime darkness. My pursuers had reached the sidewalk, stopped about fifty feet away from me, and turned toward the north side of the *jardin*.

I checked their position and saw two more men with the dangerous, *je ne sais quoi* quality typical of spies for hire, entering the *jardin* from the north side.

I still had a clear line of retreat down the Champs-Élysées. But I would only succeed in getting way if I were faster than all four of the Privatus guys chasing me. And only if none of them was armed. The chance that I could escape them if they were armed was *très petit*. I'm not without some serious skills of my own, but I was unarmed and at the wrong end of a 4-to-1 ratio.

The guys on the sidewalk had slowed down but

were still moving closer to me; their hands empty. Their team mates in the *jardin* were also moving slowly in my direction, but unless the dark was playing havoc with my eyes, both of their hands held automatic pistols.

I double-checked the position of the sidewalk pair. They had stopped and were scanning the *jardin*. If they had a pair of night-vision goggles they would have spotted me in two seconds, but night-vision goggles are not particularly sleek and fashionable. In fact wearing a pair of these goggles gives a person the look of an insect's head: the Goggle Mantis, which does not meet the fashion standards of Paris. Nor are they inconspicuous.

After a long moment, I noticed the sound of laughter, voices, and hurdy-gurdy music. I turned to the east and spotted a small carousel, the kind that gets towed into place by a truck and set up for street fairs. This carousel sat in an open space about two hundred feet away from me to the east. It was directly in front of the Théâtre Marigny, whose original architect Charles Garnier designed the magnificent Paris Opera House. The Marigny was nowhere near the size of the opera house, but it provided a nice backdrop for the carousel. Maybe I could ride to safety on a carousel horse. If only. It would have been so cool to escape the bad guys to the notes of the hurdy-gurdy machine.

Returning my attention to my pursuers, I noticed that the Privatus men in the *jardin* had spread farther apart; no doubt to cut down on my escape path and to avoid shooting each other or catching the boys on the sidewalk in a crossfire. And unless I was imagining things, they were screwing suppressors onto their pistols. Good move, I thought. When you're going to kill someone in a public place, you don't want to make too much noise—it might disturb the carousel riders.

One of the men, with a pathetically wispy mustache and goatee, was getting very close to my hiding place. The other man, with a prominent hooked nose, remained in place to cover Mr. Goatee. Staying within the cover of the shrubs, I dropped to the ground and slithered silently toward Mr. Goatee. Yes, *toward*. This seemed like one of those moments when the best defense was a good offense. He obligingly came closer and closer, peering this way and that, doing his absolute best to find *moi*. Being the thorough type, he crouched down to check the ground. His stance wasn't balanced and his feet were tight together under him. Highly unstable. I swept my right leg in a hard kick, as hard as I could manage lying on my left side, catching him directly on the backs of his ankles.

Mr. Goatee flipped onto his back, and I jerked myself upright then lunged on top of him, grabbing his gun hand, his right, with my left. I jerked the gun up and fired at the other Privatus guy in the *jardin*. It was a tough shot because Goatee's finger was still on the trigger—I missed. But the other guy scrambled for cover and aimed in my direction.

I slammed my right fist into Goatee's chin, and the

290

back of his head bounced off the ground. He was out. I rolled again, yanking Goatee on top of me at the instant the other guy's bullets thudded into Goatee's back. I tugged Goatee's gun free from his now lifeless hand, pushed his body off me toward the shrubs, while I rolled in the other direction and fired. I fired six times, and I hit the other guy twice. He went down.

There was no sign of the sidewalk team. I wished they had disappeared into the night, running in fear from Tyrrell the Terrible. Running from the Magic Warrior. But they were pros. They weren't running away. They were probably in the bushes, staying hidden, guns in hand, moving closer to me for a kill shot. Damn.

I crawled on my belly to Goatee, checked to see if I could spot the sidewalk team and couldn't, patted down Goatee's pockets, and found a phone and two extra magazines with ten rounds each for his Beretta M9. I hadn't fired this model Beretta since my time in the Army, but after the events of the last couple of minutes, I was inclined to give it my personal endorsement.

Staying hidden behind Goatee's body, I tucked the phone and clips into one of my cargo pants pockets. It was a tight fit and not very comfortable, but running out of ammo would be much more uncomfortable, so I told myself to shut up and deal with it. I scanned the *jardin* very slowly, looking for the remaining two men. Still no sign of them. That was a problem.

The other dead man was about twenty feet away,

closer to the carousel, which continued to turn while the hurdy-gurdy music played. More crawling for me. I reached him without anyone trying to shoot me as I wriggled along. It's not easy crawling around on the ground, when your pockets are full of ammo and a phone, but it gets much tougher when someone shoots at you while you do it. Sometimes, you just have to be grateful for the little things. And I was grateful for not having been shot. Yet.

The hooked-nose dead man's pockets also produced a phone and a wallet, both of which I took and was about to shove into my pocket, when I realized he was wearing a lightweight rucksack. Perfect for carrying guns, ammo, and spare phones. It took me a minute to get the rucksack off him—in my experience dead men are not very cooperative about someone looting their corpses—and loaded all the ammo, phones, wallet, and Goatee's Beretta into it. I had to paw around on the ground to find the other man's gun, a Sig Sauer P226 9mm, which I also packed inside the rucksack.

I crept into the nearest clump of bushes and checked the *jardin* in every direction. Still no sign of the two guys who had been on the sidewalk. Which meant, they could be near the carousel, enjoying the horses in their endless circling. Or, it meant they had departed the area to go enjoy some wine and cheese at a local bistro, which is what I would have done if I were them. Or, it meant . . . they were still lurking nearby, hiding, waiting for me to make a move.

If I had to bet, and it just so happened that I was betting my life, my Privatus buddies were still lurking in the immediate vicinity. But since I had no idea where they were, I had no idea if I had a clear escape route. I scanned the area again, very slowly, and still couldn't find the twosome. I opened the rucksack, took everything out, and laid it all on the ground to take a quick inventory. I put the Beretta and its magazines back into the pack along with the phones. The Sig, with its large-capacity magazine, I kept in my right hand, and a spare mag went into my pants pocket.

I wriggled over to the hooked-nose man, rolled onto my left side, unscrewed the Sig's suppressor, pointed it at his back, and whispered, "Sorry about this, but you won't feel a thing." His body and my body would screen most of the muzzle flash when I fired, which I hoped would keep the two guys from spotting me. If, however, they were hiding only a few feet away from me, they would see the flash, and I'd be dead before I could relax my trigger finger.

I inhaled deeply then slowly exhaled. Now or never, Tyrrell. Now. I pulled the trigger three times. Lots of noise. The area around the carousel erupted in screams and shouts of fear and confusion. Feet pounded in every direction.

Two men jumped out of the bushes about fifteen feet away from me, between my position and the carousel.

I leapt to my feet and hurtled across the walkways

under the trees and ran directly across the Champs-Élysées, a panel van barely missing me. The Privatus guys' bullets popped through the van's metal panels but I kept moving onto the Place Clemenceau then down the Avenue Winston Churchill, running as fast as I could past the elaborate facades of the Grand Palais on my right and the Petit Palais across the street on my left.

Bullets whined by both of my ears. One shot pinged off an ornate street lamp. Keep running, Tyrrell, the Seine's about three hundred feet in front of you.

My pursuers stopped firing and concentrated on chasing me. I raced across the walkways of the Cours la Reine and out onto the Pont Alexandre III, a Beaux Arts style bridge that—in my humble opinion—is the most extravagantly beautiful bridge in Paris.

A bullet ricocheted off the walkway near my feet. Another hit the railing to my right. I ignored them. I paused and peered down over the stone railing at the Seine. My prayers had been answered: A glass-enclosed riverboat was gliding east under the mid-span of the Pont Alexandre III. There was no time left to think or come up with another plan—there was no cover on the bridge, no place to hide.

I shoved the Sig into my pants pocket, planted both hands on the railing, and vaulted over the rail toward the glass dome of the boat—

I landed smack in the middle of the long glass dome of the boat. My feet hit part of the metal frame that supported the entire length and width of the dome, probably fifteen-feet wide by eighty-feet long. That was only a guess as to the dimensions, and a very rushed guess at that. As soon as my feet touched, I rolled forward, dispersing the force of the landing, like a paratrooper hitting the ground. Then I was scrambling to grab on to something to keep from sliding off the dome. My roll had prevented me from breaking my ankles, but I also had no secure footing whatsoever. I was about to slide off the riverboat's roof and fall into the Seine.

My fingertips caught a piece of the metal frame's edge, and it was a microscopic edge. Steady there, Tyrrell. Nice and easy. I tried not to flinch or flail about and waited for my body to stop sliding. At that point, I was clinging to the starboard side of the dome, my feet slightly above the eye-level of the passengers inside. I began to pull myself to the top of the boat.

A bullet whizzed past my head. I heard a tiny plop as it hit the water. A second bullet followed. It sounded closer, but who the hell could tell if that was the case. I couldn't. I was just a guy clinging for life to a glass boat, hoping not to get shot.

There was a jarring vibration from the glass dome. One of my Privatus pursuers had made the same leap I had made, landing near the stern. A second man had his arms braced on the rail of the Pont Alexandre III and was firing his pistol at me. Then he realized the boat was clearing the bridge and taking his opportunity to leap onto the dome with it. He jumped atop the railing and awkwardly plunged face first toward the glass dome of the riverboat. He slammed into the stern-end of glass dome as if belly flopping into the neighborhood pool. He lay there for a long moment, obviously unconscious, then began sliding off the side of the dome. His feet caught the rim of the deck, arresting his downward progress. I hoped he would tip over into the river, but no such luck.

The first pursuer had used my technique, rolling forward as he hit the dome. He was standing in the center of the dome's arch when his partner belly flopped. He took a few steps back toward the second man, crouched, gripped a bit of the metal frame, spread himself out flat on the dome, and extended his arm as far as he could. He was able to grip the hand of his unconscious partner.

Looking through the glass dome at the passengers dining at their tables, I could see that the passengers had summoned the crew. The passengers at the table just the other side of the glass from me had stood up and backed to the other side. I wondered that they didn't take their dinner plates with them—what if I shattered the glass and sprinkled shards of it all over their food? Would the riverboat company refund them their fees for this ride?

I succeeded in reaching the top of the arch. Below me the crew members were gesticulating wildly that I should come down. Yeah, right. Just how was I going to pull off that little journey?

At the other end of the boat, the belly flopper was now conscious and was working with his partner to clamber up the side of the dome. I didn't have a lot of time before the two would join me on top of the arch and then I'd have no place to go.

I stood up, wobbled as I tried to balance myself on the arch, ignored my terror at possibly toppling off into the Seine, and ran toward the stern and the Privatus pursuers.

Belly Flopper shouted to his partner, warning him of my approach. That was bad news from my standpoint, since I would have loved to catch them as they struggled to get Belly Flopper to the top of the dome. But it was really bad news from the standpoint of Belly Flopper. His partner released his grip on the flopper just as the riverboat cruised beneath the Pont de la Concorde, an arched bridge built of stone. Belly Flopper slid down the glass of the dome. His feet hit the rim of the deck on the starboard side, his knees buckled, and he tipped away from the glass and out into the water. He splashed into the Seine and disappeared.

The riverboat glided under the center arch of the Pont de la Concorde; the boat's lights casting a soft glow on the arch's underside. Inside the boat, the passengers and crew were excited about the action above their heads. On top of the dome, the last Privatus pursuer didn't spare Belly Flopper a glance. He was too busy pulling his gun on me.

I dove at him, full out, a complete extension, catching him at the waist and pinning his gun hand to his side as I wrapped my arms around him. We crashed down, our bodies sprawled on either side of the arch. For a second, we were perfectly positioned to counterbalance each other. No one was sliding. Then the Privatus guy just had to go and ruin everything by trying to shoot me. He began to yank his gun hand around to point his pistol at me, but I was gripping his right wrist with my left hand, holding the gun down and away from me. The jerk fired anyway. I guess he was hoping to hit me someplace. Anyplace. Instead, he literally shot himself in the foot.

He screamed with pain. I took a chance, released my grip on his wrist, pushed myself upright with my left hand, and slammed my right fist into his jaw. For good measure, I slammed him twice more. He went limp; his gun clattered onto the dome and slid out of sight, splashing into the water. Fortunately for him, I tugged him to the middle of the dome, exactly where he needed to be to ride the boat in comfortable unconsciousness.

As we emerged on the eastern side of the Pont de la Concorde, I carefully straightened up onto one knee. I couldn't help noticing the ornate clock towers on either end of the Musée d'Orsay to my right. I also felt a heavy, thud on the dome behind me. I twisted toward the riverboat's stern. Daryl Hawkins had leapt from the bridge to the glass dome of the riverboat. He stood up carefully.

"Jack Tyrrell," he said in recognition as he took a tentative step toward me. "We were in Afghanistan at the same time."

"Yup."

"I'm guessing you're the Magic Warrior."

"I could use a little magic right now," I muttered to

myself. I dug in my pocket for the Sig Sauer.

Hawkins was coming directly at me, walking slowly and steadily while sliding his hand inside his jacket. It didn't take a clairvoyant to know what he was reaching for.

His eyes locked on mine, and we both froze, holding our weapons but neither of us ready to fire. Both afraid the other guy might be the tiniest fraction of a second quicker. Well, I was afraid. Hawkins's emotional state could probably be better described as concerned.

The frozen moment ended as I began to pull my gun and Hawkins lunged at me. I dove forward, hoping to go under him, but it didn't work. He landed on the back of my legs, and we both started to slide down the starboard side of the dome.

I released the Sig and desperately scratched for any kind of grip. The passengers were pointing and shouting, and two crew members—on the verge of apoplexy judging by their bulging eyes—were screaming and cursing.

Hawkins had let go of my legs, and like me, he was clawing for purchase. We both found the upper edge of the dome's metal framework and hung gasping. After a three-second session of panting for breath, I kicked him with my left leg, and he returned the favor by kicking with his right. When you are trying to stick to the side of a sloping piece of glass, you can't generate a lot of power. The only thing we managed to accomplish was to annoy each other.

A minute's worth of futile kicking was more than

enough. We inched away from each other then painstakingly pulled ourselves to the top of the dome. We weren't in a race, but both of us were determined not to let the other guy achieve the top before we did. We succeeded in getting there at the same time.

"You want to go for your gun?" I asked. "Or maybe we should slug it out until one of us falls into the river and drowns?"

He grinned. "Or maybe I should let one of my guys shoot you."

I felt a heavy, thumping pain in the middle of my back. I had to fight to maintain my balance. A second thumped me in the back of my head. My eyes lost focus, my breath came in hard, short gasps, and I fell onto my knees.

I twisted around, and saw that the riverboat had almost reached the Passerelle Léopold-Sédar-Senghor, a metal footbridge that crossed the Seine in a long, single span. A man was crouched in the middle of the bridge, holding a shotgun and looking at me

"Bean bags," Hawkins said. "Don't worry, the bruising isn't too bad."

"You have got to be fucking kidding me," I muttered and passed out.

15

Things were blurry. I was semi-conscious. Hawkins reached me, and gave me a few slugs of some bad-tasting liquid from a small bottle.

"It's a mild tranq. No hangover. Enjoy the high." he said.

I had only of vague awareness of what was happening, but I did know that the riverboat pulled over to a *quai*—I had no idea which one or which side of the river we were on. Hawkins flashed some kind of credentials at the crew, and they helped him carry my almost-dead weight off the boat. Police cars with lights flashing were parked at the *quai*, and four police officers took me from the crew and carried me to a passenger van.

Hawkins was speaking to Capitaine Dantin, one of the police captains that Senior Investigator Montesquieu had introduced me to. Gee, was Dantin working with Hawkins? Was Hawkins working with the international task force? I tried to analyze the situation, but I could barely focus my vision, never mind comprehend Hawkins's fluent French.

The police officers lifted me to the van's back seat. It felt as if they heaved me onto the back seat, but they wouldn't do that to an American government-trained private detective cum troubleshooter, would they? Maybe they didn't know I was the Magic Warrior. I tried to speak, but the only sounds that came out of my mouth were, "Buh de flew flew." No one noticed. I tried to sit up and only succeeded in rolling off the seat and landing on the floor face first. No one seemed to care. I had to admit I didn't care. Tranquilizers were wonderful. Nothing bothered me. Nothing at all. The van door was closed, leaving me in the dark on the floor.

Someone climbed behind the wheel. "I see you've found a comfy spot on the floor," Hawkins said. "Can I get you anything? No. Okay then, we're off."

I passed out. Or fell asleep. Then someone was helping me out of the van and up a short flight of metal steps. There was a lot of noise. Was I at the airport? It sounded like jet engines. If I could have forced my eyelids open, I would have done a visual check of my surroundings, but opening my eyes was impossible. My eyelids weighed a couple of tons each.

Someone led me inside—inside what? Who knows?—and set me down on a large, soft cushion. It was much quieter inside.

"Is that everything?" a man asked.

"He's it," Hawkins said. "Let's get the hell out of here."

"You're the boss."

Whatever I was inside was rolling—I felt the rhythmic vibration. Then there was a roar from outside, and everything tilted. And I passed out again.

Two minutes later—or two hours later?—I woke up. I was sleepy but relaxed, sitting in a comfortable chair with a seatbelt fastened across my lap. My right wrist was handcuffed to the arm of the chair. That's not very hospitable, I thought. Damn.

"Give him some more propofol," Hawkins said from behind me. "I don't want any trouble in the air."

A slender African-American woman in her twenties appeared at my side. She gave me a half-hearted smile, swabbed my arm with alcohol, then injected me with "some propofol." I was unconscious before anyone even asked me to count backward from one hundred. . . .

*   *   *

I came to in a room that looked like it had been purchased at Dungeon Depot. The windowless walls were dark-gray cement. The floor was black cement. The better to hide the blood stains? A camera was mounted high on the wall above the steel door—the lens pointed directly at me. Me, who happened to be sitting in a plain, steel chair, each wrist handcuffed to the armrest, each ankle duct-taped to a chair leg. I craned my neck to look at my feet. This was a more difficult maneuver than you might imagine—moving my head made me dizzy. Probably an after effect of way too many drugs. I finally managed to look at the left, front chair leg. Yup, the damn thing was bolted to the floor.

There was no other furniture in the room. There were no other people in the room.

At least I was still wearing my clothes. I had awakened naked in a torture cell marginally more interesting than this room, and believe me, it is no fun at all to wake up without your clothes. Exposed. Humiliated. But not this time. I had my clothes, and I was feeling clearer by the second. In another minute I'd be ready to trade witty repartee with the bad guys.

The dungeon had no clock—it's a staple of torture that the victim is deprived of any sense of time—so after what I guessed was a few minutes and no bad guys, I whispered, "Harry?"

He appeared. You might think my heart leapt for joy at Harry's arrival and the prospect of escape, but I knew better.

"I'm guessing," I continued to whisper, "that you're not going to help me escape unless the Chairman feels I *need* that kind of help."

"You are correct. And you don't *need* that help."

I swallowed my frustration. "Do you think we—you, me, the Chairman—could sit down sometime and define 'need' a little more precisely?"

"No." Harry scanned the dungeon cell.

"Yeah, terrible décor," I said.

"You don't need to whisper. They can't hear you or see me."

"Isn't this cell wired for sound?"

"It is, but they can't hear us."

"Lucky for you."

"Luck doesn't enter into this. Now, did you summon me to have a discussion about the Chairman's decision-making process regarding 'need'? Or is there something important you would like to discuss?"

"Well, I'd love to talk about world peace. And the rising number of strikeouts in major league baseball."

"Really?" Harry replied in a flat voice.

"I'll settle for help with Kim. I need you to get her home. Tell her I'll be okay—I will be okay, won't I?"

Harry shrugged.

"Right," I said. "You're an angel not a prophet. Okay, just tell her something comforting, but get her home safe and sound."

"I will."

"Thanks."

Harry disappeared in his sudden yet smooth fashion.

I wasn't feeling particularly chipper about my immediate future, but knowing that Harry would get Kim home safely made me feel as if everything could be all right. I was ready for whatever was coming my way. Sort of ready. Okay, to be honest, not ready at all. . . .

Since there was no way to tell time in the dungeon, I had to guesstimate how long before the bad guys would show up. Would they wait for the drugs to wear off completely? Or get in here soon while the lingering effects of the chemicals dulled my brain? Maybe I had blabbed while under the influence when they flew me to this lovely destination. Maybe they knew everything they wanted to know and torturing me was just a fun time for everyone. All I needed to do was get into the spirit of the proceedings.

With my wrists and ankles were secured to the chair, my movements were extremely limited so I was stiffening up. I flexed as many muscles as I could and slowly rolled my head to stretch my neck. All of which helped my body relax. For about thirty seconds. I wished the bad guys would show up soon. They could distract me from my aches and pains.

Eventually, I heard a pair of dead bolts being withdrawn on the outside of the door, then it swung open. Hawkins walked in followed by a woman and a man.

"Hey, Daryl," I said. It was a good idea to get in the first word in a situation like this. Showed I wasn't intimidated. "And do I have the pleasure of addressing Madame Desjardins and *Herr Freund*?" I pronounced "*Herr Freund*" with every bit of Prussian crispness I could manage, snapping off the final "d" with a distinct "t" sound.

The woman gave me an icy smile that clearly was not meant to comfort. "You seem very well informed."

"You bet. I could go on and on about all the things I knew about you and—" I nodded at Freund, "your kraut friend there."

"Oh?" Her smile grew wider. And icier.

"Sure. And I know a lot of inconvenient truths about Privatus. And about your client, Waronov-Tybalt. But, then again, so do you."

"Are you suggesting that there's no point in our having a discussion because we share the same knowledge?" she asked.

"No, I think you should feel free to share whatever you like."

"How considerate. But what I really want to know is not what you know—"

"Great. Release me, and I'll be happy to get out of here."

"You're not very subtle."

"Yeah, I'm like a restaurant waiter dropping a tray full of champagne flutes."

None of them seemed amused by me. Tough crowd. Desjardins stepped closer to me and stroked my left cheek with the backs of her fingers. She had a gentle touch, but I had to admit it scared the hell out of me. There was something alarmingly impersonal about her intimate little gesture. I realized that Desjardins would smile calmly regardless of what Hawkins did to me.

She leaned over and whispered in my ear, "I want to know the names of anyone who gave you information about us. I want to know how you found out what our plans were and how you managed to be at the right place at the right time, every time. And, finally, I want to know where

George Morita is."

"Let me set your mind at ease about George," I said. "He's completely safe. And I haven't the faintest idea where he is. That's part of keeping him safe. His whereabouts were kept from me."

"Just in case you were captured and forced to talk."

"Exactly. See how easy that was?"

Freund interjected, "He's probably telling the truth. It is standard security procedure to compartmentalize all vital information."

Desjardins nodded and asked me, "Who knows about us?"

"Why not ask your buddy Capitaine Dantin? He's on your payroll isn't he? Isn't he the one who gave me up when I left the police station in Paris?"

"What?" Desjardins turned to Hawkins but pointed at me. "How does he know about Dantin?"

"He must not have been completely out when the riverboat docked at the *quai*. Dantin was there to smooth our way with the uniformed police officers who responded to the incident on the boat. Couldn't be avoided."

Desjardins returned her attention back to me, "Who knows about us?"

"Dantin can give you some of the names. But who can I tell you about? Let's see, you probably already know of Senior Investigator Montesquieu of Interpol. And Smith, that CIA jerk in the gray suit. Is he on your payroll, too? You used to be CIA, didn't you? Did you infiltrate the

Company?"

"Who else? Who is your contact in Washington?"

We had arrived at the sticking point. They probably didn't know about Joanne Agar since she hadn't been in the meeting with Dantin. I wasn't going to give her up. Which meant they were going to torture me to get her name.

I twisted my head toward Hawkins then toward Freund. "Maybe we could break this impasse the good old-fashioned way?"

"What would that way be?" Desjardins asked.

"Well, Waronov-Tybalt's coffers are very deep. Lots and lots of cash. Offer me a bribe. A huge bribe. I'll tell you everything."

"Interesting," Freund said. "If we funnel money in your direction, you'll cooperate. How much money?"

"Don't waste your time," Hawkins said and jerked his thumb at me, "He's yanking your chain."

I stared at the three of them. They stared back.

After a long moment, Desjardins broke off and looked at the two men. "I think we should use your approach."

I couldn't figure out which man she was talking to. "Is this the point where one of you gentlemen instructs me on the finer points of enhanced interrogation techniques?"

Hawkins pulled a quarter from his pocket, flashed it at Freund, and said, "Flip for it?"

"No, please," Freund replied, waving Hawkins off,

"indulge yourself." He stepped to the door and pressed a small button. The door opened. Freund stepped half out of the door, then came back, pulling a small stainless steel cart on wheels. There was a white surgical towel on the top of the cart, with a number of gleaming, sharp implements spread out. Since it was impossible to imagine that Freund and Hawkins had the slightest concerns for sterility, I guessed that the white towel was for display purposes only. The implements of torture gleamed under the harsh ceiling lights. The idea was to scare the victim-to-be. It worked. I had to breathe deeply to keep from squirming.

Freund rolled the cart to within a foot of the right side of the chair. Easy reach for Hawkins to do his work, but just out of range of my handcuffed hands.

"Enjoy yourself," Freund said to Hawkins as he walked toward the door.

"Please feel free to have a good time." Desjardins added, "As long as you make sure you get what we need."

"Of course," Hawkins responded.

Desjardins shut the door behind them, leaving me alone with Hawkins. He pulled off his sport coat, revealing a shoulder holster with what looked like a 9mm Sig Sauer in it and a mag pouch with two magazines, and hung up the sport coat on a small, pull-down hook on the back of the door. Then he took off the holster and draped it over the sport coat. Having finished dealing with his wardrobe, Hawkins paced up and down the cell and rolled up his shirt sleeves.

"Holy shit, is this some kind of ritual with you guys?" I asked. "Rolling up your shirt sleeves like you're about to put in a day's work? Maybe you should put on a white butcher's coat and black, rubber boots? You know, keep the blood off of you."

He grinned and, as he stepped over to the cart, asked, "So, what's your story, Tyrrell?" He idly touched one bladed tool after another as he waited for my answer.

"Oh, you know, I was in the Army, did a bit of work with the CIA in Afghanistan, had the good sense to avoid working with the Company after I returned home. Became a Deputy Marshal. Kinda like you, only I knew better than to work for the CIA after the Army. And there's no way I'd ever become a private spy-for-hire."

"Too stupid to seek employment with substantial remuneration?"

"Look at you with the five-syllable words."

"I went to college just like you. Army ROTC, just like you. But I didn't turn into drunken bum and get dumped by the U.S. Marshals Service."

"Just like me."

"Just like you."

"The Marshals Service didn't dump me, but you already knew that, didn't you?"

"Yeah . . . such a sad story. You were shot and went out on disability. Although I have to say, you don't seem very disabled to me these days."

"I'm not. Haven't collected disability in a long

311

time."

"That makes you honest *and* stupid."

I tried to shrug, but it's very hard to do that when your hands are cuffed to a chair.

"What was with all the drinking?" he asked.

"Listen, if you're trying to establish a rapport with me before you go to work on me, you're wasting both of our time."

He ignored me. "Was the drinking a symptom of PTSD?"

"Sure. So was my compulsive gambling and my addiction to peanut M&M's. And my need to wear leather mini skirts and fishnet stockings between the hours of 2:00 and 3:00 A.M."

"You're not as funny as you think you are."

"It breaks my heart to hear you say that."

Hawkins picked up a long, curved scalpel. He turned it over and over, admiring it. I had the feeling this little show was entirely for my benefit.

"So . . . was the drinking a symptom of PTSD?"

"Why? You worried that you have PTSD?"

He smirked.

"Don't worry," I said. "You don't have PTSD. Your diagnosis is: C – A – S."

"What the hell is CAS?" Hawkins grunted.

"Chronic Asshole Syndrome. You undoubtedly were an asshole before you ever joined the service, and now you're an asshole with serious skills. But in the end, you're just an asshole."

"Can you give me one reason why I shouldn't cut you into little pieces?"

"Actually, I can."

"Yeah, what?"

"You want to prove that you can take me man-to-man."

"Is that right?"

"Without a doubt." I paused for a second, then, "Asshole."

"You're trying to goad me." He laughed. "Pathetic effort. Why shouldn't I just cut you up, get the information Desjardins wants, then beat you to a pulp?"

"Even an asshole like you can't prove himself by beating a tortured, broken man."

Hawkins leaned over, an ugly grin on his face. His eyes were level with mine, his nose just millimeters from mine. The scalpel was an inch or two from my chin. "Why are you so intent on pissing me off?"

"I don't like you."

"Am I too much like you?"

"You're exactly like me. That is like me if I were a complete ass—"

In mid-word, I jerked as far up as my cuffs would allow and headbutted Hawkins. I felt the scalpel point scrape under my chin. The headbutt caught Hawkins on the bridge of his nose. His head snapped back, his arms dropped to his side, the scalpel fell to the floor, and he folded over at the waist. His head and shoulders sagged into my lap.

"Please don't bleed all over me," I said as I grabbed his biceps with my cuffed hands and held him in place. He moaned but didn't move. I kept my grip on him with my left hand, stretched my right as far as I could through the cuff, and patted down the pockets of his pants. I found the key for the handcuffs and freed myself. It was a lot harder than it sounded to control Hawkins's unconscious weight, find the key, and use it in the cuffs. It took a minute. Maybe two. I couldn't tell since the dungeon had no clock.

I pushed Hawkins off of my lap. He groaned as he hit the floor. Blood was flowing from his nose. I looked down at my lap. Yup, he'd bled on me, damn it. I scooped up the handy-dandy scalpel and cut my ankles loose from the duct tape. I rolled Hawkins over onto his back, grabbed his hair, and banged his head off the floor a couple of times. Then I rolled him over onto his stomach and cuffed his hands behind his back. I shoved his body close to the chair and used the other cuffs to lock his right wrist to one of the chair legs. I yanked the belt out of his pants and secured his legs together.

Still crouched near him, I used the scalpel to slice off a strip of his shirt sleeve and dabbed at my chin with the strip. There was a little blood, but not much. I'd had worse shaving cuts.

I looked skyward and said, "Thanks."

Turning my attention to Hawkins's unconscious

body on the floor, I focused on him, then on the scalpel, then back again. I would be doing the world a huge favor if I killed this guy, right here, right now. He had tried to kill me several times. He had been on the verge of torturing me to death. God only knew how many people he had slaughtered in the past for no other reason than greed. He was an amoral animal without any redeeming qualities of humanity. On the other hand . . . if I killed him now, when he was completely helpless, I'd become his true evil twin: A murderous piece of shit.

"You are one lucky son of a bitch," I said. I returned the scalpel to the towel on top of the cart and wheeled the cart to the corner farthest from the door, away from Hawkins's position on the floor. I didn't want him to kick it over and use one of the instruments, like a surgical pick, to open the handcuffs.

I slipped into his shoulder holster and pulled on his sport coat—I found it was really convenient when my kidnapper was the same size as I was, and that didn't happen all that often for me. I checked the pockets of the sport coat. Jackpot: a cell phone—with no service down here in the dungeon—a wallet with a credit card and a driver's license with a photo of Hawkins. The name on the license and credit card was Howard Watkins. And there was cash: about three hundred dollars. Dollars, not Euros. I guessed I wasn't in France anymore.

In addition, there was a light-gray plastic magnetic-card key with Hawkins's photo on one side but no name. Speaking of keys, there was the car key fob. Not just any car—a Porsche. If I ever managed to escape this place, I could drive home in style. And since my pants pockets were empty, and I had no idea where my jacket was, discovering Hawkins's stash of cash, phone, and mag card was a bonanza. I put everything back into the sport coat's pockets and stepped toward the button Freund had used to exit the cell. As I did so, I glanced up at the camera. Had someone seen my antics? Or was Harry covering for me?

"God, thanks for the help you've given me and please continue doing so," I said softly. "I think I've got a long way to go."

Pulling Hawkins's Sig from the holster, I held the gun at my right side and pressed the door button with my left index finger.

The deadbolts drew back with with heavy, metallic thuds. I didn't open the door but waited behind it.

"What's up?" a man said as the door was pulled open from the outside.

I smashed into it with my right shoulder. The door swung quickly outward, catching the left arm and shoulder of the security guard in the hallway. He spun halfway around, and I grabbed the hair on the back of his head and slammed his face against the far wall. He dropped to the floor like a sack of potatoes. He moaned, which compelled me to hit him in the head with my pistol and knock him out once and for all. I tugged off his shoe and wedged it under the door to ensure it stayed open. Then I dragged him into the dungeon. Not too surprisingly, this Privatus security guard was equipped more like a cop than a shopping mall's private police force. He had a Sig Sauer like Hawkins, and handcuffs, which I used to cuff his wrists behind his back. I shoved his gun into my belt at the small of my back, took off his belt, and used it to bind his legs.

When I'd sliced off the duct tape that had secured me to the chair, I left strips of tape still attached to the chair legs. Perfect for gags. I taped Hawkins's and the guard's mouths, kicked the shoe out from under the cell door, and closed it. Now all I had to do was get the hell out of this place, wherever it was. Probably have to escape more armed guards, more spies-for-hire, and Desjardins and Freund. I wondered if the two Sig Sauer pistols were enough.

16

The hallway outside the cell door had gray-cement walls and floor just as the cell. The interior decorator for this place had a taste for the color gray and for extensive use of steel and cement. I'd visited prisons that were cheerier. There were two metal doors on the opposite side of the hall from my cell, and one more door on the cell's side. To my right, the hallway ended about six feet away in a blank wall. To my left, the hallway stretched ahead about thirty feet to what looked like elevator doors. There were cameras mounted near the ceiling at either end of the hall.

"Harry, I hope you're blocking those cameras. I'd really like to blow this pop stand."

I walked toward the elevator doors and noticed that one of the doors in the hall had no doorknob. I stopped and scanned the other doors. Yup, all had knobs. I dug into the left pocket of Hawkins's sport coat and pulled out the mag card with his picture. I slowly waved it over the left side of the door frame at waist height. Nothing. I repeated the procedure on the right side. There was a soft buzz and then a click as the lock turned. The door popped open about a half inch. Pistol in hand, I opened the door wider.

"Wow. Christmas in July," I whispered in awe.

The room was an armory, full of weapons and

318

tactical gear. I stepped in, flipped a light switch just inside the door, closed the door behind me, and went shopping. The room was pretty much your run-of-the-mill walk-in closet with shelves full of guns, grenades, knives, tactical vests and belts, and bullet-proof vests.

I pulled on a tactical vest and loaded it with eight grenades, four each of the smoke and flash-bang varieties, and extra 9mm mags for the Sig Sauers I had appropriated from the ever-cooperative Privatus employees. Finally, treating them like Fabergé eggs, I took two Mk3A2 offensive hand grenades and tucked them into the vest. Like all grenades, they are stable as long as the pin is in place, but the concussive blast from these babies could blow doors off their hinges. Or take out a car full of bad guys. In other words, they were handy things to have while trying to escape the lair of spies-for-hire.

My vest bulged due to all the lethal hardware. I returned two grenades of the smoke and flash-bang types to their shelves and regretfully gave up one of the Mk3A2s. I tucked the extra mags into my sports coat, which I wore under the vest. Not fashionable, but effective for close-quarters combat.

In the hallway, I moved toward the elevator doors. So far, no alarms, no sign that anyone had seen anything on the security cameras. I swiped Hawkins's handy-dandy mag card in the card reader on the right side of the elevator doors and heard the whir of moving elevator cables. When the car arrived and the doors slid open, I had a Sig in my right hand. The elevator was empty.

I stepped in and the doors slid shut. There was a panel to my left as I faced the doors, but no buttons. I swiped with the mag card, and a touch screen illuminated. I pressed "1" and hoped it was the ground floor.

As the car rose, I grabbed a smoke grenade in my left hand and a flash-bang in my right. The elevator finished its ascent, the doors rolled open, and first I tossed the smoke then the flash-bang grenades out of the elevator.

There was a hail of gunfire. I dove for the front left corner of the elevator, swiped the control panel with Hawkins's card, and pressed the only button I could see when I twisted to look up at the panel. I hit "4"—I wondered what kind of reception would be awaiting me there. The elevator arrived at the fourth floor, and I tossed my remaining grenades out of the elevator.

No gunfire. I poked my head out the elevator door, and reconnoitered. No bad guys. Yet. But I could hear feet pounding up stairs. Or down stairs. Probably the fire stairwell.

The elevator doors began to slide shut, but bounced back because I had my left foot firmly planted in the doorway. The hallway on the fourth floor stretched out in front of me, just like the dungeon hallway. But the walls were painted a pastel blue, and the overhead lights were recessed and less harsh than on the dungeon floor. There were two doors with knobs. And near the end of the hall, a door without any obvious way to enter. Since I had had good fortune with the mag card before, I made directly for that door, swiped the card, and the door popped open.

I stepped inside quickly and went into a shooter's crouch. There were three people inside a windowless, very chilly, computer-filled room. To my right, behind glass doors, there were racks full of servers. There was a hum of air-conditioning, and the door to the room was very thick. I doubted the noise from the flash-bang had been audible in this room.

In front of me was a long, array of monitors in a large curve above the three-station desk where a team of classic nerds sat: an Asian woman, one pudgy white guy, and one Indian man. They all wore sweaters and glasses. The two men both had scruffy, wispy facial hair—an obvious attempt to confirm that they were actually adults. All three were in their twenties, all bad dressers. Then again, who was I to talk? I had just burst into a room with a gun in my hand and a tactical vest over a sport coat.

"Is this the Privatus data center?" I asked.

"Who the hell are you?" asked the woman.

"I'm the guy with a gun. Is this the data center?"

"Yes."

Since I wasn't in any immediate danger from a trio of computer nerds, I stood up from my crouch and said, "Are any of you armed?"

They shook their heads.

"Are there any weapons in this room?"

"Just the computers," the woman replied. Her

acidic tone suggested I was a complete moron.

"Is there data here on Privatus's operations? Evidence of criminal activities?"

"Criminal?" asked pudgy white guy nervously. "We didn't break any U.S. Laws. Seriously."

"Shut up and answer me. Is there proof of Privatus operations here? Connections to shell companies? Offshore bank accounts? Payroll to operatives?"

"No," the woman replied unconvincingly.

"Really?" I stepped forward and put the barrel of my Sig on the forehead of the Indian gentleman. "Sorry to do this to you, but I figure you're just dying to add something to this conversation. Is the data I asked about here?"

"Yes."

"How do I access it out? Can I e-mail it to someone? Copy it to the Cloud? Get a portable hard drive? How?"

The woman grinned bitterly, "None of those things will work. The building's network is internal only. There's no connection to the Internet, which means no Cloud, no e-mail, no VPN, nothing. The computers are custom built without USB ports for flash drives or a portable hard drive. You're out of luck."

"No, I'm not. Take the computers apart and pull out the hard drives."

"The data is compartmentalized. It's stored in thirty-six servers," the woman said. "Are you going to take all of the drives? Just walk out of the building with all thirty-six under your arm?"

I scanned the rows of servers in their racks behind the glass doors then did the same for the array of monitors. I turned back to the room's entry door. Any minute now, very nasty people were going to be coming through that door.

"Harry, a consultation please?"

"Yes?" he responded calmly the instant he appeared. He could afford to be calm. He wasn't going to die if something went wrong.

"How do I lock this door? I mean so it can't be opened from the outside by one of these cards."

Harry nodded in understanding and said, "It's locked."

"Will it withstand an assault?"

"The Privatus people will have to use an explosive like C-4 to get inside."

"Okay, great. We're safe for the time being."

"I'm always safe."

"Thanks for pointing that out." As I spoke, I noticed that the nerds were all wide-eyed as they watched me. "Are you invisible to them?" I asked, pointing.

"Yes."

"You enjoy making me look foolish, don't you?"

"It's one of the perks of my position."

"Thanks. Now . . . how do I get the evidence I need from the computers?"

Harry looked at the computers then into the air then back at me, "You only need the hard drives from computers number twelve and thirteen. They contain all the financial data that tie Privatus to the money it spends through shell corporations."

"Follow the money."

"Exactly."

To the nerds I said, "Get me the hard drives from twelve and thirteen."

They exchanged bewildered looks.

"Get the damn drives out of twelve and thirteen. Now!"

They stood up immediately, moved to the glass doors, then hesitated, completely unsure what to do next.

"Hey!" I called. "Turn off the power to all the servers. Tug out all the cables on servers twelve and thirteen. Carry them back to your desks, and pull the hard drives. Got it?"

There was a lot of affirmative-sounding mumbling as they set about the task. While they worked at disassembling, I took Hawkins's phone out of my sport coat's breast pocket. It was an iPhone 6.

"Harry, could you please help me get into this phone?"

As I addressed him, the nerds turned their attention to me, clearly wondering what was wrong with me as I talked to no one. I have to admit, I often wondered that myself. Harry closed his eyes, and, after a split second, the phone lit up with the passcode screen, and the numbers quickly highlighted in succession—all by themselves. Hawkins's home screen displayed. The background was all black. The only color was from the icons for the phone's apps.

"Geez—an all-black home screen. This guy needs to get a life," I said and pressed the home button and held, activating Siri, the Apple virtual assistant?

"Siri, what is my location?"

After a few seconds, Siri responded, "You're at 1674 16th Street, North Arlington, VA."

I spoke to the nerds, "I thought Privatus had offices on K Street. Trying to blend in with the other expensive but useless organizations in DC."

"That's the front office," pudgy white guy said. "Where they schmooze with the clients."

"This location is for operations, IT, and back offices," added the Asian woman.

I dialed Joanne Agar's number, noticing the time at the top of the screen: 12:38 A.M.

Joanne answered with a cautious, "Hello?" on the second ring.

"It's Tyrrell."

"Jack, my God, where did you go?"

"I was kidnapped in Paris and flown to the States. I'm currently at 1674 16th Street, North Arlington, Virginia."

"What are you doing there? Are you all right?"

"I'm fine. Sort of. The address is the back office for Privatus. Where are you?"

"Over the Atlantic in a government jet. Do you need help?"

"A SWAT team would be nice."

"I'll make arrangements. Where are you now? Specifically."

"Data center on the fourth floor."

"I'll tell SWAT an undercover is on the premises. Can you hang in there for a few minutes?"

"As long as the bad guys don't use C-4 on the door, I'll be fine."

"Are you serious?"

"Absolutely."

"Hang tight." She disconnected.

"How are we coming with the hard drives?" I asked.

The Indian guy handed me a small, flat metal box with a black cable trailing from one end. Maybe three-and-a-half inches by five inches, and about a half-inch deep. "That's one of them."

"The other will be out in a second," said the woman. It took a tiny bit more than a second, but I wasn't going to get upset. They were working under duress and doing a good job of it.

"Excuse me," Harry said. "The Privatus team is coming down the hallway. They've got C-4 to blow the door open. Once they blow the door, they'll enter this room with heavy fire, killing everyone."

"Then they won't find out what they wanted to know from me."

"I don't think that is their primary concern anymore."

"Right," I saw the wisdom of what he was saying. "They just want to stop me. And they don't care what it takes."

"Exactly. And you now have about two minutes."

"Have they placed the C-4, yet?"

Harry's eyes went skyward then to me, "No."

"Okay." I pulled the Mk3A2 concussion grenade out of its pocket in the vest. I spoke to the nerds, "You should get behind the desk. Stay on the floor. Stay down, no matter what."

Kneeling close to the door, I put the concussion grenade on the floor and laid the smoke and flash-bang grenades next to it, inches from the door frame. I tucked the two hard drives into the pockets that had carried the grenades. The two Sig Sauer pistols went on the floor near the grenades. All of my weapons were within easy reach.

Harry said, "Good luck."

"Thanks."

He disappeared. I took a deep breath, used my left hand to swipe the mag card then slipped it into a pocket, grabbed the edge of the now-open door with my left, pulled the pin on the concussion grenade with my teeth, and tossed the grenade into the hallway beyond with my right.

The explosion in the hall was everything I hoped for. Ear shattering. Lots of flying debris. Moans and groans from the wounded. I jerked out the pins on the smoke and flash-bang as quickly as possible, flinging them into the hall after their more deadly big brother.

I stood up, with a pistol in each hand, kicked the door wide open, and strode into the hall. A small lump of C-4 with a blasting cap sticking out of it was on the floor alongside the bodies of four Privatus security men. There was blood coming from their noses and ears, but they were all breathing. I picked up the C-4, stepped back into the computer room, tucked the explosive under the center rack of servers, and waved the nerds out of the room.

"Come on, get moving."

They hustled past me toward the elevator. I closed the door, found the detonator in the hand of one of the prone Privatus men, and flipped the switch. There was a very satisfying, deep *BOOM!*. A second later, the fire alarms went off and the sprinkler system activated, spraying water everywhere.

The nerds had made it to the open elevator but they couldn't get the doors to close.

"It won't work," the pudgy white guy called to me.

"Probably cut-off by the fire emergency," the woman said.

"Take the stairs," I replied. "Now!"

They ran out of the elevator, vainly attempting to ward off the sprinkler water by cowering under their arms arched over their heads. The woman swiped her mag card at a door, and the three of them rushed inside. I heard their feet flapping down the steps, then the door swung shut and I was left alone in the indoor rain.

"Harry?" No sign of my guardian angel. "Harry, could you whoosh me out of here? Please?"

Nothing.

"Really? Do you want me to shoot more people to get out of here?"

Still nothing.

"All right, I'll do it the hard way."

I walked to the stairway door, pulled Hawkins's mag card from a pocket, and was about to swipe it when I felt the barrel of a gun in my back.

"Drop your weapons and put your hands up," Freund said.

I dropped the weapons, put my hands up, and spun around with my right arm swinging down to sweep Freund's gun hand aside. He may have been one a terrific operative once upon a time, but he was at least ten years past his heyday, and he fired his pistol too late. The bullet went into the wall next to us.

My knee came up into his groin and made maximum contact. He doubled over, howling, and I hit the right side of his face with a downward jab. The force of my punch drove him to his knees. I yanked his chin up so I could see his face, and slammed him in the nose with my fist. His eyes rolled up in his head, and he slumped to the floor. The fire alarms and sprinklers shut off at that moment, and the hallway was quiet except for the sound of dripping water.

"Very impressive," Desjardins said. She was a few feet away near the elevators, wearing a bullet-proof vest, and aiming a Sig Sauer in my direction.

"If you make a run for it right this minute," I said, "you just might get away. As long as you don't dawdle to shoot me."

"Are you really as unafraid as you seem? Or are you a good actor?"

"Neither. I'm too stupid to realize how much trouble I'm in."

She smiled, "I doubt that." She pointed at the pockets in my vest. "What did you take from the computer room?"

"Just some peanut-butter-and-jelly sandwiches from your nerds. I'm feeling a bit peckish."

She fired—I could have sworn I felt the breeze from the bullet whizzing past my head. "Give me the . . . sandwiches."

I reached into my pockets and took out the hard drives, holding them both in my left hand.

"Hand them to me."

The yowling of police sirens and the deep, booming horns of fire engines could be heard in the distance.

"You don't have much time," I pointed out.

"You don't have a strong bargaining position," she replied. "Hand me the drives."

"What if I drop them on the floor? All this water can't be good for them."

She glanced down for a second to assess the possible damage, realized her mistake, and started to straightened up to look at me. But I had lunged in the instant that her eyes went down, and my right fist caught her on the jaw. She rocked back into the wall and bounced to the floor.

I leaned down, took away her gun, and checked her pulse. Alive but unconscious.

"Sorry," I said. "Not very chivalrous of me, but what could I do?"

The hard drives went back into my pockets. I picked up my Sig Sauers and Hawkins's mag card, swiped the card on the stairwell door frame, and headed down.

When I emerged on the ground floor, the sirens were very loud, and emergency vehicles of all shapes and sizes were stopping directly outside the glass-fronted lobby of the building. The emergency lights cut through the night, casting red and blue flashes on the walls of the lobby.

By the time I got to the front entrance, a SWAT team and a group of men and women in FBI-emblazoned windbreakers were swarming in. I had my hands up, my guns were dangling by their trigger guards from my thumbs.

"Tyrrell?" shouted an African-American man in an

331

FBI windbreaker. He approached me cautiously, with a pistol held down by his thigh.

"Yeah, I'm Tyrrell."

"I'm Special Agent Hart. Joanne Agar sends her regards." He looked around at the wet lobby area. "She texted me your photo. Told me not to shoot you. Warned me you would make a big mess. I guess this qualifies."

"This isn't all my fault."

"No?"

"Not all of it. . . ."

Firefighting crews were rushing inside. I raised my hand to halt them and explain that they probably weren't needed, but no one paid any attention. I was just a soaking wet man with a vest over his sport coat. A vision of loveliness.

I dug into the vest pockets and handed Hart the hard drives. "For Joanne. Evidence."

"Illegally obtained evidence."

"Noooo, it's evidence sourced by a confidential informant." I took off the tactical vest and tossed it into a corner of the lobby. Much more comfortable. Even if I was soaking wet. "And . . . after your best hackers have broken the encryption on this stuff, if you can't act on it, I'm sure the CIA will find it fascinating and actionable."

His eyebrows arched in skepticism. "Actionable. Hmm. Our brothers at Langley?"

"Oh, yeah. Also, there are some people upstairs that I'm sure they will want to interview. Alumni of the

332

Company and some other organizations that fall into the CIA's purview."

The in-pouring of law-enforcement and firefighting personnel had stopped. Hart and I walked outside. It was muggy and hot, just like July in the Washington, DC area is supposed to be.

"Joanne said we should let you go home. She'll debrief you when she returns."

"Are you sure?"

"I just do what Joanne tells me to do."

"Me, too."

"That's not what I heard."

"Lies," I said. "All lies."

At that moment, the SWAT team began escorting handcuffed suspects out of the building to unmarked vans.

"Ah . . . the glamorous world of espionage for hire—and profit," I observed cynically, "And top it off with a trip to your new home in the back of a police van."

Hart shot me a tart grin. "Do you need transport anywhere."

"No, I'm all set." I dangled Hawkins's Porsche key in front of me. "A parting gift."

"Nice ride. Maybe it should be impounded as evidence?"

"I'll check it out and let you know."

He grinned, "Let Joanne know."

"Right. I'll let Joanne know."

"It's a long story, but I have no idea what day and

time it is."

"It's Monday, no, scratch that, Tuesday morning."
He checked his watch, "1:15 A.M. Long day, huh?"

"It's been a hard day's night," I said.

He smirked in response.

The line of wet, shuffling arrestees continued.
Desjardins and Freund walked past us, soaked and bruised.

"Those two deserve special attention," I said,
pointing at them.

"Got it. Well," he offered me his hand, and we
shook. "Thanks for all your . . . help." He paused and
looked at the facade of the building and the parade of
handcuffed suspects walking out. "The word 'help' doesn't
seem big enough to describe what you did."

"It's plenty big. No worries. Thanks for leading the
cavalry to my rescue."

17

I walked to the back of the building where two police officers were stationed at the back entrance, a nondescript steel door with a short stairway down to the small parking lot. I heard their radios saying that I was cleared to leave. I gave them a wave, and one of them returned the wave and grunted something I couldn't really hear.

There were a dozen cars in the lot. Only one was a Porsche—an SUV, a Cayenne Turbo in silver metallic. Not bad. Not bad at all: 0-60mph in just under four seconds, 500-plus-horsepower engine. All of that power and handling for a mere six figures, somewhere in the neighborhood of $125,000. And you got four leather seats and a bit of cargo space, too.

"Harry."

He appeared in his patented, now-you-*don't*-see him-now-you-*do* method.

"I don't suppose you have my personal—"

He handed me my wallet, smart phone, and keys.

"All of my stuff in Paris? Is it—"

"In your apartment on West 76th Street."

"Wow. You are the *ultimate* concierge."

He scowled at my comment. Well, his facial

expression was a scowl by Harry's standards. With anyone else it might have been mistaken for a twitch.

"I should probably get going," I said.

"Not without me," a man growled behind me. "Hands out from your thighs, spread fingers so I can see your hands are empty. Then turn around, slowly."

Harry had vanished. "Harry?" I whispered. "Really?"

"Hands out, fingers spread," the growl repeated. "Turn around, slowly."

I did as I was told. Hawkins had a Sig Sauer pointed at my chest. I glanced over his shoulder.

"Yeah, my back is to the cops," Hawkins said. "They won't see my face, won't realize I'm not inside for for five minutes or so. Enough time to get away. You should have killed me when you had the chance."

"At this particular moment in time, I'm trying to remember why the hell I didn't."

"Cause you think you're the good guy," he sneered. It wasn't a full-out evil-villain sneer, but it was effective. His villainous aspect was enhanced by all the damage I'd done to his face.

"It's not for me to decide if I'm the good guy. I didn't want to kill you 'cause that would have made me just like you. Ugh."

His sneer wavered a fraction, and he glanced away for the tiniest second, reacting to the noise made by the fire department as they swarmed out the rear entrance of the building into the parking lot.

"Step past me," he said. "Wave at the nice firefighters."

I waved. He relieved me of the last of my guns. "Get in my vehicle," he spoke in a low voice. "Disobey me, and I'll kill a bunch of firefighters."

The cops at the back entrance were concentrating on the arriving firefighters and paying no attention to us at all.

I pressed the key fob and the Porsche's alarm beeped off, and the doors unlocked. Hawkins opened the passenger-side rear door and dumped my weapons on the floor. Then he opened the front passenger door and got in, keeping watch on the firefighters. I climbed in behind the steering wheel. Too bad, I thought I would have enjoyed driving this vehicle under other circumstances.

Hawkins had his Sig aimed at my midsection, and said, "Don't buckle up. Just pull the seat belt behind you and insert it into the clasp." He buckled himself into his seat. "I don't want you to get any ideas about taking me out by crashing the car."

"Gee, you think of everything."

He ignored that. "Get out of here, but do it nicely. Like you haven't got a worry in the world."

I drove past the firefighters, the police SWAT team, and the FBI agents. They were swarming the building from all sides, putting out fires, and checking the entire building to make sure no one was left behind. And all the while yours truly was driving out with the ultimate bad guy.

Hawkins told me we were going to "take the scenic route," which I assumed meant he wasn't instructing me to take the direct route.

"You worried about being followed?" I asked.

"Just shut up and drive."

He instructed me to head east on Wilson Boulevard, then turn left onto North Lynn Street, then get onto Route 29, which quickly became the Custis Memorial Parkway. The parkway took us over the Potomac River on the Theodore Roosevelt Bridge. Even in the dark it *was* a scenic, but once again, I found myself unable to appreciate the finer things in life with a Sig Sauer in the hand of my doppelganger pointed at me.

"Take 23rd Street to the Lincoln Memorial."

I turned right on 23rd Street. The Memorial seemed to glow softly in its night lights. Even though the dashboard clock read: 1:41 A.M., there were a few people climbing the wide expanse of the front steps. When you needed the inspiration and comfort of a great president, you went to see Mr. Lincoln, regardless of the time of day.

"Park in front."

"I don't think you can park there—"

"Shut up and park."

"You better hope you don't get arrested."

"Shut *up*."

"Sorry," I said insincerely and mashed the

accelerator to the floor.

"Slow down!" He jammed the barrel of his gun into my ribs to emphasize the seriousness of the moment. I didn't let up on the accelerator.

"Stop! You stupid fuck!"

Like I said, the Porsche Cayenne Turbo does 0-60 in about four seconds. Wow. The speedometer flashed past 60 just as we hit the short wall that surrounds most of the Memorial. The SUV's nose crunched against the wall, the windshield shattered, and the vehicle's back end twisted to the right, lifting off the ground and landing on the wall itself. The Cayenne rolled sloppily onto the lawn, coming to rest on its partially caved-in roof.

The airbags had deployed, pinning Hawkins and me to our seats. I had gambled that a head-on impact would minimize the damage to me in my seatbeltless state. The gamble had paid off. I felt as if I had been punched in the face and chest, but I was in one piece. As soon as the airbag deflated, which was practically instantaneous, I slid down to the roof of the overturned car. Hawkins was hanging in his seatbelt and tugging at the clasp to release himself. His gun was on the roof but several feet behind us, out of reach.

Hawkins freed himself from his seatbelt and thumped to the roof. We threw ineffective punches at each other, then gave up, and scrambled out of the broken windshield. He escaped the wreckage first and began running toward the Memorial's steps. I was out of the

Porsche a second later and gave chase.

He reached the basketball-court-sized plaza immediately below the first of the main flights of steps; the flight flanked by two buttresses topped with eleven-feet tall marble tripods. He hesitated for a split-second then turned to his left to run toward the traffic circle in front of the Memorial. Running all out, I leapt to the top of the low wall bordering the plaza and launched myself through the air at his back.

My tackle caught him in the small of his back, my arms wrapped around him, and we hit the ground with a tiny bit less force than the asteroid that had struck the Yucatan Peninsula and wiped out the dinosaurs.

For a moment, I thought one or both of my arms might be broken. And Hawkins must have had some cracked ribs. Or a comprehensively smashed nose. We rolled apart and struggled to our feet. My fingers were tingling, but I was able to open and close my fists. Hawkins had a bloody nose, but it had not sustained anywhere near the amount of damage I was hoping for.

The wail of sirens was faintly audible. Flashing emergency lights could be seen intermittently through the trees along Constitution Avenue, but they far away, down by the Washington Monument

"Much as I want to stay and settle this, I think I have to get going," Hawkins said.

"I'm afraid I can't let you leave."

"We've already danced this dance. Enough.

340

Goodbye."

He turned away from me and took a step toward the traffic circle. I grabbed his left shoulder and twisted him back toward me. His left arm swiped up and back, circling my right arm, trying to pin it so he could dislocate my shoulder. But I had seen his move coming —I jabbed him with my left fist, twice, a pair of direct punches to the jaw. He broke off his attempt to pin my arm, staggered, stopped, squared his shoulders, and threw a right hook at my head. I blocked his punch and jabbed again, this time with my right. Two bang-on-the-nose hits. He stumbled backward and crumpled to one knee.

The sirens were much louder and the lights were a lot closer. A minute to go, I guesstimated.

Hawkins stood up. He was one tough son of a bitch. I would have admired him for his toughness, except that . . . I didn't admire anything about him. He was amoral and corrupt.

He came at me again, feinting with his left. I hate to admit it, but it was a convincing feint—it convinced me anyway, and when I blocked it, my left side was open to his slashing right hook. This one connected on my cheek and all but destroyed me. I struggled to stay on my feet. He came at me, relentlessly, closing in for the kill.

Hawkins threw another right, and I rolled my head so the blow connected with my left shoulder. In the same instant, I hit him with a right uppercut deep into his gut. He exhaled in a sharp, sudden groan. I hit him with another uppercut. He folded over at the waist and dropped to his knees, gasping.

Police cars were screeching to a halt in the traffic circle.

I leaned close to Hawkins and spoke under my breath, "Tell me how your Chronic Asshole Syndrome works out in prison."

He began to curse, but I was done with this guy. No time. I kicked him in the face mid-curse, and he fell to the ground like a cartoon character who's been hit in the head once too often.

I looked back at the statue of Lincoln within the Memorial and was struck by the gravity of Lincoln's face. Then my attention was pulled to the traffic circle, where police officers, guns drawn, were running up the steps toward Hawkins and me.

"Harry . . .?" I whispered.

*   *   *

I was on the roof of Kim's building, near the wall on the front, the western side of the building. I inhaled deeply. The night air was a little cooler here in Manhattan than it had been in DC.

After enjoying the view of the Hudson River for a minute or two, I turned around. Harry was seated at one of the tables. I joined him.

"What time is it? What day is it?"

"It's 5:30 A.M., July 26th. It will be sunrise in

sixteen minutes."

"So, I was out for almost all of yesterday."

"Yes. Hawkins wanted to make sure you were easy to control from the time he captured you in Paris until you woke up in the interrogation cell." He waited for me to ask something else, and when I said nothing, he continued, "You found a rather interesting way to hand over the Porsche to the FBI."

"That was not exactly what I had planned." I slouched back in the chair and rested my head on the seat back. I realized that my hands didn't hurt; my knuckles were not red or bruised. I wriggled my fingers: no pain. Usually when I landed as many punches as I had on Hawkins, my hands were far from pain-free. This morning, nothing. I then noticed that my clothes were different. I was wearing one of my own T-shirts and a pair of cargo pants.

I looked over at Harry, "Did you fix me up?"

"You were dirty and bruised. You needed a bit of . . . refreshing."

"Thank you. Thank you very much."

"You're welcome."

I settled back into my slouch and looked at the lightening sky. "How is all this Privatus stuff going to play out? Is George Morita going to be able to go back to his life?"

Out of the corner of my eye, I could see Harry gaze upward and then turn to me. "George will be returning to his old life. The CIA is going to invite him to help them

343

close down Privatus's various operations. Desjardins and Freund are going to live out the rest of their lives in prison."

"What about Hawkins?"

"His future is vague."

"Vague? What the hell does that mean?"

"It has nothing to do with hell."

"What does it mean?"

"It means the Chairman is not allowing me to know what will become of Hawkins."

"Why the hell did I have to punch him out?"

"Because it was satisfying for you."

I admitted, "It was pretty nice."

"You have conquered your evil alter ego."

"Hawkins and I are not the flip sides of one coin. We never were."

"Because he suffers from C—A—S and always has?"

I grinned. "Exactly."

"But confronting him did help you renew your sense of purpose, didn't it."

"He certainly played a part in confirming that I'm doing what I'm supposed—no strike that—what I'm called to do."

Harry gave me the Mona Lisa treatment.

"Never mind me and my mission in life—is Hawkins going to rot in prison or not?"

"I do not know. As I explained, the Chairman has

not revealed that to me."

"That's not very comforting."

"My job is not to comfort you."

I stood up and paced a few steps to the north, then turned and paced south. "Has George already forgotten me?"

"You are a forgettable man."

"I didn't even get to say goodbye."

"Why do you need to say goodbye? So that George can thank you before he forgets you?"

I admitted, "I guess that's the reason."

"Our mission is not about you."

"I know that. But it's natural to *expect*—wait, let me rephrase—to *hope* for a little gratitude."

"Yes, it's natural."

We were quiet for a long time.

"What is your true concern?" Harry asked.

"Excuse me?"

"You have something you wish to discuss, but you are hesitating."

"I'm enjoying this beautiful early morning. That's all."

"Are you worried about Kim?"

"Maybe. A little. How did she seem when you whooshed her out of Paris?"

"She was very anxious about you."

"Me, too. But what about us?"

"'Us?' As in the two of you? Your relationship?"

345

"Come on, Harry. Stop making this so hard. Did she say anything about us?"

"She expressed some concern about your future."

"What?"

"I believe her exact words were 'I'm not sure I can deal with this.'"

"What did you say?"

"What could I say? Am I supposed to be some kind of couples therapist for you?"

"No. No, you're not."

"Exactly. I said nothing."

"Was that the end of your conversation?"

"Yes, of course. Where can a conversation go after a remark like that?"

Oh, shit, I thought. Oh. Shit.

"Have you asked me what you wanted to ask me? Is our conversation concluded?"

"Yes. We're done."

He vanished. Even though there was nothing left to say, I wished he were still there. I didn't know what to do with myself. I thought about Kim, our engagement, our future together. Or apart. My stomach knotted at the thought that our future might be . . . apart.

The sun rose through the towers of midtown Manhattan. I hoped it was a good omen.

*   *   *

I walked down the stairs from the roof to the tenth

floor and let myself into Kim's apartment. I could smell coffee.

"Hello?" I called softly.

Kim came out of the kitchen with a smile and watery eyes. She threw her arms around my neck, buried her face in my chest, and held onto me as tightly as I've ever been held. After a minute, she raised her face to mine, and kissed me. It was a long, soft kiss. I felt her tears as they ran down her cheeks to our lips. Eventually she relaxed her hold on me and leaned back at arms length but keeping her hands resting on the back of my neck.

"When Harry brought me back, I was so scared I'd never see you again."

"Well, here I am."

"I'm so happy you're back," she said.

"And all in one piece, too."

"Don't make jokes like that." She pulled away from me.

"Maybe it's just my distorted sense of humor, but I think it's much easier to deal with the . . . rougher side of my life if I don't take it too seriously."

Kim strode across the room to the front windows, giving me a view of her back, then turned to face me. Her tears were still running. "I'm not sure I can deal with . . . all this. I guess I thought that after you saved me when I was kidnapped by the Mafia and with Harry around . . . I guess I thought everything would be okay. But these last few days, you go off in the night and you get shot at and beaten up . . . and then we're in Paris, and it was funny and romantic and you proposed . . . and then you disappeared! Just vanished. And I know there was more shooting and killing and violence. I just . . . I don't think I can take it."

"Uh . . . I . . . I don't know what to say."

"I love you. I do. But I don't know if I can wait out these times when you . . . go into danger."

"It's like being married to a cop."

"Probably," she agreed, wiping her tears with the back of her hand. "But, even though cops' spouses must be worried all the time, the vast majority of cops do come home safe and sound. But you . . . there are no stats on what you do. You mix it up with the worst kinds of people. There's so much violence. So much death. There's nobody who does what you do."

"You got me there. I *am* probably the only person in the world who works for the Chairman in my specific job."

"And that scares the hell out of me. Harry's *not* guaranteeing your safety, is he?"

"No, he's not."

She held up her left hand and pointed with her right index finger at her purple-yarn engagement ring. "We're supposed to get married and build a life together. But who knows how much time we have before something happens to you."

"Nobody knows that," I admitted. "But there are no guarantees in any marriage. That's what makes it so exciting."

"You should write for Hallmark cards."

"Do you think they'd let me work remotely? E-mail them my beautifully expressed sentiments?"

"Jack, I love you . . . but . . . I had a friend who was married to a veterinarian. He was forty-two or three, went out for his usual Saturday golf game with some buddies. Dropped dead on the fourteenth green. Turned out he had an aneurism. She had no idea that when she kissed him goodbye that morning it was going to be the last time. But every time I kiss you goodbye, it's highly likely that it will be the last time. I know there are no guarantees. I know that bad things happen to good people. I get it. You never know. But . . . I don't think the odds are in your favor. In our favor. I'm not sure . . . I'm ready to take a chance on—"

"Me?"

"You as a person? I take a chance on you every day, any day. You as a government-trained private detective cum troubleshooter who works for the Chairman? I . . . I don't know. I'm sorry, I don't know."

I walked over to her and asked in a husky whisper, "Are you saying you want to break our engagement?"

She didn't answer for a long moment. "I think we need to take a break. Give ourselves some time to settle down after Paris. An awful lot happened very quickly, maybe a little more time to process it would help."

I stood next to her at the window, and stared out

into Manhattan's early morning. Take a break. The words hit me like a punch to the gut. It was hard to breathe. In my personal experience and the experience of my friends, when a couple started discussing taking a break, it was the awkward pause immediately prior to breaking up. Splitsville. Over and out. But . . . much as I did not want us to be over, past experience also told me there was absolutely no point in trying to persuade someone not to take a break. The phrase "take a break" was a bell that could not be un-rung.

My throat tight, I said, "Okay." I was barely able to avoid uttering the word in a pained croak. "I'll, uh . . . I'll head for home."

Kim nodded but didn't speak, didn't look at me.

I stretched out my hand and touched her yarn ring. "Please, keep this to remind you of me."

She smiled and wiped tears off of her cheek. "Thank you. Don't worry, I won't forget."

"Me either."

I placed her key on a small table near the apartment door, and walked out, closing the door behind me.

Out on the sidewalk, I stood still and took a long, deep breath. It was hot, hotter than Paris had been. In the last week, I had rediscovered my purpose in life and had recommitted myself to the mission of helping others. This latest case had had pretty good results: George Morita and his family were safe—and wouldn't have to spend the rest of their lives in hiding. The bad guys at Privatus were out of business. A bunch of idiotic-but-dangerous neo-Nazis had been killed or arrested. My evil doppelganger had been confronted and conquered. And I had gotten engaged to an amazing, completely out-of-my-league woman. But there was a sour cherry on top of it all: Kim and I were on a *break*. Maybe my fiancée and I were finished—it was hard to know. Holy shit, Tyrrell, you *do* know how to have a good time.

I walked a half block down West End Avenue and looked back and up at Kim's windows.

"Goodbye, my love," I said softly and headed back to my apartment very slowly.

ABOUT THE AUTHOR

Geoff Loftus is the author of the thrillers *Murderous Spirit, Dark Mirage*, and *The Last Thing* (all Jack Tyrrell novels), as well as the thrillers *Double Blind, Engaged to Kill*, and *The Dark Saint*.

Geoff also wrote *Lead Like Ike: Ten Business Strategies from the CEO of D-Day* and was the 2010 Keynote Speaker at the Eisenhower Legacy Dinner at the Eisenhower Presidential Museum and Library. He blogs for FORBES.com on leadership.

Like many writers, he once dreamed of writing the great American novel but gave that up in an attempt to write the great American screenplay. The closest he came to that lofty achievement was writing *Hero in the Family* with John Drimmer for *The Wonderful World of Disney*. He has been a member of the Writers Guild of America, East for more than thirty years.

He lives in Scarsdale, New York with his wife, Margy; son, Gregory (who actually resides in Brooklyn); and the family's marvelous little dog, Heidi.

Acknowledgments

Once again, I have to acknowledge the work of three men for inspiring me to write the Jack Tyrrell novels: Charles Dickens who wrote *A Christmas Carol*; Philip K. Dick who wrote the short story *Adjustment Team*; and George Nolfi, the writer-director of the great movie based on Dick's story: *The Adjustment Bureau*.

Many thanks to my editorial team: Alice Siempelkamp and Ted Berk. They are the best. However, struggle as they do to catch my many errors and to suggest many good ideas, I still mess up. Tom Seligson has been my editor and publisher at Saugatuck Books for years, and I'm very grateful for his continuing support.

Thank you to the many friends who have helped me through the Tyrrell novels and all of the rest of my life: Tom and Judy Galligan, Ted Canellas and Bob Roth, Erica Fross, Gene O'Brien, Steve Pitts, Katie Ryan, Jill Quist, Marcia Menter, Sal Vitale, and Lindy Sittenfeld.

Special thanks to my son, Greg. Being his father is a dream come true; a wonderful dream I didn't even know I had.

Finally and especially, thanks to my wife, Margy. She is, quite simply, the love of my life.

www.ingramcontent.com/pod-product-compliance
Lightning Source LLC
Chambersburg PA
CBHW071212250626
47159CB00001B/294